T0121954

ON THE STOOP

A *Peanut Butter Fridays* Novel

ROBERT S. PEHRSSON

abbott press®

A DIVISION OF WRITER'S DIGEST

Abbott Press books may be ordered through booksellers or by contacting:

Abbott Press
1663 Liberty Drive
Bloomington, IN 47403
www.abbottpress.com
Phone: 1-866-697-5310

ISBN: 978-1-4582-1650-2 (sc)
ISBN: 978-1-4582-1651-9 (e)

Library of Congress Control Number: 2014910018

Printed in the United States of America.

Abbott Press rev. date: 6/24/2014

Contents

Introduction: Read this first!

Dear John,

So, John, you may be thinking you do not know about me and probably you are saying to yourself, "Who is this guy writing me?" So I will do you the curtsy of inner duecing myself, or maybe better yet, re-inner duecing myself, because I am the very same Earnest what Bobby Anderson tells you about when he rites in his notebooks what he calls *Peanut Butter Fridays*. But you may still be axing yourself how come Yours Truly is writing to you, what with you being maginary and all. Well you may likewise be a bit confuciused about my good riting and spelling and all because Bobby Anderson always rites about me being illiterated and not knowing how to rite and spell ether.

It is true the teachers try for many years to teach me to be literated but before now Yours Truly never sees much cash value to the whole thing. But then one day or two I think maybe there is sumthin to it and maybe it is time to learn myself to be literated what with my being 11 years old and not getting any younger. So, as I am searching through a neighbor's garbage can, I happen to find a book about *Guys and Dolls* what is rote by a scriber who goes by the handle Damon Runyon and I use that book to learn how to be literated and now I also learn how something gotta be scribed and rote rite.

Well how this all leads to my riting you, that is quite a story and in my letters I splain how this unfolds and further envelops. In these letters I am telling you about adventures during one summer, with a couple of days or more added. I know you will become very exaggerated when you read about the adventures what Nicholas and Yours Truly have during the summer of 1952.

Chapter 1
A Saint in the Closet

Dear John,

Today I am in Bobby Anderson's apartment and he gotta go to the baffroom what is a very important thing for a guy to do because it is a scientifical fact that if a guy does not go to the baffroom when he feels he gotta go, something can bust open and in this way things can get very messy here and about in a small apartment such as the one where Bobby Anderson and his family resident. So Bobby Anderson goes off to the baffroom and I am standing there in the living room twiddling my thumbs. I am standing there all alone mainly because nobody else is in the apartment except for Bobby Anderson who is taking care of that very problem what I already menchun. So I start looking around a little and I jist happen to discover a notebook under more than a few dead socks and two shoes, what do not match, and some tin army soldgers in the bottom of Bobby Anderson's bedroom closet. So I take the notebook back into the living room because the light is much better near a widow and, if Bobby Anderson or one of his family members is all of a sudden to come into the bedroom, what I am doing in Bobby Anderson's bedroom closet is a thing more than somewhat hard to splain.

In that notebook Bobby Anderson got a lot of letters, every one of them addrest to you, John, and rite away I am very busy reading two and three and, because they are very short letters, I am reading more than a few. Some of them letters are about what Bobby Anderson and Yours Truly done and other stuff what I told Bobby Anderson and there is a lot of other stuff what got nothing to do with Yours Truly. But then I hear the terlet flushing and I know that I do not need to worry about Bobby Anderson busting open because Bobby Anderson jist solves that particle problem all by himself and probably jist in time. So I am about to put the notebook back in the closet under the two shoes, one black, one brown, and socks and toy tin soldgers but Bobby Anderson is out of the baffroom before I can even get away from the widow or even get close to the closet door and since I am nowhere near the bedroom closet, I stuff that notebook what I already menshun in the back of my pants and cover it with my shirt. I figger there ain't no wrong in borrowing that notebook, without Bobby Anderson's parmishun, when it got a lot to say about me.

Dear John,

I hate boring! I hate it! I hate being bored! Nothing is worser than being bored. It is a proven fact that summer is a boring time for many kids. The other part of the year is not all that much fun what with school and all but it ain't boring. School time ain't boring because Yours Truly got lots of idears about what to do to keep things exciting. But the summer can be boring. I want an exciting summer and I gotta figger out how to get it. I jist hate being bored.

As I often hear it stated within the past few days by many a citizen, young and old, here and about, "It's summertime and the living is easy." I hear this at times also coming from a Victrola in some second floor apartment and sometimes I even hear from an upstairs apartment across the street where Mrs. O'Reilly sings mostly about Irish eyes smiling and did your mother come from Ireland and stuff like that. But Mrs. O'Reilly only sings when she is happy but that ain't all that often. Her happy times are when Mr. O'Reilly is not home.

But maybe for me summertime is a time for me to jist relax on the stoop and get some reading done of my favorite riter who goes by the handle *Damon Runyon* who tells what it is like for guys and dolls to live in New York City but, as it is with me, I know what it is like to live in Williamsburg, Brooklyn. But I actually do not want to relax all summer on the stoop or anywhere else. What I really want is an exciting summer. Last summer was boring. I gotta do what I gotta do to make this a summer exciting. I hate boring.

Dear John,

I do not bother to learn how to read and rite until about a year ago, give or take a couple of months. I get along pretty good in school when teachers think I am stupid and illiterated. But I am not all that stupid. I am pretty smart but in my own way and definitely not in a school way.

I gotta give teachers at P.S. 18 some credit because they try really hardly and more than a few times to teach me but it don't never take. So this way I get to sit in the back of the room. Woird is out that I am hopeless.

But when I decide to learn to read and to rite, I do so by reading what this Damon Runyon scribes and that is likewise how I learn to rite. But my knowing how to read and rite is a most carefully kept secret, for Yours Truly has no desire whatsoever to let the teachers at P.S. 18 know about this recent development.

Dear John,

It is along about eleven bells and Yours Truly is sitting on the stoop and remembering some things what happen last year at the beginning of fourth grade. See the teachers at St. Mary's are called nuns and every Wednesday afternoon the kids what are Catholics gotta go to religion classes where the nuns torture us kids for three hours. I am remembering in particle the very first Wednesday afternoon last year at religion instruction.

These nuns hate us public school kids but Franky Alvareddi is one kid they really hate. The nun has it in for him from the start. He does not do anything to get her mad because what gets her mad is his name. The very first thing the nun does is unfold a paper and she starts reading our names. When she comes to Franky Alvareddi's name, the nun stops, looks up, and says, "Who is this Franky Alvareddi? Raise your hand."

Franky Alvareddi raises his hand. Now Franky is a real nice kid. He's real quiet and always polite and kinda shy.

The nun says, "You! Stand up when I talk to you!" Then she demands, "What kind of a name is Franky?"

Well Franky Alvareddi stands up and shakes his head and asks, "What do you mean, Sister? It is jist my name."

The nun says again but in a louder and more angry verse, "What kind of a name is Franky?"

Franky Alvareddi says, "It is an American name. I don't know. It's jist my name."

The nun says, "That is not your name in this school. There is no saint named Franky and if you are in this school, you will be called by the name of a saint. Your name in this school is Francis."

Franky Alvareddi says, "Please do not call me that name, Sister. It's a girl's name. My name is Franky."

"No, it is not! Your name is Francis. That is the name of a saint who is Saint Francis, a sissy."

Well that does not go over very good with Franky Alvareddi who jist stands there, first very still but then he starts shaking and he puts his hands up to his eyes.

The nun says, "Francis Alvareddi, stop acting like a girl. Sit down."

Franky Alvareddi sits down. He puts his head on the desk and covers his head with his hands. His shoulders move up and down shivering like. Franky is like that for the rest of the afternoon. The nun ignores him.

That afternoon I am walking home and I see Barry Dranski walk up to Franky Alvareddi and I hear him say, "Hi, Francis, a sissy."

Well Franky Alvareddi just stands there absolutely still. His face gets red. His shoulders start shivering. He looks like he is going to cry again.

I do not approve of Barry Dranski calling Franky Alavareddi "Francis, a sissy." So I walk up to Barry Dranski and I say, "Do not call Franky Alvareddi by the name Francis, a sissy."

Barry Dranski says, "Oh yeah? What are you going to do about it?"

I answer, "If you call Franky Alvareddi that name again, you will find out what I am going to do about it and I guarantee you will not like what I am going to do about it. You will never see it coming."

So for the rest of fourth grade at P.S. 18 he was Franky Alvareddi but at St. Mary's he was Francis, a sissy.

I wish I could tell that nun the same thing what I tell Barry Dranski. But at least word is out on the street and nobody in the neighborhood ever calls him Francis, a sissy, again. But Franky Alvareddi never seems to be the same kid from that time on. He was always real quiet but I never see him in the neighborhood. He never comes out of his apartment now. The nun calls what she does "Religious Instruction." I call is "religious destruction."

Things like that go on all the time at St. Mary's School but at P.S. 18 it is a lot easier. The teachers don't care what your name is and because I sit in the back of the classroom, I jist do whatever I want. The teachers think I am lazy but I am busy all the time. I am jist not busy doing what they want me to be doing.

The teachers at P.S. 18 try to get me to do homework and stuff like that. They try to scare me when they say I will grow up to be a bum. But at St. Mary's it is a lot different. The nuns do not care about my growing up to be a bum. They got bigger plans for me, like when last year that nun tells me, "Waste your time on earth and you are sure to waste your time in hell."

Dear John,

This afternoon I am back on the stoop and I am trying not to think about school but, trying not to think about it, does not work. I jist feel sorry for those kids who get tortured by the nuns every day of the week. I am very glad I do not go to St. Mary's except on Wednesday afternoons. My mom and dad want me to go to St. Mary's and get tortured all the time and they even got me on the waiting list. When my mom calls about once a week to see if I can get in, the nun, what's the Principal, always says the same thing. The Principal nun says, "Earnest is on the very bottom of the list and we have a very, very long list."

I know why I am on the bottom of the list. It's because two years ago I go to a Catholic School for one week when I used to live in Bay Ridge. Then the nuns tell my mom they only want the very best for me and that the public school is the very best for me. The next day I am out of Our Lady of Perpetual Help School and in P.S. 102.

Those nuns in Bay Ridge spred the rumor that Yours Truly does not get along all that good with nuns. So the nuns at St. Mary's hear about my rep-you-tay-shun and keep putting me on the bottom of the list and I am very happy to stay rite there at the bottom of their list.

But I digest from the topic of summertime when the living is easy and all. So for now I ain't gonna think no more about nuns what torture us public school kids on Wednesday afternoons.

Dear John,

I am sitting on the stoop and that is where you will find me every day this summer for about an hour, give or take a few minutes. I am on this very stoop in front of the apartment house where I live and I am reading about guys and dolls. But when I ain't reading about guys and dolls, I hope to be having an adventure or two or three or maybe more. I jist gotta think real hard about how to get one of those adventures going.

Dear John,

That notebook what Bobby Anderson rites is pretty good excepting for a few facts what he stretches pretty much. But that don't matter none because most everybody stretches a fact or two at least once in a while. Sometimes you jist gotta do some stretching to make a boring story inneresting, not that I would ever do anything like stretching the hard facts very far when the facts are truly hard but sometimes the facts jist need a little stretching especially when the facts are hardly true.

Dear John,

Today I am walking in front of Bobby Anderson's apartment house when Bobby Anderson appears at the top of the stoop and after some conversating about this and that and one thing and another, Yours Truly is invited up to Bobby Anderson's apartment on account of I got a secret to tell him but it is such a big and important secret that I cannot tell him about it in the open where some spy might be listening and we know from Senator McCarthy that Russian Commie spies are anywhere and everywhere. I tell Bobby Anderson that I accept his invitation and I will return shortly since I first have a very important errand to run. Although I do not mention it, the poipose for this errand is to fetch and bring back the notebook what I borrowed yesterday and I now wish to return to its riteful place under many a dead sock, shoes what don't match and toy army soldgers in the bottom of Bobby Anderson's bedroom closet.

Well after I get the notebook and slide it under my shirt, I am walking back toward Bobby Anderson's apartment house and I run into none other than my classmate, Nicholas, and since I almost always sit near him in school and since I read much about him in the letters what Bobby Anderson rites in his notebook which is presently stuck in the back of my pants, and since I think he can be a detraction while I place the notebook back in the bottom of Bobby Anderson's closet, I invite Nicholas along by saying as such, "Nicholas, you are invited to come up to Bobby Anderson's apartment and spend some time reminis sing about the good times we have in school and other stuff."

To which Nicholas responds as such, "I do not know of any good times what we have in school since that is a part of my life I wish to forget and this I make great efforts to do whenever I happen to remember."

When Nicholas states that he tries to remember to forget, such a response surprises Yours Truly since I never previously hear a statement from Nicholas that is so, as my upstairs neighbor, Gutsy Gus, would say "de profundis." But although Gutsy Gus is a most important citizen in this neighborhood, I must not spend time telling you about Gutsy Gus rite now for I intend to innerdeuce him in a later letter.

Nicholas accepts Bobby Anderson's invitation and in a short time Nicholas and Yours Truly are walking upstairs to Bobby Anderson's apartment. After we knock on the door and after Bobby Anderson opens the very same door, the first thing I say is, "Nicholas accepts your invitation and that is why he is here."

Bobby Anderson looks at me, turns his head a little to the side, lowers his eyebrows, smiles and says, "OK, Nicholas, I am glad you accept my invitation."

Bobby Anderson understands that sometimes Yours Truly invents things, such as an invitation.

After we step into his living room, Bobby Anderson closes the door and asks, "What is this big secret of which you speak?"

Because I forget about the big secret what is the reason for our visit, I start to make one up by saying, "The big secret is and it is indeed a very big secret, such a very big secret that…"

But I am saved by the bell and by this I mean Bobby Anderson says, "Hold that thought! I'll be rite back." With that Bobby Anderson is off and running down the hall and into the baffroom. That worries me when a guy can't hold it and goes running off to the baffroom like that. That only happens to me after I drain some bottles of my dad and mom's Rheingold. But it is better for a guy to run off to the baffroom than for a guy to bust open rite in front of Yours Truly.

Nicholas is now in the kitchen sticking his head in Anderson's icebox and that gives me jist enough time to get that notebook out of my pants and back under lots of socks and shoes and old toys in the bottom of Bobby Anderson's bedroom closet where I am kneeling when I hear the terlet flush and the icebox door close and that gives me jist enough time to shove the notebook under lots of socks and shoes and old toy tin soldgers but unfortunately that does not give me enuff time to make my way out of the closet and back into the living room. Nicholas and Bobby Anderson come looking for me and find me in the bedroom closet on my knees. So, since I am already kneeling on my knees, a thing what many a Catholic is likely to be doing, quick as a wink I lift my hands like I'm saying a prayer. Nicholas asks me what I am doing in the closet looking like I am praying and I look at Nicholas and Bobby Anderson and I say, "I am indeed praying for I jist have a vision of a saint who invites me to follow him into this closet and this is a thing what I do and that is the cause of your finding me on my knees in this closet. This saint tells me to follow him and then he walks rite into this very closet rite here and then he disappears."

Nicholas axes me if the saint says something. Again quick as a wink I say, "Yes. Rite! I almost forget. He tells me there are Commie spies all over and…" Then I cannot think of anything else the saint tells me so I say, "He tells me lots more, many things of which I cannot tell nobody else, except maybe Pius, the Pope."

Well that is such a good and convincing story that I build on it more than somewhat and I tell Nicholas and Bobby Anderson the saint comes to me before and that is the secret of which I wish to convoy. Then I jist keep building on it some more and I say, "The saint wants the three of us to do some important work this summer what can help save the world from the bad guys and Commie spies and all."

Well Nicholas shakes his head like he agrees immediately and speaks as such, "This is a very special and holy thing when a saint appears and tells us what it is we can do to save the world from the bad guys and Commie spies and all."

Bobby Anderson, however, speaks as such, "I am sorry to decline the invitation to save the world from the bad guys and Commie spies and all. The reason for my declining is that, as you may know, I have been chosen by the *Send this Poor Boy to Camp Fund* and tomorrow I get on a bus and head upstate to a camp in the Catskills and I will be gone for a very long time, about a month."

So I respond by saying as such, "Yes, of course, the saint what appears to me, in what is called an apparition, in the closet knows very well you are heading to the Catskills tomorrow but what he means is that you, Bobby Anderson, will have the opportunity to help save the world from Commies and other bad guys when you return in about one month and since this is jist the very beginning of the summer you will have opportunities to jern our cause when you return." So with that said and a few other things what don't amount to a hill of beans, we bid ado to Bobby Anderson and wish him luck and all that sort of thing for he is very fortunate to have been chosen by those who wish to send a poor boy to summer camp.

Dear John,

That part about saving the world from the bad guys and commie spies is a most entertaining thought. A thought such as this could lead to adventurous actions and that could make this summer a most pleasant time of the year, perhaps more than going to the camp upstate what is known as the *Send this Poor Boy to Camp Fund*.

Indeed Nicholas and Yours Truly are jist the guys who could pull off such an adventure mainly because we do not look like two guys who can pull off such an adventure. This is an invitation we are ready to accept and are more than a little willing to save the world from the before mentioned Commie spies and other bad guys. It is a very good thing to have this apparition of a saint appearing to me and telling me how to save the world and all. Now all we gotta do is to get started on this adventure.

Chapter 2

The Fleetwood

Dear John,

This very next morning I am sitting on the stoop of the apartment house on Leonard Street where I live and I am thinking about this and that and one thing or another while munching on a Three Musketeers for which I pay a hefty price of five cents. I am also opening my book, what is titled *The Damon Runyon Omnibus*, to page 102 where there is a most sorrowful discussion about what these present times lack in dolls like Cleopatra and Helen of Troy who are very well practiced in the art of knocking off guys. Then there is Lorelie who is a very beautiful doll who sings while she combs her long beautiful hair and invites sailors to turn their ship to a rocky cliff. She jist sings as she watches sailors drown. Some dolls, I guess, get their kicks in strange ways. Personally I am more than somewhat relieved these particular dolls of which Damon Runyon scribes have gone the way of the dinosaurs and Neanderthals. However, I do not believe all the Neanderthals are extinguished since every once in a while here and there I see some even walking around this particular neighborhood. Likewise even now-a-days there is somewhat more than a slight chance that some dolls get their kicks by leading guys to reck and ruin. A guy such as Yours Truly needs to be aware of dangerous dolls such as Lorelie and those other knock-off dolls who create circumstances what lead a guy to crash onto rocky cliffs.

Although holding the book and munching on the Three Musketeers requires some juggling and attention to such things as dangerous dolls, my thoughts nevertheless turn to the adventure about which I have already mentioned. As I am deep in thought, I hardly notice a big beautiful black Fleetwood turn rite from Grand Street and glide down Leonard. The streets of Williamsburg are seldom graced by such a stretched beauty with six door and I am especially speaking of Leonard where one is more likely to find mostly jalopies, many of which are lacking one thing or another like hubcaps and even tires. Some jalopies still look as if they could depart this street if only their batteries had not been snatched in the middle of a recent night. I must mention that, although this Fleetwood is a most beautiful car, it has a problem; the tailpipe is puffing out small clouds of dark smoke and this is never a good sign for an engine for it connotes a very unhealthy connotation. Well anyway, this Fleetwood, stretched into a six door limo, slows to a stop rite in front of my stoop and, after two huge puffs and one backfire, the driver shuts off the engine. The smoke gathers into a large cloud but in a moment or two, what with some help from a gust of wind, the smoke drifts up, up and away.

A very big guy with a deeply scarred mug under a black chauffeur's cap, steps out, stands next to the Fleetwood and opens the middle door. An ankle in high heels appears beneath the middle door, steps onto the street and what follows is one very classy doll, the likes of which I never see on Leonard. In fact, I never ever before see such a classy doll anywhere, not even in the Sears and Roebuck Cattle logs what contain some pictures of some very classy dolls indeed. This doll is wrapped in a coat what would make any animal happy to relinquish its fur or, for that what is under the coat, a sailor is likely to head for rocky cliffs.

After this doll disembarks from the Fleetwood and steps away from the limousine, the very big guy, with a deeply scarred mug under a black chauffeur's cap, shuts the door gently. This gentle touch is more than somewhat surprising since this big guy looks like he does nothing with a gentle touch. The doll never once looks around before exiting the Fleetwood and this is a sign that this doll is not from these whereabouts as she does not know that one should always look around prior to making any move especially when a doll is carrying a pocketbook that could be quickly snatched by a passerby moving fast on a bicycle or roller skates. Jist then the doll speaks to the driver in language I do not know, but some of what she says is in English and what I hear her say sounds something like, "Boris, back one hour, nyet! Not one voird. Da sveedanya."

With a nod of the old noggin Big Boris agrees to whatever the doll says. I think she wants Big Boris to keep it a secret that she is here but, if so, you can gather from what you just read, this secret is not in any way binding on Yours Truly. As this doll turns away from the Fleetwood and starts walking across the sidewalk, she suddenly stops after a startled step and notices Yours Truly sitting on the very stoop she is about to assent. I can hardly not mention once again what a great looker this doll is, even more so since she is about two feet in front of my Three Musketeers. Since this is a totally new experience what with having a doll such as this two feet from my Three Musketeers and since I do not know how to handle this particular situation, I do the first and only thing what comes natural. I hold out my three Musketeers and axes, "Wanna bite?"

The doll looks at me with two of the biggest britest blue eyes framed by flowing blond hair and says, "Nyet. I mean, no. I do not vwanna bite of that candy bar but I will take a big bite out of you if you breathe a voird to anyone about me here to see August Tin." With that the doll opens her pocketbook and out comes five green clams, all neat and clean and rapped in a rubber band and she hands me the roll of the finest five bucks I ever witness in all my life. It is a problem when a guy is holding a candy bar in his rite hand and a book in his left hand when offered a gift such as the five bucks. The natural solution is that one hand must sacrifice something. Thus I drop the Three Musketeers on the step beneath me and take the doll's offering of the five bucks. Five bucks for half a Three Musketeers what originally cost five cents is not a bad trade. The doll speaks with jist a little accent, "This ees vwat you call hush money. You know how to hush, don't you, Steve? You jist put your lips together and zip."

Why this doll calls me Steve is one of two mysteries I will not easily solve. The second mystery is that I do not know anyone by the handle, August Tin, in this apartment house or any of the whereabouts in this block or even in this neighborhood. The doll pronounces the name of this unknown citizen in such a way that it sounds like the gust of wind what cleared the smoke from the Fleetwood. But, at any rate, I nod in agreement which is a most unusual thing for me to do because I am not such a guy who nods and I am not all that agreeable to almost anything except maybe a greasy hamburger at Randy's Restaurant, especially if that hamburger is accompanied by a big chocolate malted, but in the case of which I am accounting, I find it somewhat safe to jist nod in agreement. But behind my back I keep my fingers crossed what cancels out the nod for it is a well-known fact that two fingers crossed beat a nod or two every time and for that reason I can tell you, John, about this event.

It is a most puzzling mystery that a doll such as this is making her way up the stoop and approaching the front door to this apartment house. But the main thing is that this door has hinges that sadly lack attention of the 3-in-1 kind and thus it does a swell imitation of the creaking door one is likely to hear if ever you have your radio tuned to Inner Sanctum. Thus from my experience, I am aware that a gentle lady-like push on the front door is insufficient to open it. So I place Guys and Dolls on the stoop, stuff the hush money in my pocket, run up the stoop and reach the door before the doll and, with a very hard shove, the door swings open but much more easily than I expect and so I land on the entrance floor with my feet sticking out through the doorway. A slight breeze whisks over Yours Truly as the doll steps over me, glances back, smiles and ascends the stairs. I look up from the floor and watch the doll take each step. The seams on the back of her nylons are straight as an arrow. The seams rise up from her high heeled shoes and disappear under her fur coat. It is good that I am already on the floor because this doll is truly such a knockout. I am feeling like a sailor what got crashed on a rocky cliff.

So after getting back on my feet, I have every intention of finding out where the doll is heading and who this August Tin person may be. However, it is a very strong possibility that this Lassie has the wrong address and is barking up the wrong stairs. Now it seems best for a guy under circumstances such as these, as what I have mentioned, to retreat and to sit still on the stoop until the coast is clear and to continue being very careful thereafter. But I do not do that. Instead I tiptoe very fast up the stairs and stop near the top of the landing of the fourth floor and that is when

I hear a door open and I hear a verse saying something that sounds like "Salvay matter." But then I hear the woirds, "De fumo in flammam" and I know who it is that speaks these woirds and it is none other than Gutsy Gus who lives in apartment 2B on the fourth floor. I do not really know eggsactly what those woirds mean but Gutsy Gus is a guy who likes to catch on to a phrase and repeat it very often and for Gutsy Gus that which can be said in Latin is a far better way to say almost anything. In fact, Gutsy Gus says these same Latin woirds, which I have already mentioned, so very often that I know the woirds but I am not so sure of their meaning. Gutsy Gus loves to say things like that in Latin and that can be a lot, really nearly all the time. To give you an example, one time we are yacking away on the stoop about one thing or another and about this and that when Gutsy Gus is telling me about some guys what lived a long time ago in Rome and Gutsy Gus lights up a Lucky Strike and he says, "De fumo in flammam." Gutsy Gus tells me it means something like you should stop smoking because you can start a fire but, more often than not, Gutsy Gus tells me it means you might go from the smoke into the fire. Why Gutsy Gus tells this to the doll about smoke and fire is another mystery for me to solve at some future time.

But then I hear the doll speak, "August tin, it is vwery portant for me to come and spake vit you todays because ..."

But then the door closes and there is nothing more for me to hear, not even by placing my ear on the hallway door of 2B on the fourth floor since Gutsy Gus and the doll are whispering in a verse so low it is a wonder they can hear each other. Therefore, I very quietly back down the stairs. There is good reason for me to back down the stairs and this is the reason: should the 2B door open on the fourth floor, I am jist walking without a care in the world up the stairs and not

18

down the stairs and thus I reduce the evidence that I have been trying to listen through the hallway door.

When I finally get to the bottom of the stairs while still stepping down backwards, I turn around, open the front door of the apartment house and I see the coast is clear because there is little chance the Fleetwood is hiding somewhere on this street.

I sit down on the stoop and consider the mystery about this doll who climbs four flights of stairs to knock on apartment 2B on the fourth floor for the poipose of telling Gutsy Gus something important. You may also wonder why an apartment on the fourth floor has an address of 2B, and not 3B or 4B, but that is jist another one of those many mysteries and suspicious goings on what Nicholas and Yours Truly need to investigate.

Dear John,

I take a fast break and go upstairs to apartment 3B on the second floor where I live and I pour myself a big glass of cold water and drink it. This is a very good thing to do on a hot day in Brooklyn.

Then I return to my seat on the stoop and start considering what is taking place this afternoon. It is a strange thing, this memory of a thing what very recently takes place because it is a well-known scientifical fact that we sometimes fail to notice something when it is taking place but remember something about it after it takes place. So, to give you an example of such a memory, as I am still sitting on the stoop looking at the five bucks in my hand and the Three Musketeers melting on the stoop below, my thoughts are returning to the events of the past few minutes. I am remembering, when the doll pulls out the wad of bills, I see something shiny sticking up out of the doll's pocketbook and it looks like this doll may have something big and heavy with a very shiny pearl cover or maybe a handle. I do not know what this heavy and shiny something is but I also remember the doll quick as a wink shoves it back into the bottom of her pocketbook and covers it with a hanky. I do recall the doll saying, "You never see that" and she looks at me in a most unpleasant way which is quite a turn around, for this doll has a most pleasant face under all other circumstances, what I thus far notice, accept for this first time unpleasant face. Well to promise her I never see that, I shake my head this time from side to side and shrug my shoulders. In this case I do not even have to cross my fingers because I do not know what the shiny something with a pearl cover is and so I never do see it.

Dear John,

It is now fifty-five minutes after Big Boris drives the black six-door Fleetwood down Leonard and turns left onto Montrose, and I am downstairs on the stoop with my notebook and I am busy writing about what is taking place as events unfold. I am expecting the doll who is visiting Gutsy Gus in 2B on the fourth floor to appear any second.

Jist as I am completing that last sentence, a black cloud of smoke turns rite from Grand Street and slowly coasts down Leonard and stops in front of the apartment house where Yours Truly lives. Three unfortunate citizens are crossing Leonard in back of the Fleetwood and are now standing on the sidewalk, holding onto a lamp post while coughing and brushing soot from their clothes. Although there is a parking space directly in front of this apartment house, Big Boris double parks, exits and leans against the front door of the black six door Fleetwood awaiting his passenger who is nowhere to behold. I look at the parking space and attempt to measure the length of the Fleetwood and I realize that Big Boris is wise not to park in the open space which appears to be long enough for a Studebaker or maybe even a Packard but not a six door Fleetwood.

Big Boris removes a pocket watch from his vest and shakes his head. He has been leaning against the Fleetwood for about five minutes, give or take a few. Then a green DeSoto suburban drives down Leonard, stops in back of the Fleetwood and gives Big Boris three very loud long beeps and a hand gesture demanding that the Fleetwood gotta get out of the way and then he includes another hand gesture what is actually a finger gesture what I do not wish to describe further.

Big Boris opens the Fleetwood's front door, climbs back into the Fleetwood, starts the motor resulting in a very thick cloud of smoke what shoots black soot all over the DeSoto's windshield. The driver of the DeSoto gets out of his car with a baseball bat swinging from his rite hand. Jist then the Fleetwood backfires and the driver ducks back into the DeSoto. The backfire sounds a lot like three bullets firing from a very big gun.

The driver of the DeSoto sits still and watches the Fleetwood drive down Leonard and turn left onto Montrose. Then the driver gets out and with his shirt sleeve wipes some of the black soot off the windshield. After that the driver walks over to the stoop and asks, "Kid, you see what dat guy in the Caddy done?"

I answer as follows, "Sir, as you can see, I am reading this here book what is called *The Damon Runyon Omnibus* and as a result I do not see anything at all what happens. I do not even see the smoke what comes out of the Fleetwood. In fact, I don't even see any Fleetwood."

He asks, "You don't see the Fleetwood?"

I answer, "What Fleetwood?"

As the DeSoto drives down Leonard, it slows at every intersection and the driver is looking real careful both rite and left.

After a few minutes the cloud reappears on Leonard and stops for jist a short time in front of this apartment house.

Without exiting Big Boris sits for about five minutes, give or take a few, and then drives away. Big Boris and his black smoking Fleetwood repeat this activity about five more times, give or take a few.

I hear the door open at the top of the stoop behind me and, since I am sitting on the third step from the bottom of the stoop, when I turn, I see only an ankle in high heels on the top step. I do not hesitate to mention that this is indeed a most attractive ankle. The doll steps down from the top step, floats onto the sidewalk and looks up the street and, without moving her lips, her face asks, "Where is Boris?" I respond in as kind a verse available to me, "Boris has been driving around for almost an hour."

The doll looks at her wristwatch and then at me and speaks but she is such a doll that I am detracted and I am not able to remember eggsactly woird for woird what lovely woirds she speaks. I am only able to state that she does not want me to speak a woird to anyone that she is here and, if I do say anything, Big Boris will return and cut out my tongue. So I nod in agreement but I have already prepared my two fingers behind my back and I thus cancel out the agreement that I am not speaking a woird about this. But in any case I do not feel deposed to speak about such a matter as this because Big Boris would leave me speechless. For that reason it is a very good thing that I am not speaking about it but then there ain't no harm in my writing about it.

Dear John,

These goings on are indeed very mysterious and so suspicious that it takes two investigators to solve such mysteries. So I walk over to Nicholas's apartment and inform him about the mysterious goings on what I jist witness.

I splain to Nicholas as such, "An adventure or two can develop from such mysterious and suspicious goings on."

Nicholas agrees by stating, "I am all up and ready for an adventure or two because a summer in Brooklyn can be boring."

I say, "Well then I hereby invite you to help with an investigation about these very mysterious and suspicious goings on."

I am indeed glad Nicholas agrees to this investigation. Such goings on can usher in the beginning of the very adventure of which I previously proposed to Nicholas.

Nicholas suggests as such, "What is needed thus far is one or two more appearances of that saint what appears in the closet and evaporates into thin air."

I agree and say, "I will do my best to conjureate up another meeting with the saint whose advice I will seek and most certainly follow. It is likely that this saint will appear to me the very next time I step into a closet. Therefore, I will leave you for now as I am in search of a closet."

Dear John,

But I forget to tell you about how earlier today Big Boris and the doll exit Leonard. Well it happens that the doll stands in front of the apartment house looking up Leonard and sometimes down Leonard but it is a very unlikely that the Fleetwood is coming up Leonard unless Big Boris drives the wrong way for Leonard is a one way street going south. All the while the doll is looking at her wristwatch which appears to be a very expensive time piece indeed. She wraps the fur coat tight around her and this is also very suspicious mainly because this is a very warm afternoon in June and a sweater is more than what is needed since the air is quite warm, some might even say it is a hot day. But I mention this doll looking both ways and looking at her watch and doing these other suspicious activities because they suggest that the doll is more than a little nervous about standing outside this apartment house.

Big Boris seems to have taken a coffee break or is otherwise occupied because the doll is waiting more than a few minutes and her patience is not holding up all that well. The next suspicious activity is that the doll is walking down Leonard in a very quick click of her heels what are very long and very thin heels indeed. And before long the doll is looking over her left shoulder and crossing the street. At that very moment I look up and see none other than the mother of Gutsy Gus, who is otherwise known here and about as Mrs. Manichy, walking down Leonard from Grand Street. It appears that the doll does not wish to meet and greet the mother of Gutsy Gus.

Jist as the doll is on the other side of Stagg, a cloud of smoke chugs up and pauses in front of the stoop. Big Boris is looking around but I catch his eye by waving my hand which he has difficulty seeing until the smoke disperses with the help of a gust of wind. I point down the street toward Scholes and Big Boris sees the doll walking at a very fast clip. Jist as Big Boris drives off, Mrs. Manichy is standing in front of the stoop and although she is coughing more than somewhat, she stops and watches the Fleetwood drive down the street. The Fleetwood stops on the other side near Scholes and through the cloud of smoke I can barely see the doll opens the middle door, gets in and with another cloud of heavy black smoke the Fleetwood exits Leonard.

Chapter 3

Gutsy and Mrs. O'Reilly

Dear John,

It is along about that time for me to tell you what I know about Gutsy Gus who is a resident of the before mentioned 2B on the fourth floor in this apartment house where he resides with his mother and there is a rumor that Gutsy Gus has a father who resides also in 2B on the fourth floor. I think I see him one time about a year ago but it is generally agreed by citizens in and around here that Mr. Manichy is more fictional than factal.

However, be that as it maybe, the first thing to tell you is that at first I do not know who the doll is talking about when she says my upstairs neighbor's name because nobody around here knows him by that name, August Tin, and she pronounces his name like a gust of wind followed by the woird, tin. In contrast, Mrs. Manichy, the mother of Gutsy Gus, calls him by a name what ends in teen, something like August Teen. In this neighborhood he is known as Gutsy Gus and that is what all the citizens in the hereabouts call him and more often than not he answers to the shorter name, Gutsy. There is good reason for this moniker since Gutsy Gus is well known for his gutsy attitude and more than that by his gutsy actions.

Why he lives with his mother and maybe a father is an easy answer on account of Gutsy Gus, having graduated from St. John's Prep just last year, is about seventeen or eighteen and now a student at St John's University which unfortunately for Gutsy Gus is no longer located nearby on Lewis Avenue rite here in Brooklyn. Not so long ago, St. John's College was situated near St John's Prep which was an easy stroll from Leonard but St. John's College has moved way out to a place called Queens and that makes it a very long walk from Leonard. St. John's has also been promoted from a college to a university and such a promotion from college to university is more than a big deal for Gutsy Gus who now finds it worth his while to travel by train and bus for about two hours each way to St. John's University and back home. I know a thing or two about such matters mainly because more than once or twice me and Gutsy Gus kill time sitting on this very stoop upon which I am presently perched and we chew the rag. At such times I splain why going to school is a boring waste of time and Gutsy Gus splains the meaning of life and similar matters what are, to me, not all that important. But I pretend matters such as the meaning of life are important. But that is a secret what needs to be kept from Gutsy Gus.

I will splain more about Gutsy Gus later but it is now suppertime as my mother informs me by yelling out the front window of apartment 3B on the second floor.

Dear John,

Today me and Nicholas are holding a special meeting at Randy's Restaurant. Yours Truly is chowing down a delicious, greasy hamburger with chopped roar onions and sucking up a chocolate malted. I can afford such a meal what with the five smackers I earn from the doll. I earn this do-re-mi by promising the doll not to say a woird about the mysterious events what take place on the stoop yesterday afternoon.

At this meeting in Randy's Restaurant I am informing Nicholas of the mysterious goings on what take place on the stoop yesterday afternoon. I am next telling Nicholas about the Saint what appears to me last night when I am standing in my bedroom closet.

At this point in the conversation Nicholas axes a very good question which he states as such, "Does this saint in the closet inform you of his name?"

Such a good question deserves an equally swell answer but before responding, Yours Truly stops to think. I am thinking. I am still thinking when Nicholas looks at me, leans his head in, as if he is waiting for an answer, but I am still thinking. The following is what I am thinking. Gutsy Gus says more than a thing or two in Latin, and many a saint is called by a name what sounds more than a little like a Latin woird, and many of the woirds what Gutsy Gus says, in this Latin language, end with a sound like *us*. By now Nicholas is leaning his head so far antiseepating my answer that he is just about to fall on top of the table. I look down and then up with my eyes raised high giving off just as spiritual a look as I can muster and I respond to Nicholas's question in this manner, "I ask the saint in the closet this very question just last night and he informs me of his name what is Saint Closétus."

I must pause here to inform you that I pronounce the saints name so that it does not sound like closet but it sound more like Clo see tus and the see part is louder than the Clo and the tus, just like what I hear in a Latin woird. So when I spell the name, as you may notice already, I place an accent mark above the *e* and spell our saint's name as Saint

Closétus. That way it fits both with the closet and with a sound much like Latin about which I already mention. It also has a classy style what with the accent over the *é*.

Well getting back to the conversation, Nicholas smiles and nods showing that he is very pleased indeed with knowing the saint's name what is to be Saint Closétus and we are both happy about that proposition what has now been clarified and all, for it is always unsettling to know a fact without having a name for that fact.

So while munching on the last hamburger bite, Yours Truly is thinking up and figgering out what else Saint Closétus tells us. To this end I begin with another fact what Saint Closétus tells me which is about the Fleetwood driver's name which is Boris when Nicholas stops me in mid-sentence. It is not even a second later Nicholas and Yours Truly say at the eggsact same time, "Boris!" and we shake our heads because we know Boris is a Russian name.

Nicholas puts in his two cents, "Remember a couple of Sundays ago the priest gives a sermon? He says that Senator McCarthy is making a black list of all them Commies what are infilterating the government and movies and even the Catholic Church."

Although I do not actually remember that sermon or almost any other sermon, I wish to support Nicholas for his attempt to think and to remember some things. Because this thinking and remembering is a rare thing for Nicholas, I respond as such, "I remember and it all fits together."

Nicholas buts in and says, "Rite! It all fits. Boris is a Commie and you saw the doll wearing the fur coat in the summer and that cements it! That the doll is from Russia and every Russian wears big coats and everybody from Russia is a Commie."

Nicholas is getting very excited while conversating about this subject so in the interest of continuing his excitement Yours Truly adds as follows, "And sometimes the doll speaks like with a Russian accent."

Nicholas can hardly stand the excitement so he stands up and nearly knocks the table over and says, "The doll speaks with a Commie accent. Then I hear just the other day on the radio that Senator Joseph McCarthy is investigating the un-Americans and he is writing a list in black ink so people know that some movie stars are Commies. Even Charlie Chaplin and Edward G. Robinson and about 300 others are on the Commy black ink list."

I ask, "How do you know Charlie Chaplin and Edward G. Robinson are Commies?"

Nicholas answers, "Senator McCarthy writes their names in the black ink list. That's why. But it's even worser than that because Senator Joseph McCarthy says there are 205 card players at Commy parties having a good time and all when they are supposed to be working in the government of the United States." Nicholas adds in a whisper, "But it's even worse than worser if these Commies are rite here and one of them is Gutsy Gus who goes to St. Johns and maybe he is a Commie infilterating the Catholic Church."

I am impressed that Nicholas listens to sermons and even tries to get something from them. While in church Yours Truly has other very important things to think about.

Nicholas then tells me more, "Last Sunday the priest says this Russian woman named Bella Somebody one night leaves the party what the Commies are having and takes a bowl full of beans with her and then she goes off and joins the party down the street at the Catholic Church and that's where she spills the beans. Bella tells the priest that the commies are taking their beans and going to universities and even becoming Catholic priests by joining seminaries where they eat lots and lots of beans."

Because I need time to figger out what Nicholas just said and because I hope to keep this enthusiasm on the up and up but still have a little fun with the whole thing, I add, "Maybe Gutsy Gus eats beans. Have you ever seen any of this un-American behavior?"

Nicholas seriously shrugs his shoulders, shakes his head and says, "Maybe." But then Nicholas stops talking and puts his hand to his chin and asks, "But beans? Is that what the soldgers eat like most of the time?"

"Rite!" I answer. "Do you think the commies infilterated the army too?"

Nicholas responds, "Maybe."

But then I get back to thinking what Nicholas says about that sermon and it takes me a couple of more minutes to desifer Nicholas's interpretation but when I figger out what the priest probably meant, I put in my two cents, "And that is why the doll is so secret about everything and telling me not to spill none of the beans about this to anyone or else Big Boris, the Commie, is coming back to cut out my tongue."

"Golly gee wilikers! That's rite. I seen that in the movies where Commies and other bad guys cut out peoples' tongues when they spill the beans what are filled with commie secrets."

I notice for some time that Nicholas has intelligent idears only some of the times but then some of the other times his idears are not all that intelligent. His intelligence has ups and downs. With Nicholas you just never know about his ups and downs.

Then I remember Saint Closétus and I think up a great

thing he tells me that helps the commie story more than a little. I tell Nicholas what the saint tells me and I use a spooky verse to say, "You and Nicholas have to save the world from commie spies who live in your very own neighborhood and they are doing bad things like infilterateating the Catholic Church."

Well that message from Saint Closétus does the trick for Nicholas, especially the way I say it in a spooky verse. So Nicholas and Yours Truly make a pledge to do everything we can to save the world from these commies, especially these very ones what are infilterating the Catholic Church rite here in our very own neighborhood of Williamsburg, Brooklyn. Although Nicholas agrees, I can see from the look on his face he is not totally sure about what I just say and what he agrees to but one good thing comes out of it and that is he says nothing more about beans.

Dear John,

Today about eleven bells Nicholas and Yours Truly are out taking a walk around the neighborhood in search of an adventure or two. Well when we pass rite in front of Randy's Restaurant, one whiff from whatever is on his grill informats us about our first adventure. See in Randy's Restaurant you can get the best greasiest hamburgers you ever want. Well since I am still in some of the do-re-mi as a result of my earnings from the doll, I invite Nicholas to partake of one of Randy's burgers and a malted is included in the invite. My poipose is to talk Nicholas into one or more adventures so we can both get through this summer without being bored. Nicholas and Yours Truly agree that last summer was not all that much fun so between chowing down and sucking up we are planning to make this summer just a bit more adventuresome. This summer is off to a good start what with a hamburger and a chocolate malted at Randy's Restaurant.

Dear John,

This whole Commie conspiracy fits together except for Gutsy Gus who earns that handle because all the citizens here and about consider Gutsy Gus to be a very upstanding citizen and indeed a very brave guy since it is well known here and everywhere, at least in walking distance, that Gutsy Gus defends people what need defending and he is quite capable of doing so since he wins both the wrestling and boxing championships for all of Brooklyn when he attends St. Johns Prep. As to how he defends people what need defending, I will give you a very good example. I already mention Mrs. O'Reilly who lives upstairs across Leonard, and may still be choking on the smoke from the Fleetwood which I describe in some detail in my epistle as of yesterday. However, about a month ago, give or take a day or two, Mrs. O'Reilly is screaming out her window and the woird she states repeatedly in a most loud verse is, "Help!" No one on the street pays much attention because people on the street conclude that since there is no smoke there is no fire and therefore no hurry. It's like Gutsy Gus says, "No fumo, no flammam," what means no smoke, no fire! Actually I made that up. Gutsy Gus never says that but I like the way it sounds.

So most people just continue walking to their planned destinations and do their best to ignore the screaming from the upstairs window. It is also not the first time Mrs. O'Reilly is heard screaming for help along about this time of day shortly after Mr. O'Reilly staggers up the street while grabbing lamp posts along the way to keep from falling flat on his face which happens more than once in the last few weeks. I too can hear Mrs. O'Reilly screaming, "Help!" but there is little for me to do about it as I am sitting on the stoop very much interested in a story by Damon Runyon. But my interest is interrupted when the window in apartment 2B on the fourth floor opens and Gutsy Gus sticks his head out and looks to see if Mrs. O'Reilly needs help. By this time several citizens are standing around and debating if Mrs. O'Reilly needs help since she is screaming, "Help!"

Shortly after the front door of the apartment house opens fast, Gutsy Gus jumps down from the top of the stoop and, just missing my head by an inch or two, he lands with both feet on the sidewalk. He and his feet are immediately racing across the street and up the stoop and into the apartment house where Mrs. O'Reilly is screaming.

This is shortly followed by much louder screaming coming from the apartment window but this screaming does not sound like that of Mrs. O'Reilly. Then all the screaming stops like as if someone turns off a radio. In a minute or two Gutsy Gus appears on the stoop of that apartment house and he is holding Mrs. O'Reilly in his arms and he walks into the middle of the street, puts his hand up and stops a black Ford. Gutsy Gus says a woird or two to the driver who gets out and opens the back door and Gutsy Gus with Mrs. O'Reilly still in his arms sits in the back seat and the Ford drives off. In less than half an hour a paddy wagon comes screaming down the street and two cops jump out and in no time at all they are hauling Mr. O'Reilly into the back of the wagon and locking the door.

Since the events at that time are very exciting indeed, I accidentally close the book and lose my place in the Damon Runyon Omnibus and I am paging through to find where I leaf off when Mr. Pitsacola, who owns the apartment house where much activity has recently taken place, drives up in his grey 1950 DeSoto Custom hardtop, 4-Door Sedan, and parallel parks without tapping bumpers either on the car in front or the one behind. I am always impressed when I witness parallel parking such as accomplished by Mr. Pitsacola. After this impressive accomplishment, Mr. Pitsacola steps out of the DeSoto and walks into the apartment house while all the time he is carefully watching where he is stepping. After several minutes, give or take a minute or two, Mr. Pitsacola exits the building, walks to the rear of the DeSoto, and opens the trunk. He then takes out a bucket and a mop. He opens a faucet on the side of the building, fills the bucket with water and with mop in hand Mr. Pitsacola reenters the building. About fifteen minutes later, give or take a minute or two, Mr. Pitsacola exits the building with the bucket and the mop and he pours out the water into the sewer on the street corner. I can see the contents of the bucket and the water is pink with real dark red spots.

Dear John,

I do not hear a woird about the events of that day until the next day when I am sitting on the stoop thumbing through the Damon Runyon Omnibus while continuing my search for the place I leaf off in the story when Gutsy Gus walks down the stoop and I ask, "Gutsy Gus, what happens yesterday when I see you running into the apartment house and coming out with Mrs. O'Reilly neatly tucked away in your arms?"

To this Gutsy Gus responds, "When I get upstairs, I hear very loud screaming and so I kick in the apartment door and see Patty O'Reilly punching Margaret O'Reilly in the face and she is bleeding pretty bad. So I grab Patty O'Reilly by his collar and with one punch to his fat belly and another to his chin, he is on the floor screaming his own head off but then he gets up off the floor and tries to take a punch at me but he misses. As I step back Mrs. O'Reilly slams Patty with a frying pan. He then sinks to the floor and is quite unconscious. Then I get Margaret to the Emergency Room at St. Mary's Hospital. They sew up her face with twenty stitches and I guess she'll be OK in a couple of days."

I tell you about this event as one example as to why my upstairs neighbor is known as Gutsy Gus by citizens here and around Williamsburg, Brooklyn. Although there is much evidence to the contrary, it is not easy to believe that Gutsy Gus is a Commie who is infilterating the Catholic Church. But then being a gutsy guy may be just the kind of cover for a commie spy.

Chapter 4

Party Line

Dear John,

Nicholas and Yours Truly are having an emergency meeting at Randy's Restaurant and we are each sucking on a two cents plain mainly because, after adventures what include several hamburgers and malteds at Randy's Restaurant in the last two days, we are just about flat broke and are definitely flat broke after we pay the check on these two cent plains.

So we propose what we call a proposition and that means we propose to get to the bottom of this mystery of the doll and Gutsy Gus and Big Boris although we already know activities such as what we see are about Commies infilterating the Catholic Church and becoming priests and nuns.

Nicholas adds to the already proposed proposition by stating, "It is indeed important to follow up on this investigation with lots of action but first of all it is totally necessary that we have a code name for it is a routine thing to have a code name for an investigation of such importance, which of course is saving the world from all them Commies, especially those we already know to be Commies namely Big Boris and the doll."

Nicholas further suggests, "We should also have important secret spy tools."

I agree and ask, "Do you have a secret decoder ring?"

Nicholas answers, "No, not any more. I had a very good secret decoder ring that worked real swell but I no longer own it due to my meeting Lucky Luigi on Grand Street. About a month ago I am walking along minding my own business when Lucky Luigi along with two of his very big friends admire my secret decoder ring and Lucky Luigi and his two very big friends ask me to take the ring off my finger so Lucky Luigi can admire the secret decoder ring. But then after Lucky Luigi admires my secret decoder ring, he just walks away and forgets to give the secret decoder ring back."

Although I personally do not encounter an incident such as this involving Lucky Luigi, I hear from several other young citizens who are at a loss of one thing or another because of Lucky Luigi's bad memory.

Although Nicholas no longer possesses a decoder ring, I ask, "Nicholas, may you be in possession of a Captain Midnight decoder badge?"

But Nicholas answers, "That is another unfortunate incident. See I do have in my possession a Captain Midnight decoder badge until one Wednesday afternoon at religion class. At the time I am somewhat bored so I take out my Captain Midnight decoder badge but I do not have it in my hand for more than a minute when I look up and see the nun heading rite to my desk. I do not have time to put the decoder badge in my pocket or anywhere else out of sight so I just try to hide it in my hand. But the nun is standing rite in front of me and she asks, 'What is in your hand?'"

I shrug my shoulders like I do not know what she is talking about but she says, 'Let me see your hands.'

So I show her my hands but I keep my fists closed real tight until I see the yardstick come out from nowhere and she hits my hand so hard the Captain Midnight decoder badge drops to the floor and breaks in half.

Then the nun says, 'Pick that up and give it to me.'

Well that was the end of that. I do not care all that much if I get it back because it is smashed pretty bad and would not be a very good secret spy tool."

I splain to Nicholas, "With regret that, although we are lacking these important secret spy tools, the investigation nevertheless must proceed for the good of one and all."

So Nicholas and Yours Truly lower our heads to concentrate on a code name. Nicholas lifts his head and says, "I got it! The code name is 'Secret Spies'."

Sometimes Nicholas makes a good suggestion but there are other times he makes a suckgestion and this is one of those times. Personally I do not think Nicholas's suckgestion is a good one but after the two sad stories of loss he has just related, I do not wish to cause Nicholas any further grief and I do need a companion for adventures because it is a well-established fact that an adventure by one person is only half as good as an adventure shared by two persons.

So just then, after Nicholas suckgests "Secret Spies" as the code name, it becomes real important for me to go to the John which one would do only in an emergency because the John in Randy's Restaurant is indeed a very unclean John. So I am in the John which is actually about the size of a small closet. I am standing in front of the terlet, which I do not need to use as such because the emergency previously mentioned has nothing to do with my needing to use the terlet, at least not in the usual way. The emergency is about the code name what Nicholas suckgests which in my opinion is a code name that lacks dignity but, since I do not want to offend Nicholas, I am buying time in the manner I have just described because I see no cash value to entering into a beef with Nicholas about the code name what he suckgests. I am thinking about another code name because the Secret Spies code name just ain't gonna do the trick for such an important investigation. It is at that very moment that I realize I am standing in a closet and, although this is a closet with a terlet, it is nevertheless a closet and it is in a closet where Saint Closétus is likely to appear and give Yours Truly instructions about saving the world from Commies and about other things like a really swell secret code name.

Upon returning to the booth, where Nicholas is sucking up the last drops of his two cents plain with a straw and looking more than somewhat desirous of the remaining two cents plain still in my glass, I inform Nicholas as such, "Saint Closétus appears to me just now in the terrlet. I am just standing there doing what a guy has got to do when all of a sudden Saint Closétus appears sitting on the top of the water tank above my head and he says the name of the operation has got to be, 'Operation Top Secret.'"

To which Nicholas puts in his two cents and makes a great contribution what truly amazes me because Nicholas making any contribution is a thing what I am seldom experiencing in the presence of Nicholas who now offers his great contribution by saying as such, "We can make Operation Top Secret a really secret code by using just the first letters of each woird and we can call it *OPTS.*"

Well that almost done the trick but after I splain and clarify that the first three letters are *OTS*, we are in total agreement about naming our adventure *OTS* and we are also in agreement that Saint Closétus would accept our amendment.

Whereupon Nicholas asks, "What are we going to do for our first OTS adventure?"

Well I must admit this is a very good question and one that needs further consideration so we both lower our heads and think about what we are going to do for our first OTS adventure. Nicholas raises his head and states, "I know! We should go to the church rectory and tell Father McNulty about the Commies what are infilterating the Catholic Church."

Upon this suckgestion I once again have an urge to relieve myself and I head back to the terlet closet where once again I conjurate Saint Closétus who appears to me and informs me about what we are to do for the first OTS adventure.

When I return to the table, I encounter a situation which perplexes me for I notice my glass, what previously contains some remaining two cents plain, is now empty. I am quite certain that I do not drink the remaining two cents plain before my visit to Saint Closétus in the terlet closet. However, I decide there is no cash value to beefing about this. The bigger concern is that Saint Closétus tells me what we are to do for the first OTS adventure. I inform Nicholas thus, "When I am in the terlet closet just now standing there doing what a guy needs to do when he has such needs, Saint Closétus appears to me sitting once again on the water tank above the terlet and he tells me we must follow Gutsy Gus and see where he goes."

Well that done the trick again and Nicholas puts in his two cents, "Now we're cooking with grass! Yes! We need to follow Gutsy Gus and see if he is one of them Commies infilterating the Catholic Church."

Nicholas and Yours Truly shake hands and agree about three important matters, one being the name of our adventure, OTS, the second being that we follow Gutsy Gus and the third thing is that we agree to resolve any and all differences of opinions we may encounter in the future by agreeing to follow the advice of Saint Closétus. On this note we unfold a paper towel what previously hung on a rack in Randy's closet and mark it with our secret code sign, OTS, and then we sign with our very secret signatures, one X for Nicholas and XX for me. With this signing of our secret code we conclude our meeting.

Dear John,

I forget to tell you, at our meeting of OTS yesterday, Nicholas agrees to follow Gutsy Gus tomorrow but that is today and I do not see Nicholas hanging around waiting for Gutsy Gus to exit our apartment house and, since Nicholas lives a block away and around the corner, it is important to have a way to signal when Gutsy Gus exits the apartment house. But we agree that in a situation such as this, we make use of a new top secret spy device what is called the telephone. Nicholas's family just got a telephone installed and there is another new telephone installed in a phone booth on the corner. I can run down to the telephone booth and call Nicholas and let him know when Gutsy Gus exits. I do not even need to waste a nickel doing so because I put the nickel in and after two short rings on his phone, I hang up and that way I get the nickel back and Nicholas gets the signal that Gutsy Gus is on the move.

Dear John,

So I am sitting on the stoop reading about Guys and Dolls and I am indeed happy to find the place in the book where I leaf off. Then I hear just a slight squeak as the front door opens and Gutsy Gus stands on the top landing and lights up a Lucky Strike. "Hi, Gutsy Gus," I say. "Where are you off to?" Gutsy Gus, who is generally a most amiable guy, looks at me and I am not sure if he is squinting because the sun is in his eyes or his squint may indicate that I have just raised some suspicion on his part. So to catch him off guard, Yours Truly follows up with, "I myself am heading for the pool at McCarren Park and I thought you might want to come with me for a cool dip on this very hot summer day."

Gutsy Gus responds, "No, thanks. I have some business I need to attend to. Maybe next time." Then Gutsy Gus takes a drag on the Lucky Strike and offers me one but I slip into my mouth a rather large piece of Salt Water Taffy what is now stuck to the roof of my mouth and I say, "Na tanks, I ged zem candy in my mout what I am walking on."

So Gutsy Gus looks at my mouth, shakes his head and walks off south on Leonard. It looks like he's heading for the elevator train down on Broadway. So I run to the telephone booth, dig in my pocket for my last nickel and place it in the coin slot. I dial Evergreen 8-4905 what is Nicholas's number, but then I hear a conversation between two lady verses what are talking about being blue in heaven. Well that bothers me more than somewhat because I know that being blue is a sad thing for one and all but then I hear they mention some stupid movie called *My Blue Heaven* and since I know by now I lose the nickel and I am indeed feeling blue, I ask politely, "Hey, hang up. I got an emergency call what I gotta make to Nicholas rite away."

They just laugh and one says, "Listen, kiddo, this a party line and we got the rite to talk as long as we want because we got on this line foist.

I answer in a very loud verse, "Lady! When a guy uses

the woid emergency, you gotta hang up because I hear that is the law and, when a guy says the woird emergency real loud like what I am doing just now, you gotta hang up or you can go to jail."

One of the ladies says, "Emergency! Emergency! I just say it twice. So you hang up. If you do not hang up, I am sending my husband to track you down and cut you up into little chunks and you will be stinking along with the dead fishes."

After listening carefully to this woman's suckgestion, I decide to politely bid goodbye but first I do so by saying, "Twice? Well do you know what D.D.T. means?"

"What? And look like you? Hey kid! Yeah, I know. You are gonna drop dead twice, one time before and the other time after your pieces are sinking to the bottom of Newtown Creek."

So I hang up as fast as I can and then I put my finger on the receiver handle and click away three times but my nickel is indeed swallowed up by Ma Bell and not to be regungitated. Since there is no possibility of signaling Nicholas to get moving for this important mission, I decide to follow Gutsy Gus myself, a proposition what may not be all that difficult because Gutsy Gus is wearing his St John's brite red shirt. By now Gutsy Gus is hoofing it halfway to Broadway and Yours Truly is in no less of a hurry. My guess is that Gutsy Gus is heading for the J line at Lorimer to take him to his destination which may be out to Parsons Blvd. in Queens and then a bus to St. John's University. I am now running out of breath more than somewhat but I am too busy to notice it, at least not all that much, because my mind is focused on these suspicious goings-on. I am considering the proposition that if Gutsy Guts gets on the east bound J which is the express train out to Queens, he is most likely heading for St. John's but if he boards either the J or the M train going west, then my suspicions will grow to an all-time high.

Not to cause attention to my need to catch up with Gutsy Gus I am alterating between running and walking while trying to catch my breath and at the same time I am also digging into my pockets in search of a subway token which unfortunately is nowhere to be found. Before I know it, I am now standing at the bottom of the stairs on the north side of Broadway and Gutsy Gus is now ascending these very stairs in much of a hurry to catch the train. It is certain now that Gutsy Gus is not heading to St. John's University but that he is heading west toward the city and that elevates my suspicion in no uncertain terms.

Although I have been unable to find a token in my pocket, I do not give up hope because I believe it is my duty to follow Gutsy Gus and help save the Catholic Church from the Commies. It is a likely bet (I give it 5 to 1 odds) that one of several solutions will occur to allow me to continue trailing Gutsy Gus. The first solution is that the toll booth is unoccupied and I can jump the turnstile. But by the time I reach the top of the stairs I can see very plainly that the first solution is not available because the toll booth is occupied not only by the pretty young doll who on more than one occasion exchanges fifteen cents for a token but also by a transit cop who looks quite menacing to say the least. But then I look much closer and I see that these two have eyes only for each other and there is much more going on it that booth than I wish to relate here. So without hesitation I jump the turnstile and no one is the lesser off because I am on the other side of the turnstile and the two what have eyes only for each other are undisturbed by the likes of me. Everyone benefits from what I just done, especially the

Catholic Church, the USA and OTS and thus there is no need to present the other possible solutions.

Well, by the time I get up to the station platform the M train is arriving and I watch Gutsy Gus step in before the doors close and I am also stepping in the said train just before the doors close but I am two cars away so I do not blow my cover. Now this M train is a local so I surmise that the station from which we will exit is not a very great distance. I grab hold of the bars as I walk through the car and open the door, step across the grating between the cars and enter the next car. The train is swerving back and forth and I feel like a monkey swinging from branch to branch as I grab from one bar to the next until I arrive at the next door. I can see through the window Gutsy Gus sitting in the next car and he is deeply into reading a book. I can see the big print on the cover and it is called *Philosophy*. A book with this title is not unusual for Gutsy Gus to be reading because almost every book he reads has that as the title or at least part of the title. One time a few weeks back Gutsy Gus lends me a book what is called an *Introduction to Philosophy*. Although many woirds in that book are longer than the M train, I find books such as this to be somewhat interesting but *Guys and Dolls* is more to my liking.

I wander off the present concern. So getting back to my account of the subway ride, I notice there is more to the title of that book. Just below the woird *Philosophy* there is smaller print what is hard to read. I squint and get really close to the window and I see the woirds *of Karl Marx*. Now I do not know who this Karl fellow is since the book I mostly read is by Damon Runyon who does not mention this guy what goes by the handle, Karl Marx.

I now understand why Gutsy Gus chooses the local because it gives him more time to read. After stopping at each station the train finally pulls into the East 34th St. Station. I am just twenty-feet, take a foot or two, behind Gutsy Gus but he double steps up the stairs onto East 34th St and takes off at such a clip he is clear up the stairs before I place my foot on the first step. After taking one step at a time as fast as I am able, there I am standing in Herald Square which is a very fine square indeed especially to find oneself standing in but I do not have the time to admire my surroundings. So after taking a minute or two for checking my whereabouts, I look up and down East 34th St. but Gutsy Gus is nowhere to be found. But then the sun flashes off a bright red shirt turning the corner onto 5th Avenue and, since this is a block away, I am off and running and before long I am standing on 35th Street, once again about twenty feet in back of Gutsy Gus, a little too close. So as fast as I can I jaywalk onto the other side of 35th St. and I succeed in not drawing attention except for the delivery truck driver who jams on his squeaking brakes and is yelling at me and blowing his horn to which nobody pays any attention because this yelling and horn blowing is a generally accepted practice in NYC. So from the other side of 35th Street and, in between trucks passing and sometimes stopping in traffic, I can see Gutsy Gus who walks down an alley and up to a door on the side of an office building and the door opens and Gutsy Gus is getting a big hug from, you guessed it, none other than the doll. So I am standing there taking in this action when I happen to notice I am not alone in taking in the action. Someone is watching Yours Truly. There parked in the alley is the big black six-door Fleetwood and who is sitting in the driver's seat, no one else but Big Boris who, much to my discontent, immediately recognizes me and we are both off running, Big Boris on one side of 35th Street and Yours Truly on the other. So I get to 5th Avenue and I turn right and keep running. I have always considered myself to be a rather fast runner but when I feel a hand squeezing the back of my neck I am convinced that Big Boris, although apparently somewhat over weight, is in fact a faster runner. Although Big Boris is a faster runner, he is not a louder screamer and I discover this when I start screaming at the top of my lungs, "Help me. I'm being kidnapped by the Russian Commies!"

A crowd of well-meaning citizens surrounds us. Big Boris tries his best to set the record straight by yelling something that sounds like, "Nyet! Nyet! Mal chick isht loosed end pomoshchnik doma. I helper him go home!" One of the men shouts, "That's a Russian Commie kidnapper. Get him!" Well Big Boris takes off and indeed he is quite fast on his feet. I walk back to the corner and watch all the commotion without getting personally involved. I can see Big Boris makes it back to his big black six-door Fleetwood but he soon finds this is not a safe base and he quickly runs up to the side door of the previously mentioned building and he is repeatedly and frantically knocking on the door which opens just in time before five well intentioned upstanding patriotic American citizens reach out and almost grab the Russian Commie kidnapper. I consider this a very good time to head back to Brooklyn and, after a hop and a jump over the turnstile at the East 34th Street subway station, I soon find myself back in our safe neighborhood what is Williamsburg, Brooklyn.

Chapter 5

Suspicions Increase

Dear John,

It is a couple of hours later and I am sitting on the stoop with Nicholas and recounting the adventure of which I have just related in my last epistle when I see Gutsy Gus strolling up Leonard. I excuse myself for the moment and run up the stoop and up the stairs to 3B on the second floor because this is not the most apropos time for me and Gutsy Gus to have a conversation mainly because I do not yet think of what to say to him about why Big Boris and Yours Truly did not eggsactly get along earlier today.

I am standing just inside the door to apartment 3B on the second floor and listening for the front door of the apartment house to screech open and slam shut what would thus indicate that Gutsy Gus is ascending the stairs but there is not even the slightest squeak. So I shut my door and move to the window and look out onto the street and there I see Gutsy Gus standing across the street in front of an apartment house two doors down the block. Gutsy Gus is across the street conversating with a neighbor who goes by the handle Mr. Joey Pits. This neighbor's name is much longer than Pits but since not one citizen in the entire neighborhood can pronounce that longer name, Mr. Joey Pits and his wife, Mrs. Joey Pits, agrees to the shorter version. However, since Mrs. Joey Pits is deceased for quite a spell, Mr. Joey Pits spends much of his time looking out the window. He is a very lonely windower.

When Mr. Joey Pits is not looking out his window, he is often walking up and down the street and around the block and he stops to talk with many citizens who live in the neighborhood. But Mr. Joey Pits's way of talking is strange, more than somewhat. Most of the citizens he greets are young ladies and Mr. Joey Pits most often attempts to compliment these young ladies by saying things such as the following, "Hi ya! You with your beautiful gams. Would you like to come up to my apartment for a splash of a vwadka?" Sometimes Mr. Joey Pits offers help such as, "Hi, young lady, you are very beautiful but you look a little zonked. Would you like to sit and chat up?" Although Mr. Joey Pits is very complimentary and generous in his offers, the young ladies do not see it that way and they always decline his invitation by saying things such as the following, "Put an egg in your shoe and beat it." And I hear on more than one occasion, "Hey old man. What do ya think? I ain't all that hard up." I often hear citizens who are confuciused ask Mr. Joey Pits, "Who let you out of your cage?" One time I hear, "I ain't no pushover but I will push over you if you don't get out of my way." The young ladies are of such a mind that they do not accept compliments and they almost never stop walking. Some act like they don't hear Mr. Joey Pits's compliments but they are not eggsactly deaf because after a compliment or two, they start walking really fast.

At such a time Mr. Joey Pits waves to them and offers them some breakfast by saying, "Well Cheerios then."

When Mr. Joey Pits is not walking up and down the

street, he is sitting on the stoop of the apartment building in which he resides where he compliments young ladies as they pass by. I usually pay no attention to Mr. Joey Pits because of my head being buried in my book about Guys and Dolls what was scribed as I have mentioned by Damon Runyon. But I notice Gutsy Gus spending some moments with Mr. Joey Pits as they are often involved in conversations as is the present case as I already describe.

So I continue peeking out the window until the conversation between Gutsy Gus and Mr. Joey Pits ends. Soon thereafter the long awaited screeching front door slams shut and in a very short time I hear the door to 2B on the fourth floor shut and I conclude that it is safe for me to rejoin Nicholas on the stoop. So I do just that and as I am continuing to recount the adventures of earlier today, who appears at the top of the stoop without any screech from the door, none other than Gutsy Gus himself with his arms folded looking a little like Captain Midnight in his Ovaltines. Fortunately he is without his secret squadron, but nevertheless this is quite a perdickamint because I am not eggsactly open to confronting the likes of some uberman what I read about in that book what I loan from Gutsy Gus a month ago, give or take a day or two.

But then Gutsy Gus lowers his arms and asks, "What are you two guys up to?"

"No nothing! Not a thing. We are sitting on this stoop chewing the fat all day except for a baffroom break every once in a while. Ain't that rite, Nicholas?"

Nicholas backs up my story by stating, "Well that's not eggsactly rite. But it's close enough to be true. We are sitting rite here for a little while. What we are doing is …"

But then I interrupt before Nicholas spills all his beans and I add, "You know, Gutsy Gus, there is many a guy who looks just like me and I see quite a few young handsome guys who look just like me and they hang around midtown and thereabouts in Manhattan."

Gutsy Gus now squints his eyes and wrinkles his forehead and that indicates to me that he is very confuciused and his confuciun is affirmed when he asks, "What are you talking about? You two guys seem nervous about something. What's up?"

Nicholas and Yours Truly look at one another and at the same eggsact moment we say, "Nothing!"

Just along about that time Gutsy Gus's mother opens the window on the fourth floor and yells to Gutsy Gus, "August Teen, supper is ready all ready. Come on and get it while it's hot."

At this Gutsy Gus looks directly into my eyes and then into Nicholas's eyes and says, "You guys need to relax." Gutsy Gus then exits and runs up the stairs to apartment 2B on the fourth floor to get it while it is hot.

I look at Nicholas who has his mouth open wide and is about to say something but I get my two cents in first and in a whisper I say, "Gutsy Gus does not know I am there earlier today. Big Boris never tells him what happens."

That my encounter with Big Boris is a secret increases our suspicion that Big Boris does not want to let some cat get out of the bag. Commies know how to keep secrets because they are trained so that it is nearly impossible to brain wash a commie, especially a Russian Commie!

Dear John,

This is quite a mystery that is bugging Yours Truly more than somewhat. Why does Big Boris not tell Gutsy Gus about the events what take place on 35th Street? Indeed whenever secrets are kept, there is a plot than runs deep and this is much more of a mystery than I previously contemplicate.

Dear John,

So today Nicholas and Yours Truly are having a meeting of OTS but this is such a top secret meeting that we do not even have this meeting in a public place such as Randy's Restaurant. We are having this super-duper top secret meeting of OTS in a bin in the cellar of Nicholas's apartment house. One reason for having this meeting in the cellar bin is that it is unlikely any citizen interrupts us for only a very courageous citizen comes down here, not even once in a while, what with all the roaches and rats. The other reason for holding the top secret meeting in this location is that we are no longer all that welcome in Randy's Restaurant. Why we are not welcome in Randy's Restaurant is a long story what I will relate on another occasion.

At the very beginning of this top secret meeting Nicholas makes one very good suggestion and it is such a good suggestion that it is not necessary for me to consult Saint Closétus who would agree anyway since Saint Closétus and Yours Truly generally agree at all times about all things.

Nicholas suggests, "We can both go to that building on 35th Street what is probably the Commie Headquarters."

I nod my head and say, "You may be correct. That building is probably the Commie Headquarters."

Earnest continues, "We need to investigate those Commies and see what's up with the doll but we have to be careful not to meet up with Big Boris. But then if we both run, we can run twice as fast."

I ask, "Nicholas, are you telling me that if two people run, they can run faster than one person."

Nicholas puts his hand up to his chin and utters. "Hmm.

Twice as fast? Well if two is twice, then one is half of twice is... I do not know but …. No... Yes! I think two run faster than one. Yes! Twice as fast."

I look at Nicholas and shake my head.

Nicholas continues to explain his meaning of twice, "It is just like the number thirteen. Everybody knows that is an unlucky number. Right?"

I nod in agreement.

Earnest states, "The number twenty-six is twice as unlucky because it is twice the number thirteen."

I ask, "Does that mean the number fifty-two is twice as unlucky as the number twenty-six and four times as unlucky as the number thirteen?"

Earnest says, "I am not sure about those higher numbers but personally I try to stay far away from any one of them."

I should tell you a little about Nicholas. He is a very nice kid and is somewhat fun to pal around with. But is he smart? When they were giving out talents to the newborns, Nicholas got niceness and a really big smile. Girls like his big smile but he never notices them. Nicholas has brains what work but only ups and downs. By that I mean Nicholas surprises me a lot because sometimes he says something very smart and then there are the other times. For example, in school Nicholas just sits a little like a frog on a log. If nothing is moving, he does not see it. This summer I am planning to keep things moving.

So hanging around with Nicholas during a summer is a good thing to do but it also means being responsible so he does not kill himself during one adventure or another. Sometimes Nicholas gets confuciused about things and it is good for him to let his brain relax this summer. Fortunately this summer Nicholas will not be making all that many decisions because most decisions will be made by Saint Closétus.

I believe the main reason for Nicholas's suggestion to travel to 35th Street is that he wants to take a gander at the doll. After all, the doll who visits Gussy Guts is a very classy looker and that is more than somewhat but Nicholas has yet to set eyes on her. Nevertheless this suggestion offered by Nicholas is an up one. The only problem is that the purchus of subway tokens will take a major addition to our present funding which at this moment amounts to zero. Although I have my own way of traveling the NYC subway system, Nicholas is very reluctant to jump turnstiles since the last time he does so, he is so nervous he trips and falls on his face but the worst part is that it is a transit cop's foot what he trips over. Soon thereafter Nicholas discovers the inside of the 69th Precinct is a very unpleasant place. So I make a suggestion that can either earn us some cash or can make us both very sorry. I make such a suggestion what I will describe in depth shortly.

Nicholas makes another up one, what is a wise suggestion, as he says, "Before we do this, because this is a very daring thing to do with possible results we may both regret, I suggest we consult Saint Closétus."

Well this is a suggestion to which I immediately agree because, as I already inform you, most decisions, and all the really good ones, are now made by Saint Closétus.

Nicholas and Yours Truly look around the whole cellar but, although there is not one closet to be seen anywhere, we find many bins that are very dark and look somewhat like closets. So I tell Nicholas, "Go upstairs and be a look-out and I will try to conjurate up Saint Closétus."

Nicholas disagrees and says, "I want to see what Saint Closétus looks like so I'm staying rite here."

That sounds like a problem to me at first but then I think it is not such a big problem as I first suspect because it is a well-known fact, when saints and angels and such appear like in Fatima and Lourdes, no one can see them except for a few people who, in the case of these two miraculous apparitions, are three kids. So it is the same way for me and for Saint Closétus who Nicholas is guaranteed not to see because he is not supposed to witness the miraculous apparition what involves Saint Closétus.

But then I remember the nun on one of those Wednesday afternoons tells us about the miracle what happens at Fatima when the sun rolls all around in the sky. So just like at Fatima Nicholas does not get to see the apparition in person but he can see a little miracle what can help. Fortunately, while searching for a closet, I find a flashlight hidden in a crack at the bottom of the stairs and, although the batteries are weak and the bulb is not very bright, it works and that is a most useful thing to find in circumstances such as this. So I walk into an empty bin what has no bulb. Now this is a very normal thing because everyone steals bulbs from cellars, especially from empty bins. So I find an old ripped bed sheet and put the flashlight under it which I keep off for the time being. Then I walk up to a wall in the bin and I say, "Saint Closétus, we have quite a perdickamint and we need your advice about saving the Catholic Church from all the Commies what are trying to infilterate." Then I click on the flashlight and move it around in a circle and I listen to what Saint Closétus says. I bend my head so Nicholas can see I'm listening real close to every woird what Saint Closétus speaks.

Then I hear Nicholas tiptoeing toward me and I click off the flashlight, put the bed sheet with the flashlight wrapped in it on a table, and turn around. Nicholas is standing in back of me so close that we bump heads but that is not of major concern because it is much more important that I relate the message I just receive from Saint Closétus that concerns how we are to add cash to our funding which as previously mentioned is zero.

Nicholas is pacing up and down and stamping his foot and saying, "I did not see Saint Closétus what you were talking to. Nobody was there."

Well I figure rite away that Nicholas is having serious doubts about these apparitions and having such a doubt as this can be a very serious problem that can lead Nicholas to becoming a non-believer in many other things spiritual and all. So it is an obligation on my part to come to the aid of one who is having doubts about spiritual and religious matters. I must steer Nicholas away from such doubts. Nicholas is more than somewhat upset that he is not able to see Saint Closétus but then I ask him, "Nicholas, do you see anything strange going on when I am talking to Saint Closétus?"

Nicholas stops pacing the floor and stamping his foot and responds, "Well I did see some kind of a light rolling around on the wall and ceiling."

I say, "You saw that? You saw a light rolling around? Well that is just like the miracle of the sun at Fatima what the nun told us about. That light was Saint Closétus's halo and that is a great thing that you see that. You know most of the time when saints appear, they do not let anyone in the audience see anything. So it is a very special thing that you see the light from Saint Closétus's halo."

Well that does the trick and Nicholas calms down and says, "O.K. I remember the nun telling us about the sun rolling around in the sky when those kids are talking to the Blessed Virgin Mary. I guess I do see something and it is a good thing too because, if I do not just see the light from Saint Closétus's halo rolling around, I am much inclined to believe you are having hallucinations."

I turn to Nicholas and inform him that I am shocked, not just at his lack of trust in me, but more importantly his lack of belief in things spiritual and religious. Nicholas lowers his head and states as follows, "I do believe in things spiritual and religious but I wonder about whether you are having apparitions or hallucinations. But now, when I see the light from his halo rolling around, I no longer doubt. It is a real and true apparition and not a hallucination."

Well when Nicholas says such woirds, I am truly shocked because I never before get the idear that Nicholas has such a swell vocabulary and knows these two woirds, apparition and hallucination. I can tell from Nicholas's remark that I need take a trip to the public library and do some research about apparitions and hallucinations so Nicholas continues to have faith in Saint Closétus and other spiritual and religious matters. It is not rite for me to lead Nicholas into questions about apparitions and hallucinations that may lead to doubts about faith.

So in this way and in many other ways I perform a most worthy act for I lead Nicholas away from doubting in the miraculous apparition of Saint Closétus and other religious truths.

Chapter 6

Lucky Luigi

Dear John,

Nicholas is a constant surprise this summer because in school he seldom shows any signs of intelligence. But then the same is true for Yours Truly but my lack of intelligence is a very deliberate shenanigan con on my part. Teachers and nuns at St. Mary's School pay little attention to the kids they consider to be stupid and Nicholas is seen to be most certainly one of those kids. However, Nicholas has more of a brain during summer than during any other season of the year. Nicholas' intelligence is seasonal.

Dear John,

Now that the question concerning Nicholas's faith has been cleared up, Nicholas brings up another topic. Here I will provide you with one more example of Nicholas' seasonal intelligence.

Today Nicholas and Yours Truly are having an OTS meeting on the stoop of my apartment house when Nicholas puts his two cents in by offering a suggestion as follows, "I know about spies and detectives because I see many a movie with Sam Spade and Philip Morris. I have also seen the movie *My Favorite*

Spy. In many of these movies one or more of the people keep secrets by doing things like changing their names. So now that we are spies, we should likewise change our names."

This is such a good suggestion from Nicholas that it almost puts me flat on the sidewalk. I can hardly believe I am dealing with the same Nicholas who sits in the back of every classroom and fails every test ever devised by any teacher. For a minute or two I just say nothing. Then I tap my head with my fist to make sure I am not hallucinating and that Nicholas actually says what I hear him say. Then Nicholas who is sitting back on the third step and looking like he is in deep thought continues and states, "We should definitely change our names because this is a thing undercover spies do when they are investigating a top secret operation. We should definitely do this."

I smile and shake my head in agreement and respond as follows, "Definitely! We should definitely change our names and this is definitely the best suggestion I have ever hear from you or just about anyone ever."

Nicholas puts his thumb up to his mouth, licks it and then places his thumb on his chest like he is giving himself a medal.

Well after this short discussion about acquiring new names Nicholas suckgests the following, "I can change my name to Joey and you can be Johnny."

When Yours Truly hears this second suckgestion, there is little doubt that we need to conjurate Saint Closétus concerning such an important matter. So I excuse myself by stating the following, "Nicholas, your idear about changing our names is such a great idear what excites me so much that I have an urgent need what I must take care of upstairs and, unless I immediately take some action about this urgent need, this stoop is soon to be baptized."

Nicholas looks at me like I am speaking some language other than American. I can see he is very confuciused about what I am saying. So I state what I mean by using the following woirds, "I gotta go to the baffroom."

After I return from a visit to the nearest available closet which is upstairs in my apartment 3B on the second floor, I inform Nicholas that Saint Closétus has just appeared to me and the message what I receive is as such, "Saint Closétus is very proud of you and he agrees with you that it is indeed and definitely a very good thing to change our names. He further states that I am to be called *Turnstile Tommy* because I have a talent for jumping turnstiles. Saint Closétus also instructs that you are to be known as *Two Cent Sam* because you are very good at helping yourself to a two-cent plain whether it is yours or another's."

Nicholas smiles a little and says, "I guess Saint Closétus watches everything we do."

I say, "Yes! Saint Closétus is always watching and that is why we have to do the rite thing by investigating the Commies and other bad guys. He wants you to know that he is very pleased with your suggestion about changing our names to undercover top secret names."

Nicholas smiles, a big smile, and says, "We should immediately start using our top secret spy names, Turnstile Tommy."

Dear John,

At our next OTS meeting what will take place tomorrow morning, Two Cent Sam, previously known as Nicholas, and Yours Truly, Turnstile Tommy, plan to take up the issue of a budget for OTS. But formulating a budget is a problem more than somewhat due to the fact that a budget involves money and that is one thing OTS is in sorry need of. Two

Cent Sam and Yours Truly, Turnstile Tommy, are working out the details of a plan for the poipose of enlarging our OTS budget from zero to more than zero.

Dear John,

I already mention a guy who goes by the handle Lucky Luigi. He is just a little squeak of a guy but he is also one hard-bearled thug, who lives on Bushwick Avenue in a big beautiful three story brownstone but one finds him more often than not in this Williamsburg neighborhood for three reasons. First reason is because Lucky Luigi loves to gamble and finds easy marks in Williamsburg. Reason two is he finds young guys, like Nicholas, are willing to give over their valuables to avoid being beaten up by Lucky Luigi's two very big gorilla-looking pals. The third reason is that his dad is none other than Mr. Pitsacola who owns many apartment houses and several business buildings and at least two, maybe more, factories in this very neighborhood. This includes two apartment houses on this very street. So Lucky Luigi thinks he owns this neighborhood and he can come here and do what he wants and take what he wants. But Yours Truly intends to change his thinking about that subject and perhaps a few more subjects.

It's just like when I hear when one Dapper Dan who gets an invite to go to Carnegie Hall, he says, "This is a great operatoonity!" So Two Cent Sam, and Yours Truly, Turnstile Tommy, can use this operatoonity to solve two problems. One solution is to put and keep Lucky Luigi in his riteful place what is Bushwick Avenue and the other problem to be solved is that of funding OTS. Lucky Luigi loves to gamble and got the do-re-me to gamble every day and he is well known to take a gamble on almost anything, sometimes more than a few times a day. But the problem, and this is what makes this plan more than somewhat of a challenge, is that Lucky Luigi is not a happy loser and when he makes a bet, it is very seldom he loses. Lucky Luigi is often seen to win even when the dice say he loses. For example, it is rumored that on more than one occasion Lucky Luigi rolls snake-eyes on the come out roll and says, "I win." It is also rumored that not one guy argues with this claim of winning. See Lucky Luigi secures his bets by having two very big gorilla-looking pals always standing on both sides of him and there is a general consensus that these two guys are paid by Lucky Luigi's dad, Mr. Pitsacola, to make sure no ill befalls his son, Lucky Luigi, and that includes losing a bet. So you may gather that any suggestion concerning Lucky Luigi may either earn us some cash or might get us both very sorry I make such a suggestion and even more sorry that Two Cent Sam and Yours Truly, Turnstile Tommy carry out this suggestion. To further explain our plan I will just let it be known that it also involves the absence of Randy from Randy's Restaurant since we have recently learned that Randy is off to Italy to visit his relatives for about a week or two and Hamburger Henry is running Randy's Restaurant in Randy's absence.

Now Hamburger Henry is known by that handle, not because he flips hamburgers, but because his face looks more like a hamburger than anything else. But that does not mean a thing to Two Cent Sam and Yours Truly, Turnstile Tommy, because Hamburger Henry is a most pleasant fellow. The most important thing is that Hamburger Henry does not know that Nicholas, I mean Two Cent Sam, and Yours Truly, Turnstile Tommy, owe Randy a dollar or two when we recently exit in quite a hurry and forget to pay our bill on more than one occasion. It is also to our advantage that Hamburger Henry does not know our names, either one of them, and this is most fortunate at a time such as this.

Now that you have some idear of our plan I will go off with Two Cent Sam and upon my returning I will relate what we accomplish. I must tell you I owe this plan, upon what we are about to embark, to that Guys and Dolls book what was scribed by this fellow Damon Runyon. So you can plainly see Yours Truly, Turnstile Tommy, gives credit where credit is do.

Dear John,

Our little caper is finished earlier today and I will now inform you about the pacifics how we come about getting sufficient funds to continue our investigation of the Russian Commies and how Gutsy Gus is involved in this matter.

Two Cent Sam and Yours Truly, Turnstile Tommy, confirm that Lucky Luigi will dine at 2 p.m. this very afternoon at Randy's Restaurant but this is no big surprise because it is well known in and around Williamsburg that Lucky Luigi dines at said fine establishment at 2 p.m. on most Friday afternoons.

Randy's Restaurant is a rather empty establishment on Friday afternoons for two reasons; one of which is that hamburgers contain meat, a product most citizens who reside in this neighborhood refrain from eating on Fridays. Just walk around this neighborhood at about twelve bells on any Friday and you will smell lots of peanut butter. The other reason is that most citizens in this neighborhood avoid being in the presence of Lucky Luigi and his two very big gorilla-looking sidekicks. These three guys do not smell of peanut butter but they are most unpleasant in many other ways.

So Two Cent Sam and Yours Truly, Turnstile Tommy, enter Randy's Restaurant at about one and a half bells on this Friday afternoon and I strike up a conversation and I ask as such, "Hamburger Henry, I am a very inquisitional guy so I am wondering about many things such as how many hamburgers are sold in this establishment on a regular day?"

Hamburger Henry shrugs his shoulders as if to say he does not know the answer to my question but then he opens a drawer under the counter and looks at a yellow paper and answers as such, "Let me take a look at this form which is a summary of Randy's sales for last month. I can see on most days we sell about 55 hamburgers except for Fridays when we sell maybe ten."

Hamburger Henry and Yours Truly, Turnstile Tommy, discuss other things as well like how many hotdogs, orange juice and coffee cakes he sells in a week and other things like that just to keep the conversation moving along since this is a very quiet afternoon in Randy's Restaurant and time goes somewhat slow when you are awaiting the arrival of a particular customer.

So along about the end of our conversation I can see Hamburger Henry turns his attention to some glasses which he places first into a pan of soapy water and then into a pan of clear water. These glasses he wipes dry and places on the shelf on the back wall but every minute or so he is turning his head to look at the clock on the wall where the hands are approaching two p.m. and I also notice the glasses are rattling because Hamburger Henry's hands are beginning to shake more than somewhat.

So we, Two Cent Sam and Yours Truly, Turnstile Tommy, can see that Hamburger Henry is more than somewhat detracted so we order a two cent plain for each of us. After Hamburger Henry agrees to run a tab for us, we walk to the back of the establishment. After a short walk we are sitting in a booth at the rear of a very quiet Randy's Restaurant, quiet that is except for the rattling of glasses in

Hamburger Henry's shaking hands. We each are sucking up a two cents plain and hoping to increase our budget enough to pay for these two cent plains and also to have a little extra cash in our pockets when we exit this fine dining establishment. We are sitting in a back booth and waiting for more than a few minutes while very slowly sucking up our two cent plains as we are killing time. I am sitting with my back to the front door and Two Cent Sam is seated across the table. Although I am seated with my back to the front door, I can see all the action behind me since there is a very large mirror on the back wall. In between sips, what are now mostly bottom of the glass gurgles, I pick up a green napkin, a left-over from St. Patrick's Day, upon which I am writing numbers and I say to Two Cent Sam, "So they sell about 55 hamburgers five days a week and 10 on Fridays and since Randy's Restaurant is closed on Sunday..." I am calculating here and thus I briefly pause and then I finish my thought, "They sell in one week approximately 285 hamburgers." I then slide the napkin across the table and say, "Here, check my math."

Two Cent Sam holds the napkin up to the light so he can see the pencil marks on the green napkin with a shamrock in the middle he says, "I am truly surprised you can perform such high level mathematics. Certainly you did not learn this high level arithmetic such as multiplication in school since I remember you failed almost everything last year."

"So did you! But we both got promoted anyway," I respond and restate my request, "Just check my math and someday I will explain to you more about how I get by in school but since this is not presently a conversation about school, just check it."

At my request Two Cent Sam picks up the pencil and

places a check mark on the napkin. There is too little time to explain to Nicholas the ordinary meaning of checking math because just then I hear the door squeak open in back of me and I see Two Cent Sam's eyes open wide and his head tilts up and then down and thus, without necessarily intending to do so, he signals our mark has entered the scene.

I am seated in such a location that although my back is turned away from the door and thus my back is to Lucky Luigi, nevertheless I can see every move he makes due to the mirror on the wall in front of me. So I can see Lucky Luigi and his two very big gorilla-looking sidekicks, who might otherwise be called thugs, are seated comfortably on three stools at the counter and they are ordering hamburgers and this indicates that they are either non-believers in the Catholic tradition or they do not care about their sinful ways. But that is of little matter at this time and location. Hamburger Henry slaps five hamburgers on the grill and excuses himself to get hamburger buns, although quite a few buns are clearly visible on the back shelf.

So since it has been previously decided as directed by Saint Closétus that I am the one to approach Lucky Luigi with a proposition, I rise to my feet and in a loud verse I say, "Two Cent Sam, I am so ankshits to see if you are correct in your estimate that I am going to ask Hamburger Henry just how many hamburgers he sells in a week."

To which Two Cent Sam responds in a loud verse as such, "O.K. Turnstile Tommy, I will even bet you a dollar that this establishment sells about 300 hamburgers a week."

As I approach Lucky Luigi I act surprised to see him and I say, "Lucky Luigi, what a surprise it is to see you especially since my friend, Two Cent Sam, sitting over there has just bet me that Randy's Restaurant sells almost 300 hamburgers a week, give or take twenty five, and I bet him a buck that it is more like a hundred hamburgers a week. What do you think?"

Lucky Luigi swivels around on the stool and says to me as such, "If you are attempting to sucker me into a bet on how many hamburgers are sold at Randy's Restaurant in one week, you make a very big mistake. See I am the kind of a guy who's been around the block more than a few times and on one occasion a guy comes up to me and offers me a proposition that is too good to turn down and the proposition is a bet that Running Ragged in the third at Aqueduct will jump the wall and sit down in the bleachers, light a Chesterfield, and watch the rest of the horses pass by and, as sure as you are standing here, Running Ragged does every one of the aforementioned. And now it is my assumption that you two already gather ample information about how many hamburgers are sold at this establishment each week and, if you think I am a chump to go for such a proposition, you are wrong, maybe even dead wrong." Then Lucky Luigi smiles and looks at his two gorilla thugs who smile back and shake their heads in agreement. Lucky Luigi repeats, "Maybe dead wrong."

I cannot help to notice that the smiles on the two gorilla thugs are bigger than most but that is because there are not all that many teeth to get in the way.

Lucky Luigi continues, "But since you are interested in a bet, I will bet you a buck that two hundred hotdogs are sold each week at this establishment and you can choose another number and which number is closer to what Hamburger Henry says will be the winning bet. If you so agree, take one dollar out of your wallet, place it on the counter as I will do likewise, and we will inquire about the number of hotdog sales when Hamburger Henry returns." With that said, Lucky Luigi takes a dollar from his wallet and places it on the counter, looks at me and points to the counter indicating that I should do likewise.

Of course, this is more than somewhat of a problem for me because I have not a dollar nor any other form of currency in my wallet nor anywhere else on me, but since I am a fast thinker, I remember Two Cent Sam has a green napkin upon which I have just recently completed some mathematical calculations and upon which there is also a recently placed check mark. So I say to Lucky Luigi, and I say it loud so Two Cent Sam can hear every woird, "I personally am flat broke at the moment but my friend is flush with the green stuff. Ain't that rite, Two Cent Sam?"

Two Cent Sam looks confuciused more than somewhat.

Then I call back to Two Cent Sam and I tell him, "Take one of the many dollars out of your pocket and hold it up in front of you so Lucky Luigi can plainly see the green."

Well, Two Cent Sam looks at me with mouth open and hands in the air as if silently expressing, "What? I have no money." But fortunately Two Cent Sam does not utter such woirds and just before he is about to say such woirds, I say, "What are you waiting for, the St. Patrick's Day parade?"

Two Cent Sam now closes his mouth, nods his head and makes like he is taking something out of his pocket but what he does is fold the green napkin in such a way that it looks like a dollar bill sticking out of his hand and he says, "Here in my hand I am holding just one of my many dollar bills to cover your bet, Turnstile Tommy. I am placing it on the table before me."

I say to Lucky Luigi, "I bet they sell only about 100 hotdogs each week give or take about 10."

Just then Hamburger Henry enters from the back room with a bag of buns in his arms and stands in front of the grill which is crackling more than somewhat as five hamburgers are spouting grease in every direction. Hamburger Henry flips the hamburgers and opens the bag of buns.

At this moment Lucky Luigi asks, "Hamburger Henry, we have a bet going on here about how many hotdogs are sold in one week in this establishment. I say you sell about 200 hotdogs a week and Turnstone Tommy here says you sell only about 100 hotdogs a week. Which one of us is closer to the actual number?" But Lucky Luigi does not stop there and he looks to the sidekick thug on his left and then to the sidekick thug on his rite and then continues as such, "It would be a very good thing for you to agree that this establishment sells 200 hundred hotdogs a week, if you get the picture."

Hamburger Henry stutters, "W…w… w…wuh…we sell lots of hotdogs a week. M… m…m…muh…maybe you are rite, Lucky Luigi. M… m…m…muh… maybe we do sell about 200 hotdogs a week."

With that Lucky Luigi jumps off the stool, looks up at me and states, "You lose! Ante up!"

But then I say, "Wait just a minute here, Lucky Luigi. We cannot just go on some opinion expressed in the form of a maybe when it comes to a matter of such high stakes. We need to see the facts." Then I turn to Hamburger Henry and I ask, "Do you have any basis for your estimate of how many hotdogs are sold in this establishment in one week? Did I not see a form here that looks like it may have a summary of sales in this establishment each day?"

Hamburger Henry nods his head up and down just a little as he reaches under the counter and hands me a form with sales for the last month.

So I say, "Let us take a look at these numbers and see how many hotdogs are sold each week for the last month."

Well I add up the numbers and I say, "It turns out that

about 106 hotdogs, take a few here and there, are sold each week in this establishment."

With that, as Lucky Luigi grabs the yellow paper out of my hand and, with the help of his two thugs, tries to do the higher math of addition. While they are busy counting on their fingers and, before they start taking off their shoes to start counting on their toes, I grab the dollar bill off the counter and I am quick as a wink at the back table and Yours Truly and Two Cent Sam take off out the back door.

It is indeed a fact that we now owe Randy's Restaurant more than before due to another hasty departure from these premises but it is an easier proposition to pay Randy than to settle with Lucky Luigi and his two gorilla thugs.

Dear John,

Woird is out on the streets that Lucky Luigi is looking for two young guys who go by the names Two Cents Plain and Tombstone Tony but the two guys who go by such names are not known to the citizens of this neighborhood.

Chapter 7
Joke Book

Dear John,

So I will catch you up on the events following our winning the hotdog bet. After our hasty departure from Randy's Restaurant, we run to the adjourneying apartment building which fortunately contains the apartment where Two Cent Sam resides with his family. Although these two building appear to be two entirely different buildings with entirely different front stoops, the wall between them is so thin that every sound and even every woird spoken in one can be heard in the other.

So we tiptoe up the stairs very slowly so no creak of the stairs can be heard on the other side of the thin wall where one can hear much disgustion taking place about Lucky Luigi losing the bet about how many hotdogs are sold in Randy's Restaurant in a week.

I must pause here on the stairs to splain to you, John, a difference what I make between a discussion and a disgustion. The difference is that a discussion is more or less pleasant but that is not the case for a disgustion.

So anyways, the disgustion is only between Lucky Luigi and Hamburger Henry because there is no one else in the establishment at this time and this is because Lucky Luigi's two gorilla thugs have stepped out and are looking up and down the streets.

So Yours Truly and Two Cent Sam continue tiptoeing up to Nicholas's apartment. We can still hear Lucky Luigi's two gorilla thugs, using very loud and excited verses, asking questions of citizens concerning the whereabouts of two guys who go by the names Two Cents Plain and Tombstone Tony. This we continue to hear when we open the front window after arriving at Two Cent Sam's apartment where for our safety we decide to spend the remainder of the afternoon.

To kill time we get to talking about our adventure and we are enjoying our escapade so much so that Two Cent Sam's mother, Mrs. Foley, walks in and with a frown on her face asks, "Sure and begorrah! What now is so funny? Why are you laughing so loudly?"

But Two Cent's Sam is prepared with an answer as he holds up a joke book what he just recently places on the table in front of us. Personally I do not think this particular joke book is appropriately placed on the table in this family's living room because this is a joke book what I give to Nicholas for his very personal amusement. I do this about a week ago for the poipose of helping Nicholas improve his illiteratsy by enjoying some jokes what he is not likely to hear elsewhere, especially in a family situation.

But before I have any opportunity to change the subject and also the joke book, Two Cent Sam explains, "Mom, we are telling jokes what we read in this joke book which is before us on the table and that is why we are laughing so loud."

Then Mrs. Foley reaches for the joke book but I beat her to it and I open the book, close my eyes, put my finger on the page, point to a joke and I say, "It is now my turn to read the next joke."

Nicholas and his mom seem very surprised when I say I am going to read something other than a Dick and Jane first grade school book mainly because I have acquired quite a reputation here and about of being illiterated and for some time now I cultivate this reputation because it helps me do whatever I want to do in school. However, about a year ago or so I make a decision to learn to read and since many a teacher has tried and failed to teach me to read, I decide to teach myself by finding something to read that is of interest and entertaining. So in addition to finding the book by this Damon Runyon guy I also purchus this very joke book which now rests on the table before us and since I read every single joke and therefore no longer have any need for it, a few weeks ago I give it to Two Cent Sam to help him find something fun to read and thus to improve his reading. But I also suggest he keep it buried in the bottom of his closet or elsewhere out of sight, a suggestion what Two Cent Sam seems to forget.

However this results in quite a sacrifice for the good of all since I am now willing that Mrs. Foley and Two Cent Sam know my closely held secret what is that I can read. I am just hoping that they do not let the cat out of the bag by telling the nuns at St. Mary's. So I open a page of the joke book and I read as follows, "A traveling salesman's car breaks down. So he goes to a farmhouse where he sees the farmer's daughter. But the farmer…"

Mrs. Foley shouts, "Stop! Do not be readin any more of that manky joke. What age are ya to be readin as such? Actin the maggot, are you?"

Even though I do not fully understand the foreign language what Mrs. Foley speaks, I do know right off the bat I make a bad choice when I start reading that joke since it does not go over all that well in this Foley home. So I turn the book over on the table and I smile and laugh a little and I say, "O.K. that one is not all that funny anyway but I hear many jokes about farmers." So I remember a joke what I already know and although it has not one thing to do with any farmers and their daughters, I adapt it for this special occasion and I say, "A skunk walks into a farmhouse and asks, 'Where did the farmer's daughter go?'"

Nicholas looks at me with his nose all wrinkled and his mouth open like saying, two stupid jokes, which, of course, they are. Nicholas picks up the book, which is still open to that page.

But just then Mrs. Foley steps quickly across the room, grabs the joke book from her son's hands, looks at the page, puts her hand to her mouth and exits the room with the joke book held out straight by the tips of two fingers like she is carrying a bag of dog poop. I can also see her face is more redder than her hair. Mrs. Foley looks like she puts some rouge on her cheeks what ladies are known to do to make themselves look pretty, except at the moment Mrs. Foley is not all that pretty what with her nose wrinkled like she is actually smelling crapomundo.

Mrs. Foley is soon carrying a big bag out the door with the urgent need to take garbage down to the alley where the big garbage cans are stacked in the rear of the building. Just as she is closing the apartment door I see the before mentioned joke book is sticking out of the top of the garbage bag.

When she returns, Mrs. Foley holds the hallway door open, points to Yours Truly, and says, "C'mere 'til I tell ya.

So I think Mrs. Foley is saying that I should walk toward her. So I do just that.

But then Mrs. Foley points to the hallway and says, "I'll be seeing the back of ya now and forever more."

I think that is her way of saying goodbye. So I step out into the hallway and the door slams behind me.

Dear John,

Today before I can even ring the buzzer to Two Cent Sam's apartment house, he surprises me by opening the front door, and informs me that I am no longer welcome in his apartment. This

I understand what with the joke book incident of yesterday. So before long Yours Truly and Two Cent Sam are sitting on the stoop of his apartment house and talking about this and that and one thing or another. Two Cent Sam interrupts and makes an excellent suggestion and it is as follows: "I suggest we consult Saint Closétus and hear what he advises so we can get back to our investigation and save the Catholic Church from being infilterated by Commies." But then Nicholas continues and says, "But first I have to run upstairs and go to the baffroom."

As he is returning from the baffroom, I am backing out of a basement door under the stoop and I look up and inform Nicholas that I just now receive a message from Saint Closétus and I tell it as follows: "Saint Closétus instructs us to change our names again for the poipose of conducting our Operation Top Secret, what we now call OTS, and Saint Closétus is indeed pretty proud of you for suggesting we change our names and it is indeed a very good thing what we do because otherwise Lucky Luigi has quite an easy time finding us. So as per instructions from Saint Closétus you are henceforth to be called Hotdog Harry and I am to be called Hasty Departure Dan and from this moment on we must address each other by these names."

Although Hotdog Harry is not at all pleased with his new spy name, I explain as follows: "It is a far better name than the first one Saint Closétus proposes which I immediately negotiate on your behalf for that name was Weeney Willy." This explanation helps Hotdog Harry feel more comfortable with his new name because he now understands things can always be much worse than they are.

Dear John,

A bit later on this same day we agree to another requirement as suggested by Saint Closétus who is able to consult with me when Hotdog Harry has to excuse himself once again to go to the baffroom. This need of Hotdog Harry's is a problem that increasingly concerns Yours Truly, Hasty Departure Dan, because it could be very inconvenient for Hotdog Harry to go searching for a baffroom when we are working undercover as spies for OTS. However, this is not my present concern and since we previously agree to follow all requirements set forth by Saint Closétus, I inform Hotdog Harry that we are to pick up the lead and go to that building on 35th Street and, if the doll or Big Boris exit, we are to follow and spy without being seen.

Hotdog Harry enthusickly says, "I agree! We should go to that building on 35th Street and get a good looking at that building."

I do not think it is the building what Nicholas wants to get a good looking at. Nicholas wants to get a good looking at the good looker otherwise known as the doll.

With this agreement we conclude the meeting of OTS. Before exiting that apartment house stoop, I do a thing what I am beginning to get accustomed to be doing what is to look up and down the street. I cautiously walk up the street to my apartment house and again I look up and down the street to see if the coast is clear. Then I smile a little and ask myself, "Where did that farmer's daughter go?"

Chapter 8

Officer Clancy

Dear John,

This morning along about eleven bells Yours Truly, Hasty Departure Dan, is standing at the bottom of the elevator train station when Hotdog Harry comes strolling along and we actually pay for four tokens at the booth and legally board the J train to Manhattan with the intention of transferring trains and heading up to the East 34th St. Station. But to poichase tokens with real money at the booth and then to put a token into the turnstile rather than just jumping it, I personally consider this to be a waste of moola but it helps Hotdog Harry who has previously experienced hard luck when it comes to jumping turnstiles.

Well the ride to the East 34th St. station is mostly uneventful but that is only in the beginning of the ride. Things get very eventful during the second half of the ride when the subway train comes up out of the tunnel into Manhattan. The eventful thing has much to do with the old dame who gets on at The Bowery station where so many people come on board there is not one more seat left. So the old lady stands right in front of where Hotdog Harry and Yours Truly are sitting and she is holding on to the strap with her left hand and swaying back and forth more than somewhat. She is holding a small brown paper bag in her right hands and she is looking at us like we should get up and give her a seat and, since Hotdog Harry is a very polite young citizen, he is rising from the seat but just as Hotdog Harry gets up, the train makes a sudden turn and the old lady hits against Hotdog Harry and winds up on my lap which ordinarily would not be a big problem except when she lands, I feel something sharp and real wet on my lap. Well at first I think it is either me or the old dame what is bleeding or maybe both but then I look down at my pants and I am somewhat pleased to see that the liquid spreading across my pants is not red. It is a clear liquid but I can easily identify its true nature because the smell is definitely that of wine. The old dame, who is now standing, swaying back and forth more than somewhat, looks down at the brown paper bag crushed on my lap and grabs it. At that instant the old dame begins screaming such woirds what are best not quoted here. The train pulls into the Canal Street Station and the doors open. The old dame turns around and, although the train is not moving, the old dame is still swaying from side to side as she departs the train. The old dame sways across the platform, bumps off a pillar, reaches a bench, and collapses onto the seat. Then she looks up at the train window, points a finger at Hotdog Harry and yells some of those same woirds with a few added. These are woirds what I do not repeat here or anywhere and in fact I am so concerned that I am thinking maybe I should put my hands over Hotdog Harry's ears. When the train doors close, the old dame is sitting quietly on a bench, holding her head in her hands and looking at the bag, ripped open, exposing the red and gold label of Thunderbird wine what is dripping onto the subway platform.

Following that most sorrowful accident, Hotdog Harry and Yours Truly have no trouble keeping a seat for the rest of the ride because every time passengers come near, they back away quickly and quite far.

I am still smelling much like Thunderbird when we exit the train at the East 34th St. Station. We walk along the platform and up the stairs and there we are standing in Herald Square. Hotdog Harry is looking all around and up and down and saying things like this: "Wow, Holy Mackerel! Jeepers creepers! These buildings are really big! These buildings are really, really big. Are these buildings not really big, Hasty Departure Dan? Look at that one there!"

Well Hotdog Harry goes on and on about how big the buildings are here and there all around us in Herald Square and of course the really big one he is pointing to is known to one and all as the Umpire State Building but I figure Hotdog Harry is new to the city because it is no surprise that many buildings here and there, up and down Broadway and even off Broadway are indeed really big. This is a thing well known to citizens one and all except maybe to a stranger and I am finding that there are few citizens stranger than Hotdog Harry.

So I say to Hotdog Harry, "I cannot argue with you about these buildings being big and tall because they are such as you describe so accurately but we do not have time to admire our surroundings." So after a minute or two, which I grant Hotdog Harry for his need to admire the big buildings, I point and say, "I think it is this way to 5th Ave. So we should proceed in this direction."

However, because I do not sound certain of the way we should proceed, what Hotdog Harry does is to call out to a cop and ask, "Excuse me, officer, which way to 5th Ave.?"

The cop, who is standing on the corner about 15 feet

away, is not able to hear the question so he walks over to Yours Truly, Hasty Departure Dan, and to Hotdog Harry and before the question is posed again by Hotdog Harry, the cop leans toward me and sniffs and then sniffs again. The cop then has a question all his own which he addresses to me as such, "You been drinking wine, kid?"

I explained as such: "No, Officer, the wine you smell is a result of a train accident." Unfortunately my initial attempt to explain the reason I smell of wine does not help as much as I hope.

The cop at this point takes out a little notebook and asks what would ordinarily be a simple question with an even simpler answer but things are not always as simple as they seem. The cop asks the following simple question, "What are your names."

My traveling friend answers promptly, "My name is Hotdog Harry and his name is Hasty Departure Dan. May I ask what your name is?"

The cop shakes his head and answers, "Clancy, Officer Clancy." But then Officer Clancy asks another simple question, "Where are you two guys from."

I am not very fast to reply mainly because I am considering possible answers to this question since the one and only correct answer is not always the best answer in situations such as this. Before I can stop Hotdog Harry, he answers honestly. I recognize immediately that this honesty is a recurring problem I notice about Hotdog Harry. Hotdog Harry states, "We come from Williamsburg, Brooklyn and we are …" But Hotdog Harry fails to complete his thought when he is interrupted by Yours Truly, Hasty Departure Dan. For I consider it to be a very wrong thing what Hotdog Harry just now does and that is to give any information beyond our name, rank and cereal number. So Yours Truly,

Hasty Departure Dan, in as subtle a way as I can think of, interrupts Hotdog Harry by stamping my foot on top of his left toes. Hotdog Harry jumps around on his right leg while holding the other leg and reaching for his left shoe and in this way he is somewhat detracted and fails to complete his sentence.

But anyways Officer Clancy ignores Hotdog Harry jumping around and says, "Williamsburg? Oh! I know where that is because I read a book about a tree what grows in Williamsburg, Brooklyn. Do you guys live near Manhattan Ave and Maujer or around about there? That is where the tree grows."

Well, by this time Hotdog Harry has quieted down but, before I can clamp my hand over his mouth, he says, "That is eggsactly where we live but, although I wish not to disappoint you, there is actually more than one tree in our neighborhood. There are even two trees growing on Maujer Street."

Well just then a patrol car pulls up with sirens blasting and the cop who is driving shouts, "Hey, Clancy, somebody just blows open a safe on Broadway and 22nd St. The guy is fast on his feet and heading this way with some bags stuffed with C-notes. Hop in and let's be the ones to grab him."

Officer Clancy is no longer interested in our names nor where we come from, nor does he care one bit about the train accident. So Officer Clancy opens the passenger door of the patrol car and, with the siren blasting again, the patrol car heads down 6th Avenue which is also known as the Avenue of the Americans.

So Hotdog Harry and Yours Truly, Hasty Departure Dan, stand there watching this action and waiting for the light to change before crossing East 34th St. when a guy, racing faster than Seabiscuit, crashes into Hotdog Harry and they both go sprawling out into the traffic. Two cloth bags full of greenbacks break open and flood the street as a third bigger cloth bag goes bouncing and rattling across the street, slides directly over a sewer grate, finds the opening under the curb and falls into the sewer below.

Brakes screech and cars skid to a stop but more than a few fail to do so and there is many a collision of front bumpers hitting rear bumpers and much glass breaking and very much smoke from cracked radiators filling the street. But most drivers are far less concerned about damages because they are now out of their cars and pocketing many C-notes what are blowing all around in the middle of the street.

Well after the noise and smoke clear the air and most of the C-notes have vanished from the scene, I can see Hotdog Harry lying out on the street with the Seabiscuit guy spread out on top. Hotdog Harry attempts to slide out from under Seabiscuit just as a patrol car with the siren still blasting skids to a stop and Officer Clancy jumps out with his revolver pointed at both Seabiscuit and at Hotdog Harry.

Officer Clancy shouts, "Don't make a move." Officer Clancy walks over, bends down and puts handcuffs on Seabiscuit during which time Officer Clancy's partner handcuffs Hotdog Harry.

Dear John,

So this morning I am back on the stoop reading about guys and dolls but, of course, I am no longer reading because at the present moment I am writing as you can easily see. But it helps me, more than just a little, to read from this book what got the title the *Damon Runyon Omnibus* and reading this book gets me very much in the mood for writing which as I have previously stated I am now doing.

Dear John,

It is now after lunch and a quick nap on the living room couch. Last night Hotdog Harry and Yours Truly arrive back in Williamsburg late. So this afternoon I will catch you up on the events what follow the incidents as described previously.

Fortunately Officer Clancy says to his partner, "I know this guy who goes by the handle Hot Time Harold and he is not one of the thieves. As a matter of fact I was just investigating him and his friend standing over there for P. I. or underage WWI." And with that Officer Clancy points directly at Yours Truly.

To this accusation I respond as follows, "Officer Clancy, I was never involved in any war, neither WWI nor WWII and I am not a sp… sp…" I am about to say I am not a spy but telling a cop a lie is a sin against the Constitution and can land a guy like me in the cooler for a century or more. So, the fast thinker what I am, I am quickly thinking of how I am to change the ending to my sentence mainly because I am a spy for Operation Top Secret or what is now known as OTS. So I begin to say, "I am not a …"

But just then Officer Clancy puts up his hand to stop me from uttering another woird for which I am thankful and he says, "Kid, WWI means Walking While Intoxicated. What is your name? Oh, I remember. You are Hastily Disturbed Danny."

I do not think there is any cash value in correcting Officer Clancy concerning my name or that of Hotdog Harry so I just respond in the following manner, "Oh! Right! That's what WWI means and so I am innocent of that too. See the wine you smell is not the result of my drinking. It was a result of the train accident what …"

Then Officer Clancy stops my explanation in

mid-sentence by raising his hand and says to his partner, "Murph, uncuff the kid."

After Sebiscuit is packed safely away in the back of a paddy wagon what recently arrives on the scene, Officer Clancy gets out his notebook again and starts writing. Along about this time Hotdog Harry and Yours Truly are very, very slowly walking away but just then Officer Clancy in a loud verse says, "Just wait a minute, you two. We need witnesses to this crime of theft and how we capture this guy. Wait! I need to get more information from you."

Well, more information is something Hotdog Harry and Yours Truly are inclined not to offer especially after Hotdog Harry is informed in no uncertain terms by Yours Truly that honesty is not the best policy in some cases and this is one of those cases.

So Hotdog Harry and Yours Truly, Hasty Departure Dan, take off running east on East 34th St. against the traffic and we figure that is the best way out of this proposition as offered by Officer Clancy. Hotdog Harry and Yours Truly have the advantage of being faster on our feet than either Clancy or Murph, and, if you add both their speeds together and give it all to one of them, we are still more than somewhat faster, and since we are running east and against the traffic, the patrol car is not about to give a very successful chase.

But speaking of being successful, that is a thing Hotdog Harry and Yours Truly definitely are not. This lack of success is that we do not get to follow the plan to spy on Big Boris and the doll. After our encounter with Officers Clancy and Murph, we decide Saint Closétus would not mind one bit if we retreat. So we enter the nearest subway and take the first train that comes along what takes us to Van Courtland Park. Since we have no idear where Van Courtland Park is, we go up one flight of stairs and walk down onto the other platform and take the train that takes us away from Van Courtland Park but after some time we arrive at South Ferry. To make the telling of a long ride short, we get home quite late but one good thing is that we are now better acquainted with the NYC Transit System.

Chapter 9

A Spoon for a Horse

Dear John,

This morning at about ten bells I am sitting on the stoop when I see Lucky Luigi along with his two gorilla thugs turn the corner and start walking up Leonard. In no time at all you will find Yours Truly, up in apartment 3B on the second floor, watching Lucky Luigi stop citizens and ask a question or two. I know these are questions because all the citizens what are stopped shrug their shoulders and shake their head to say no to whatever the question may be.

After Lucky Luigi and his two gorilla thugs pack themselves into a grey 1950 DeSoto Custom hardtop, 4-Door Sedan and leave the neighborhood, I go downstairs where I see Katy Brown and Mr. O'Reilly walking down Leonard Street. Katy Brown is carrying a shopping bag with some Wonder bread sticking out of the top. Now Katy Brown is one of the citizens Lucky Luigi recently stops and asks a question.

When Katy Brown and Mr. O'Reilly approach the stoop on which Yours Truly is sitting, I say, "Katy Brown, I see Lucky Luigi asking you a question just a few minutes ago. Please tell me what question he asks of you."

Mr. O'Reilly puts his two cents in first and says, "That is none of your freaking business what anyone asks, son of beach party."

I must admit that, although I do write quotation marks around that last sentence, Mr. O'Reilly does not exactly say what I just right but I do not wish to quote the exact woirds because, well, just because. Well OK I will tell you. I substitute the word *freaking* and *beach party* for different words.

But Katy Brown says, "That's OK, Patty. I mean, Mr. O'Reilly. I can tell this kid what Lucky Luigi asks because I do not like Lucky Luigi. If it does Lucky Luigi no good by my telling this kid what Lucky Luigi asks, I do not mind that one bit." Then Katy Brown turns to Yours Truly and says, "Lucky Luigi asks if I know any kids who go by the names, Two Penny Sam and Turntaker Toni. I tell him I never hear of any kids who go by those names."

Dear John,

Woird is out on the street that some cops are knocking on doors and stopping people on the street and asking if anybody knows the whereabouts of two guys who are known as Hot Time Harold and Hastily Disturbed Danny. We further hear that no one in all of Williamsburg ever hears of guys with handles such as these.

Dear John,

WNEU News reports a robber blows up a safe yesterday belonging to Carmine Decrepio, a major crime boss, and gets away with two bags filled with hundred dollar bills.

But Carmine Decrepio responds by stating, "Get this straight! You got it all wrong. I am not a crime boss. I am a legit business man. The rest of your story is false too and, although my safe is blown, it is empty at the time."

The announcer states, "The thief is in custody but the cops are not releasing his name. The cops are searching for witnesses to the crime and if anyone has any information about the robbery, they should call the cops right away."

Ring! Ring! Ring! Bam! Bam! Bam! Hotdog Harry is ringing the bell and knocking on the door and appears to be a most excited guy. I will let him in and tell you what further events unfold.

Dear John,

Hotdog Harry and Yours Truly discuss the events of yesterday and we agree that WNEU does definitely get it all wrong. At the time Seabiscuit collides with Hotdog Harry he is holding not two but three cloth bags, one of which goes sailing across the street and down the sewer drain on the other side of East 34th St. Hotdog Harry and Yours Truly are now wondering just what it is that makes two bags break open and spill C-notes all over but a third cloth bag does not break open and keeps going across the street and down a sewer drain.

Well my reading about guys and dolls offers a very helpful clue because, in one of the stories by Damon Runyon, a guy who goes by the handle Big Sky makes a bet he can throw a peanut very far when everybody knows a peanut is too light for a long trip through the air. But Big Sky wins the bet for he switches a regular peanut for one loaded with lead and it is the lead what carries the otherwise light as a peanut across a very far distance. So with that as a clue, Yours Truly concludes that bag number three contains something much heavier than C-notes. It is also known to Seabiscuit and most likely to Carmine Decrepio and some friends of his that a cloth bag containing something, what is heavier than paper, is down the drain.

Dear John,

As I am sitting on the stoop this afternoon deeply involved in reading about guys and dolls, a police car slowly drives up Leonard, passes right by without even a glance and stops in front of an apartment house about a block away. The cops get out and a citizen, an old guy what I see around from time to time, comes out and greets the cops. This is followed by a conversation and a lot of pernting up to the windows and the old guy does a lot of shaking of his head back and forth. I do not know what the deal is here but it looks like it has nothing to do with Yours Truly.

Dear John,

Since not one citizen in all of Williamsburg ever hears of these two guys who go by the handles, Hot Time Harold and Hastily Disturbed Danny, the cops have given up looking and so it is safe for Yours Truly to be sitting on the stoop catching up on my reading about guys and dolls.

Dear John,

Along about ten bells Hotdog Harry comes walking down Leonard, sits on the stoop next to me and whispers another very good suggestion which is to seek further advice from Saint Closétus and to this good suggestion I agree mainly because I am just about to make that very same suggestion when Hotdog Harry beats me to it. All we need is a closet but this happens to be a problem since, for reasons what I need not go into at the present moment nor perhaps at any other moment, Hotdog Harry is no longer invited to my apartment and, of course as you know, Yours Truly is no longer welcome in his apartment.

But quick action is needed immediately and I whisper to Hotdog Harry, "Just a few minutes prior to your arrival on this stoop, Saint Closétus appears inside the front door to this apartment house and I can see him through the glass window motioning to me with his finger to step into the vestibule which with a little imagination could be a closet. Well I do as Saint Closétus beckons and he tells me that it is very urgent that for the time being we drop our spy names and return to our original names."

Although I intend to add further explanations for this advice, just at that very same moment Gutsy Gus walks across the street after having a conversation with Mr. Joey Pits who is sitting on his stoop doing what he does mostly every day and that is complimenting young ladies as they pass by.

Gutsy Gus asks, "What are you too guys whispering about?"

To which I answer in a whisper, "We got laryngitis so it is important that we speak in a very quiet verse or else we can permanently get a horse in our throats."

As previously stated by Yours Truly, Gutsy Gus is well known in this neighborhood for his gutsy attitude and more by his gutsy actions and even more than that for his gutsy helpfulness. So Gutsy Gus insists that we walk up to his apartment, 2B on the fourth floor, for the poipose of administering a medicine composed of a spoonful of honey mixed with lemon juice and also mixed with a few drops of whiskey. This does sound like a swell medicine, especially the whiskey part. So while continuing to whisper about one thing or another, we climb the stairs, and enter 2B on the fourth floor.

Gutsy Gus says, "Wait here and I will get two teaspoons."

Nicholas suggests, "Two soup spoons are better."

Yours Truly agrees, "Two soup spoons are better because the medicine could spill out of the little teaspoons and what with the honey and lemon juice that can get pretty messy."

Gutsy Gus is smiling when he returns with two soup spoons each filled with a drop of honey, lemon juice but the spoon smells more like whiskey than any of the other ingredients.

After swallowing this medical brew, Nicholas talks without any hint of a horse in his throat when he says, "Well that is really good medicine. See it chased that horse right out of my throat."

Gutsy Gus says, "I am happy to help."

Then Gutsy Gus decides at the moment to tell us about stuff what he reads in a book what is called filosofy. But then he explains that this woird means in Greek the love of wisdom and it is spelled not the way I just spelled it but it is spelled as philosophy because philo means love and the sophy part means wisdom. Just about everything Gutsy Gus says after gets wasted because Nicholas got no idear about philosophy and Yours Truly presently has more interest in a more practical matter like another spoonful of that medicine. Well Nicholas has a similar interest what is demonstrated by his whispering again as if his horse returns to the stable and as a result Gutsy Gus offers another soup spoon of the medical brew.

Nicholas, in a horsey verse, speaks as follows, "Although this is a soup spoon, it is still a little spoonful of medicine and there is still the possibility of some medicine dripping onto the floor. The other problem is that the medicine does not last long enough and the horse returns too soon. So I suggest a small cup what will hold a little more of the medicine than a soup spoon."

Well Gutsy Gus smiles at that suggestion and says, "For a cup of this medicine, you will need show me evidence that you are 18 years old. Medicine like this comes only on a spoon."

Then Gutsy Gus goes into the kitchen and finds a much larger table spoon and pours the medicine as requested. Very soon thereafter Nicholas speaks with a clear and horseless verce. But soon enough the horse returns to his stable and this opening the gate for the horse and the horse returning goes on for quite some time and as the clock ticks away Nicholas's interest in philosophy increases and so does anything else Gutsy Gus wishes to discuss while administering a large table spoonful of medicine.

Well one thing leads to another as we are discussing this and that about the right way to think and the right way to do things what Gutsy Gus calls ethics. Just then the horse releases Nicholas's tongue and he asks, "Gutsy Gus, what is the right thing to do if you know a secret what is really a big secret, and you gotta tell somebody but not telling and telling is both bad and bad. There just ain't much good gonna come out of it neither way."

Gutsy Gus answers as such, "That is a matter of ethics where you must choose the lesser of two evils. So you must ask yourself which is a little bit better, telling or not telling?"

Well, in my opinion this is not a good time for Nicholas to be spilling the beans about any number of secrets and so I look at the clock on the wall and I say, "Look at the time! It's late! It is time for us to get downstairs and …"

I don't get a chance to finish my sentence because Gutsy Gus is likewise surprised by how quickly time flies and so he exclaims, "Tempus Frigid!", a thing what he says so often that I gather it means a clock stops because it is cold. So to impress Gutsy Gus and Nicholas with my knowledge of Latin I say to Gutsy Gus, "It is not cold enough for a clock to stop." However, my attempt to impress Gutsy Gus with my knowledge of Latin is unsuccessful because Gutsy Gus explains that he does not say *tempus frigid* but he does say te*mpus fugit* means time flies. But then he decides to teach a more complete lesson in Latin and states, "What Virgil actually writes is, 'fugit irreparabile tempus' and there is much more to say but that will have to be taken up at a later time."

After that Gutsy Gus again looks at his watch and says, "I'm late for an appointment. I have to run right away. So you two shut the door when you leave." And with that said, Gutsy Gus picks up a neatly wrapped package and runs downstairs. I notice that the conversation about Latin has little or no interest for Nicholas who is busy licking all the spoons.

As I am watching Gutsy Gus open the door and close it after him I do not immediately know the reason for the loud thud in back of me. When I turn I see Nicholas crawling across the room. He grabs hold of a chair and struggles to his feet.

Just then a cloud of black smoke rises outside the open window. A gust of wind fills the window with smoke and enters the room. Nicholas staggers to the window, chokes on the smoke, grabs for the window ledge but he misses. I run to the window and grab Nicholas's feet just before his upper body exits in a sudden upside down departure. After I help Nicholas place his feet on the floor, we look out the window, which is now clear of smoke.

Big Boris is opening the back door and Gutsy Gus steps in and disappears into that very same Fleetwood. But then something else confuciuses Yours Truly more than somewhat and it is this: Mr. Joey Pits, all dressed up in a Dapper-Dan zoot suit, walks out of his apartment building two doors down the block, crosses the street, and walks right up to the big beautiful black Fleetwood. The back door on the left side opens and Mr. Joey Pits enters the Fleetwood which, after puffing a smoke cloud, slowly moves down the street and turns left at the first corner.

Nicholas says, "You sood, you shod, you should go and get some more admice from Saint Codslet. But first I have to go to the baffroom."

Well since there is nothing to do about the present mysterious goings on and since there is no immediate concern about Nicholas falling out a window, there is little else to do but to search for a closet and I find a most suitable hall closet in this very apartment. Nicholas finishes throwing up in the baffroom, flushes a couple of times, staggers into the hallway and sits on the floor, which in my opinion is a good choice for in this position Nicholas is likely not to fall on his face or out the window. From his seat on the floor Nicholas looks up and asks, "Do I see what I shee or do I not shee what I see? I mean donstes, donsars, donstairs Mr. Joey Pist gets in the Feetward, the flee, the big car. Do I see what I see or what?"

Well after Nicholas and Yours Truly agree that we both see Mr. Joey Pits enter the Fleetwood, and we agree also that this is a most confuciusing event and even a mysterious proposition, we carefully shut the door, walk down to the street and walk around the block a few times. Nicholas as a result wobbles less and he wobbles even less when he sits on the stoop. Then after I take my place on the stoop, I inform Nicholas, "While you were throwing up in the baffroom, I was looking around the apartment and I open the hallway closet and who was present in that very closet? Well it was none other than Saint Closétus." I further state the following, "Saint Closétus is very proud of us because we do what he tells us to do especially that part about changing our names and he agrees that we do the right thing by retreating yesterday from East 34th St. But then he tells me to change our names again and from this moment on you are to be known as Horseless Horace and my new name is Medicine Mike."

Chapter 10
Say Please!

Dear John,

Many a citizen in this neighborhood is very concerned that somebody is going around robbing apartments. Yesterday I tell you about that old citizen, what got the visit from the cops. Well he lives in one of the apartments what got robbed. The problem is that nobody knows how the robber gets into the apartment because there is no broken down door and the robber does not come through the window except maybe he can jump from the sidewalk up to the third floor. So this is quite a mystery here and about.

Dear John,

At our meeting this morning of OTS (Operation Top Secret), Horseless Horace announces he is more than agreeable regarding his new name and says as such, "Horseless Horace is indeed a more distinguished name than the former, Hotdog Harry, and from my point of view your name, Medicine Mike, is much easier to remember than Seriously Disturbed Donny,"

Well it is obvious to me that memory is somewhat more than a challenge to Horseless Horace for that which is mentioned is not my previous name. However, since there is no cash value in correcting Horseless Horace and since there are far more important things to discuss and plans to be made, it is time to change the topic of this conversation and to move forward to other important matters, one of which is the concern about that cloth bag what weighs more than a bag of C-notes. But first there is that which Horseless Horace and Yours Truly, Medicine Mike, observe when we are looking out the window in Gutsy Gus's apartment. This is a matter of two or three or maybe more incidents, depending on how you count something as an incident. The first is that Gutsy Gus gets into the beautiful black six door Fleetwood. This I personally observe but Horseless Horace states that he also observes Big Boris who steps out and opens one of the back doors for Gutsy Gus and there is a hand with a big beautiful diamond ring what reaches out to lead Gutsy Gus into the Fleetwood. Although I am not convinced whether sobriety is or is not a factor in what Horseless Horace describes from memory, I tend to believe it since I do now remember something shining and glistening in the sun reaching out to Gutsy Gus and I also remember, when last week the doll greets me on the stoop, she is wearing a very shiny and glistening diamond ring on her middle finger.

The next topic to be taken up during this meeting of OTS is for me to tell Horseless Horace that last night I have another visit from Saint Closétus in my very own bedroom closet and, while speaking in a low spooky verse, this is what I say when I quote woird for woird eggsactly what Saint Closétus states, "You two have to go and investigate that cloth bag what goes sliding across East 34th St. and winds up in the NYC sewer system. You need to find that bag and see its contents before anybody else and ..."

But just then Horseless Horace interrupts Saint Closétus who is sort of speaking in his own spooky verse through me like what I see in a movie about a medium lady. Horseless Horace asks a very good question and this is what he says, "How come Saint Closétus knows about the cloth bag but, if he is a saint and all, how come he does not already know the contents of that cloth bag what goes sliding across East 34th St. and winds up in the NYC sewer system?"

To this question I do not respond immediately mainly because I do not know what to say. It is such a good question that it takes me ten seconds, give or take a few seconds, to come up with an answer that is in keeping with and fitting to the present situation and therefore perfectly truthful.

After reviewing several possible answers to the question as stated above, Yours Truly answers as follows, "Well maybe Saint Closétus knows what is in the cloth bag but if he himself does not know the contents of this bag or any other bag, all he has to do is go up to God and he can ask. He can say, 'Tell me God Almightly, Creator of heaven and earth, what is …' And Saint Closétus can fill in the rest of the sentence and God will tell Saint Closétus the contents of any bag anywhere and whatever ends the sentence, whatever that ending may be, because as the nun tells us in Catchekism, God is omniscientific and that means He knows everything but he keeps most things a secret because we have to pass a test here on earth to figure things out on our own and in this way it is more entertaining for God to watch people mostly mess up. But then it does not end up all that good for people who do not figure out the right things. But the saints already passed the test and got it all right the first time so they no longer need to figure out things on their own."

Well at first Horseless Horace shakes his head and looks pretty satisfied with that answer either because it is such a good and truthful answer or because it is such a long answer that Horseless Horace is lost along the way. But then Horseless Horace looks at me, puts up his hand to stop me from further addressing this issue and shakes his head and this shaking of his head causes me anxiety more than somewhat.

So I look at Horseless Horace, squint my eyes and put my finger up to the side of my head and I say, "Oh wait! I almost forget! Now I do remember Saint Closétus does go up to God and says, 'Tell me God Almightly, Creator of heaven and earth, what are the contents of that cloth bag what goes sliding across East 34th St. and winds up in the NYC sewer system?'"

Horseless Horace asks, "Is it your honest to goodness truth that you quote woird for woird eggsactly what Saint Closétus asks?"

I answer, "It is indeed the honest to goodness truth that I quote woird for woird eggsactly what Saint Closétus asks."

"Well then it is the case that Saint Closétus does not know the contents of that bag and that is why he wants us to investigate and find out the contents."

I ask, "Why do you think God does not tell Saint Closétus the contents of that bag when he asks?"

"God does not to tell Saint Closétus and I will tell you the reason God does not tell the contents of that bag. The reason is that whenever you ask for a favor, you have to say *please.* Saint Closétus does not say *please.*"

So with a sigh of relief I add, "Right! You are right. Saint Closétus does not know the contents of that bag because he does not say *please.* He just forgets to add that most important woird and of course Saint Closétus and any other saint should start such a request by saying *please*, except maybe the Holy Virgin Mary, the mother of God, who has special privileges and does not need to be extra polite. She can ask God for anything any time and she does not even need to make an appointment or to say *please*. And if God asks, "Why do you want me to do such and such," she can answer, "Because I say so." Mary can say something like that because that's the way a mother speaks to her son. If she does not say that, then she is not acting like a real mother and since she is a real mother, she does say such a thing. Mary is the mother of Jesus, who is otherwise known as God, and she gets so many prayers with so many people asking her for a favor or two, she barely has time to get all her housework done and when she tells God what to do, she has no time to say *please*. So I am sure that Holy Virgin Mary, Mother of God, can get away with not saying *please*. Then I ask the following, "Does not your mother say, 'Because I say so'?"

Horseless Horace says, "My mom says that and then she says, 'You're being a bit dense, you are.'"

But then Horseless Horace demonstrates his satisfaction with my response by smiling and nodding his head up and down and thus this situation is resolved and the topic moves on to just how Horseless Horace and Yours Truly, Medicine Mike, are to find out what is in the cloth bag what is now resting in the NYC sewer system. There is one small problem with the location of the bag. The problem is rain. For in a case such as that, the heavy bag and its contents can be moved somewhere down the sewer and toward the East river but there is no rain for many days this summer and it is quite likely that the cloth bag and its heavy contents are resting where it entered on the corner of East 34th St. and the Avenue of the Americas.

Tomorrow morning we set out to find that cloth bag what goes sliding across East 34th St. and winds up in the NYC sewer system. If I pray and ask for God to help in finding the bag, I better say *please*.

Chapter 11
One C-Note

Dear John,

This morning along about nine bells Horseless Horace comes walking up and sits next to Yours Truly on the stoop. Horseless Horace appears to be full of questions lately for he asks one and it is also a good one which follows, "How are we to travel to East 34th St. and the Avenue of the Americans since all our money from Lucky Luigi is long gone and we do not have enough money to buy subway tokens?"

Well I have an extremely good answer to that question and I reach deep into my pocket and pull out five keys tied together with a string, one half of a Spalding ball, three marbles, one spoon with peanut butter sticking to it, one peanut shell filled with lead and finally one C-note. And I answer further, "We have sufficient funds for OTS to make many excursions to 34th and the Americans."

Handcuff Harry's eyes open wide and he asks, "Where did you get that?"

"I found it!" My answer is no lie because I did find it right near East 34th St. and I found another one too but that is to be of no consequence at this time and I therefore do not mention the additional C-note in my other pocket.

Horseless Horace and Yours Truly, Medicine Mike, head off to Woolworth's Five and Dime because such change is necessary to purchus tokens. The Five and Dime, located on Grand St. is a short walk around the corner and up a couple of blocks. Horseless Horace and Yours Truly, Medicine Mike, enter the store and go up to the soda fountain located on the right side of the store. Horseless Horace, in a most polite verse and manner, asks the soda jerk as such, "Sir, we need some dimes and nickels and since this is a dime and nickel store, we would like some change in just those coins." The soda jerk responds as such, "Whad do I look like, a banker? You wanna buy sumtin or not? I don't just give out no change widout youse buyin sumtin."

But then Yours Truly asks, "Why are you being so grumpy when all we are asking for is some change for this?" And after saying that, I hold up a C-note to demonstrate that we have nothing but good will and, of course, a C-note.

Well when Mr. Grumpy Soda Jerk takes a gander at what I am holding in my hand, he becomes more than somewhat interested and in fact he changes his tune and says, "OK, kids. I can change that into nickels and dimes but I gotta get the change from the back room so give me the dollar you are holding in your hand and I'll will take it into the back room and get you change in dimes and nickels."

I look around and wonder if we are standing near Newtown Creek. I turn to Horseless Horace and I whisper into his ear, "I am smelling something fishy here and I think it not a good idear to hand over this C-note when Mr. Grumpy Soda Fountain Jerk calls the C-note a one dollar bill. In fact I think it a very good idear to exit this establishment as quickly as our feet can travel."

Horseless Horace shakes his head up and down in

agreement and with that I stick the C-note deep into my pocket and we are out the front door quick as a flash.

As we are heading back to Maujer, we pass the Chaste National Bank. I suggest this bank may be a more suitable place for us to seek change for our C-note because they are more likely to know the difference between a C-note and a one dollar bill. So we enter the Chaste Bank for the poipose of cashing the C-note into dimes and nickels what we need for to purchus tokens. We walk up to the window and I say to the teller, "We wish to cash in this C-note and acquire an equal amount of money half in dimes and half in nickels." The teller, a very well dressed fellow with a bowtie, smiles and says, "We are not able to cash this hundred dollar bill for half dimes and half nickels because we do not have enough dimes and nickels in my drawer and most likely not in this entire bank."

So we are indeed disappointed by this answer and we leave and head for a teller at the Manhattan Company Bank and then to a teller at the Bushwick Savings Bank and the tellers at two other banks, what are in Greenpernt, a far walk outside of this neighborhood. The reason for our visit to so many banks is that at each bank we are told by the tellers that they do not have that much money in their drawers and that there are not enough dimes and nickels in their banks to fulfill our request.

So Horseless Horace and Yours Truly, Medicine Mike, are back sitting on the stoop of the apartment house on Leonard and we are very worried about these banks what are running out of money and we are thinking that this is one proposition we should not keep secret what with the worthless C-note back in the bottom of my pocket, and one more in my other pocket, and if people got money in such banks, they need to know the banks do not have much money left.

We are accustomed to believe that a C-note is a lot of loot but Yours Truly is becoming more than somewhat worried about the lack of value of the C-note since no one cares about providing change in dimes and nickels except for one jerk. Horseless Horace and Yours Truly, Medicine Mike, are not only concerned and worried about our personal funds but we are becoming very concerned that banks have insufficient funds to cash the C-note.

Dear John,

The plan of setting out early to find that cloth bag what goes sliding across East 34th St. and winds up in the NYC sewer system does not exactly woirk out. Trying to cash that C-note for dimes and nickels takes more time than we expect.

So it is now along about two bells this afternoon. Horseless Horace and Yours Truly, Medicine Mike are back sitting on the stoop continuing to talk about the problem of banks running out of money when a large cloud of black smoke comes rolling down Leonard and pulls up to the curb. After the cloud disperses, Big Boris exits the big beautiful six door black Fleetwood and opens one of the back doors and out steps Gutsy Gus who is holding and now releasing a hand what got a big diamond ring on the middle finger. I kick Horseless Horace so he looks at who is in the back seat but the door closes before we can see anything but a hand with a big diamond ring on the middle finger.

But just then the back door on the other side of the big beautiful six door black Fleetwood opens and out steps Mr. Joey Pits in his Dapper Dan zoot suit. He walks across the street toward his apartment building and then turns and waves to Gutsy Gus and then salutes Big Boris.

Well before there is any opportunity to comment on

what we just witness, Gutsy Gus steps across the sidewalk, looks at the two of us who are sitting on the stoop and sits down right in between and he talks to us in a very low and very serious verse and what he says follows, "I want you two to make me a promise never to tell anyone, especially anyone in 2B on the fourth floor, about the comings and goings of that Cadillac."

Well Horseless Horace and Yours Truly, Medicine Mike, immediately put our hands behind our backs and shake our heads like to say we promise. But that does not work for Gutsy Gus who says as follows, "Boys, I live in this neighborhood and on this very block and in this very apartment house upstairs in 2B on the fourth floor long enough to know that a promise made with fingers crossed behind one's back will buy you as much as does a wooden nickel. So, boys, uncross your fingers and move your hands to the front so I can see them."

This surprises me more than somewhat because I never think Gutsy Gus knows about fingers crossed as undoing any promise but nevertheless Horseless Horace and Yours Truly, Medicine Mike, do as Gutsy Gus says and then he continues to speak, "Now promise to keep the comings and goings of this Cadillac to yourselves and never say a woird to anyone, especially to any one in 2B on the fourth floor, about of that Cadillac."

Horseless Horace and Yours Truly, Medicine Mike, put our hands out in front and shake our heads but Gutsy Gus says, "You must say, 'I promise.'" Then Horseless Horace says, "I promise." And Yours Truly, Medicine Mike, says, "I promise never to say a woird about the comings and goings of that Cadillac."

Of course, when I promise never to say a woird about the before mentioned goings and comings of that Cadillac, the promise does not in any way obligate me not to write a woird or two or even more than a few about the comings and goings of that Cadillac.

But then I think maybe I should share the proposition that the banks in our neighborhood and one or two in Greenpernt where we walk far outside of this neighborhood do not have sufficient funds in their cash registers to cash a C-note.

So I say to Gutsy Gus that which I have just been thinking. I say to him like this, "Banks in our neighborhood and even a couple in Greenpernt, what are more than somewhat far from our neighborhood, are all out of money since they are not able to cash a C-note."

Then I demonstrate that I have such a C-note by digging deep into my pocket and pulling out five keys tied together with a string, one half of a Spalding ball, three marbles, one peanut shell filled with lead and finally one C-note. I do not bother to remove the spoon with peanut butter because it is sticking to the side of my pocket.

Well, I think maybe we should get something in exchange for that promise what we so recently make and what we now gotta keep. So I ask Gutsy Gus for some advice, "If a bank does not have enough money to cash a C-note and if a guy goes to five banks and none of these banks have enough money to cash the C-note, should we not go around telling people banks are running out of money like what I hear happens a few years ago in 1929?"

Well, after I explain the whole problem, Gutsy Gus says, "I think I may know how to straighten out the whole deal and I wish you to escort me to the nearest bank."

Well we escort Gutsy Gus for a short walk to the Chaste Bank and he walks right up to the nearest teller and exchanges the C-note for one hundred dollars in the following destinations: 4 twenties, 4 sawbucks, 4 fins, 10 singles and a pocket full of dimes and nickels. Although that's the end of that proposition, the problem is easy to see. Banks do not want to cash a C-note for kids like us but Gutsy Gus is a lot older and they cash it for him and that's what I call age disincrimination!

But later that day after we thank and bid a doo to Gutsy Gus, Nicholas asks another very good question what is as follows, "How come Gutsy Gus does not even ask us how we come about having a C-note?"

This, of course, is what is known as a ratticorical question and that means there is no need for Yours Truly to produce a truthful or any other kind of answer. So I respond by shrugging my shoulders what is generally known to be the best reaction to a question that is purely ratticorical.

Well at any rate with cold cash in our pockets, we are now ready to head off to East 34th St. and the Avenue of the Americans and to find out what is in that bag what is heavier than a bag full of C-notes.

Chapter 12

The Sewer

Dear John,

It does not take all that long to get from the Lorimer St. station to East 34th St. and the Avenue of the Americans when you practice a lot. It is also helpful to avoid train accidents by staying clear of old ladies what board the train at stations such as The Bowery and Canal Street or in the vicinity thereof. So in almost no time at all Horseless Horace and Yours Truly, Medicine Mike, are standing on the corner curb and we are gazing down through a sewer grating into which a cloth bag, what is heavier than a bag full of C-notes, slides into the sewer system below.

As the case may be, and as Yours Truly is a big thinker in such situations, we come prepared with a plan what I devise while sitting on the stoop back on Leonard and this plan involves a fifty pound fishing line with a hook strong enough to snare a giant squid, or better, a naked mermaid, although neither of these are likely to be snared under this sewer grating. Just a little wishful thinking going on, especially about the naked mermaid. However, there is a possibility that one could snare an alligator for it is a well-known fact that well-fed alligators habitate the sewers of New York City.

There is somewhat more to this plan as you will gather and as I explain the course of the events taking place this afternoon. Although the plan is as well thought out as ever a plan can be, there are unforeseen snags along the way. For example, when one looks through a grating down into a deep dark sewer, there is nothing much to see and it is such a proposition that exists this very afternoon when Horseless Horace and Yours Truly, Medicine Mike, are standing above the sewer grating at the corner of East 34ᵗʰ St. and the Avenue of the Americans. There are two other annoying concerns and one is that very many citizens walk up and down East 34ᵗʰ St. what makes it difficult to stand still for all the pushing and shoving what some citizens are apt to do and, when the traffic lights turn green on the Avenue of the Americans, an even greater number of citizens rush across that avenue and the crowds make it impossible for two guys to even stand next to one another without getting pushed and shoved here and there and back and forth.

The other problem is even more serious and that is the problem of cars driving over the sewer grating, an occurrence what makes it just about impossible to fish for a cloth bag what weighs more than a bag full of C-notes. However, for proceedings such as the first problem, that of the pushing and shoving crowds of citizens, a plan is necessary and this plan involves a diversion what in turn requires an investment of about half a C-note, otherwise known as fifty bucks what is part of the plan before we head out for Manhattan. This very afternoon at about one-thirty Horseless Horace and Yours Truly, Medicine Mike, visit the Chaste Bank what Gutsy Gus visits a couple of days ago because it is now a known fact that this particular bank, unlike others in our neighborhood, has sufficient funds to cash a C-note and thus we cash two twenties and a ten and we obtain fifty George Washingtons. So that first problem concerning the crowds of citizens, we intend to solve with a detraction and this involves Horseless Horace standing against the corner building and handing out one dollar bills to passersby and so it happens that many a citizen stops walking and a crowd gathers around Horseless Horace and such a crowd definitely has the desired effect such that the rushing and pushing diminishes more than somewhat but the second problem remains and that is the cars what drive up and onto the sewer grating as Yours Truly attempts to snag a cloth bag of unknown heavy contents from the bottom of the sewer.

So I am sitting on the curb, picking up my legs now and then so they do not get run over by some inconsiderate driver. I am thus pretending to be doing nothing of any notice and most citizens are not noticing me when all of a sudden a Cadillac La Salle pulls up and stops right on top of the sewer grating and a man jumps out from the passenger door and runs across the sidewalk, shoving citizens here and there. This man from the passenger side of the Cadillac La Salle grabs Horseless Horace and pulls him toward the Cadillac La Salle. Well this causes quite a bit of a confusion and disappointment among citizens who are about to lose their opportunities to get their free dollar handout to which they feel entitled. While Yours Truly is still sitting on the curb, several citizens are noisily complaining about their mistreatment and some even express concern about the treatment being handed out to Horseless Horace. The man from the passenger side of the Cadillac La Salle shouts, "It's OK! This kid is my son. He is trying to run away but …"

Nicholas interrupts by shouting, "He is not my father. He is kidnapping me!"

The citizens gather around and stand still because they do not know who to believe. Nevertheless the man from the passenger side of the Cadillac La Salle is shaking Horseless Horace and he sort of gives it away by asking, "What is your name? What are you doing here?"

"My name is Horseless Horace and I am here with my friend here, Medicine Mike, who as you can see, is fishing for what are in the sewers all over this fine city, namely alligators."

The crowd of citizens starts to surround the man from the passenger side of the Cadillac La Salle but they just stand there still wondering what is going on and who is telling the truth.

It must be handed to Horseless Horace for he follows one part of our plan very well and that is the fib about fishing for alligators but I am inclined to think that part what includes me in these proceedings is best omitted. However, the driver of the Cadillac La Salle steps out onto the curb and looks directly down on me and I look up into his face and this is a face I recognize for this is none other than the face of Seabiscuit who grabs me by the shoulders and begins to shake me while shouting, "Where is the bag?"

Now I look at Seabiscuit with as honestly a puzzled look as anyone can fake and I say, "What bag are you talking about? I do not know anything about no bag. I am just sitting here, minding my own business while fishing for an alligator or two."

Next Seabiscuit and his driving companion are pulling Horseless Horace and Yours Truly, Medicine Mike, into the Cadillac La Salle when all of a sudden a 1952 Packard 250 Mayfair Hardtop drives up the Avenue of the Americans and screeches to a halt directly in back of the Cadillac La Salle. Two very big thugs jump out of the 1952 Packard

250 Mayfair Hardtop and grab hold of Seabiscuit and his driving companion and these two release their grips on Horseless Horace and Yours Truly. Seabiscuit and his driving companion are then shoved into the back seat of the 1952 Packard 250 Mayfair Hardtop and indeed Seabiscuit and his traveling companion are willing to go because these two very big thugs are pointing pistols at them. Well, what with horns blowing from cars what are totally blocked by the 1952 Packard 250 Mayfair Hardtop and the Cadillac La Salle, and what with many citizens screaming about being mistreated because they are about to lose out on a dollar bill to which they are entitled, things on East 34th St. and the Avenue of the Americans are confusing to say the least.

Well, all of a sudden things go very quiet and back to normal. Once again citizens are pushing and shoving Horseless Horace and Yours Truly, Medicine Mike, out of their way as we are standing on the curb as if nothing at all out of the ordinary happens. I look around and I can Medicine Mike is smiling and pointing to the 1952 Packard 250 Mayfair Hardtop what is driving away with Seabiscuit and his driving companion in the back seat squeezed between the two very large thugs.

One might think all this excitement and confusion would add to our problems but in fact they add to the solution of one of our more challenging problems, that of the cars driving over the sewer grating. The solution is that the Cadillac La Salle is now abandoned and is blocking the way for cars to drive over the sewer grating and this provides Yours Truly with an opportunity to continue fishing for alligators, which of course is just an alibi for that which we are actually doing and that is fishing for a cloth bag, the contents of which remain unknown.

I drop the fishhook into the sewer which is now protected

by the abandoned Cadillac La Salle and immediately I snag something and it is heavy. In the meantime Horseless Horace returns to his station alongside the corner building and he once again proceeds to distribute one dollar bills to citizens and again a crowd gathers and the pushing and shoving and tripping over me decreases.

I slowly pull up what has been snagged on the fishing line and by this time Horseless Horace has abandoned the corner of the building and returns to the curb to inform me he runs out of one dollar bills and he is ankshisly standing next to me as citizens push and shove and say some nasty things as they trip over Yours Truly. Slowly I pull on the line and that which has been snagged is now at the top of the grating but too big to fit through so I suggest to Horseless Horace that he crawl under the Cadillac La Salle and stretch his arm around and under the grating and pull out that which has been snagged by the fish hook and when this is done and what I see at the end of the fish line and now snuggly clenched in Horseless Horace's hand is the biggest dead rat I ever in my life see, bigger than the biggest I ever witness in all my years of watching rats run across Grand Street in Williamsburg.

Then Horseless Horace crawls out from under the Buick, looks at the contents of his hands, and let's out quite an enthusiastic scream as he throws the rat up into the air which without much ado returns, not directly to the sidewalk, since its fall is interrupted by one citizen's little pink hat which happens to be a very pretty pink hat on a very lovely Pan American Airline stewardess. Well this creates such a diversion what with the very lovely Pan American Airline stewardess screaming and throwing the rat again into the air and thus the rat is flying and landing on one citizen's head and then flying to another citizen's head and this flying rat works well as a legitimate detraction. This detraction provides Yours Truly with the opportunity to ensnare another object which turns out to be much heavier than a very swollen dead rat. That which is on the end of the alligator fishing line again requires assistance from Horseless Horace who is more than somewhat reluctant to crawl again under the Cadillac La Salle and to stretch his arm around and under the grating and to pull out that which has been snagged by the fish hook. However, Horseless Horace is persuaded by my argument that this may be the cloth bag what is so important that Saint Closétus has sent us on the mission to discover the contents of this big what is heavier than a bag of C-notes. So Horseless Horace crawls under the Cadillac La Salle and stretches his arm around and under the grating and pulls out that which has been snagged by the fish hook and when this is done and what I see at the end of the fish line and now snuggly clenched in Horseless Horace's hand is the very same heavy cloth bag for which we are searching.

Very shortly after this, the dead rat finds its way back into the sewer with the help of a few kicks from a young sailor who is more than a little helpful to the injured party of the first part who of course is the lovely Pan American Airline stewardess with the pink hat. The very lovely Pan American Airline stewardess and her new sailor friend are standing quite still and creating a further diversion for they are striking up a conversation and blocking other citizens from interfering with our on-going rescuing of the cloth bag. While ignoring a citizen or two who continue to shout and scream about the attack of the rat, Horseless Horace and Yours Truly, Medicine Mike, decide to depart and thus we walk away quietly and as innocently as a couple of young guys can appear under such circumstances. Although we are now fifty dollars lighter, Horseless Horace is wise enough to retain two subway tokens and thus we enjoy a comfortable ride back to the Lorimer St. Station. Although while traveling we very greatly desire to open and gaze into the package what weighs considerably more than a bag full of C-notes, we do not do so on the subway. It is sufficient for us to hear the contents of the bag clinking and rattling as the train swerves from side to side. Indeed the bag is heavier than a school bag filled with a dozen or more school books. Of course, this comparison is not one I can attest to from experience for I never carry a school bag with any amount of books since I never do any homework and this is because I let on to the teachers that I am neither able to read nor to write.

In the late afternoon along about five bells Horseless Horace and Yours Truly, Medicine Mike, return to our neighborhood and since the events of the day have increased our appetites and, since Medicine Mike admits he holds out about five bucks from his handouts to citizens along East 34th St. and the Americans, we head for Randy's Restaurant for the poipose of holding a special meeting while chomping down a couple of the best and greasiest hamburgers in all of Brooklyn; although I hear it said there is much competition from Charley's Chuckburgers down in Sheepshead Bay.

While we are chomping away, I take my hand and untie the cord on top of the cloth bag what is lying on the seat next to me and I reach into the bag and very slowly, while trying not to attract any attention to the clinking sounds, I withdraw my hand and between my thumb and my index finger there is a very shiny bone. Well after I pick out about five smaller bones Horseless Horace and Yours Truly, Medicine Mike, are most disappointed at what we find in this bag. However, Horseless Horace sees some value to the biggest bone for he knows of a stray dog who loves to chomp on bones such as this.

Well we finish our hamburgers and as we are paying our bill to Hamburger Henry who is not all that happy to see us after our last visit. But then Hamburger Henry smiles when I give him a big tip what equals the amount owed from our last visit when we departed so hastily. As I am paying the bill for today along with the tip, Horseless Horace points to the New York Mirror with the headlines what says "Safe Bombing Suspects Released" Under the headline it says, "Two suspects in the bombing of Carmine Decrepio's safe are released this morning." I keep reading and it further states that the suspects' begged the judge to keep them in jail but Judge Georgio Decrepio released the two suspects due to a lack of evidence.

When we go out of Randy's Restaurant we see a 1952 Packard 250 Mayfair Hardtop parked across the street. I pull Horseless Horace back out of the street and I say, "That 1952 Packard 250 Mayfair Hardtop looks just like the 1952 Packard 250 Mayfair Hardtop that packed away Seabiscuit and his traveling companion."

Then Horseless Horace points to a guy standing on the corner and says, "That guy standing on the corner looks just like one of the thugs who convinced Seabiscuit and his traveling companion to get into the 1952 Packard 250 Mayfair Hardtop."

Well Horseless Horace and Yours Truly head down to the cellar under Randy's Restaurant and wait a while and, as we are waiting, we open the cloth bag and spill the contents out onto the cellar floor. We find a whole bunch of religious looking stuff. There are small crosses, a metal cup and more than 20 round pieces of shiny metal with glass and one big cross with jewels on the top and bottom about as long as a 12 inch ruler. Some of these things are round and look like St. Christopher medals and others look like sun rays and others are square. All are made of a shiny yellow metal and inside each glass there is either something what is tiny and yellow or a tiny piece of cloth with some woirds on them what look like Latin woirds. I copy one of them and write it here, "sancta cecilia caecilian relica patrona sancta musica. Some small bones and cloth are also on the floor and they look like they fall out of some of the metal things what got broken glass. Each of these bones has a paper stuck to it with what look like names on them. One bone is pretty big and this is the one what comes out when Horseless Horace and Yours Truly, Medicine Mike, are sitting upstairs at Randy's Restaurant.

I suggest, "Horseless Horace, I think these bones are not such as what are good for that stray dog you previously mention. Maybe there is more to these bones and other stuff than what meets the eye."

We put the bones and religious stuff back into the bag and I suggest further, "Maybe the best thing to do is to show these bones and religious looking stuff to Gutsy Gus for he is such a smart guy he may know something about these objects and why Seabiscuit and his traveling companion are so interested in recovering them."

Well after about an hour during which we look at all the religious stuff and conversate about this or that and one thing and another, we head upstairs and see the 1952 Packard 250 Mayfair Hardtop is gone and the coast is clear but everybody who is walking up and down the street is talking about two strangers who drive a 1952 Packard 250 Mayfair Hardtop and are asking the whereabouts of two guys who live in this neighborhood and are known as Horrible Horseface and Medicine Man. But all the citizens are confused because they never know nobody what lives in this neighborhood what go by those names. It is once again time to conjurate Saint Closétus.

Chapter 13
Religious stuff

Dear John,

A closet! That is what we need right away and the first thing we do is to look for a closet suitable for the conjurating of Saint Closétus, but since we are persona non greater in both our apartments, we need to find a closet what is for us persona greater without that woird *non* stuck in the middle. So Horseless Horace and Yours Truly, Medicine Mike, are out walking about looking up and down Leonard for a closet or something that resembles a closet when who should we meet but Bobby Anderson who is back from *Send this Poor Boy to Camp Fund* and he is walking this way from Grand and carrying a big paper bag of what looks like groceries. Well from past experience we know Bobby Anderson got a closet where Saint Closétus first appears to Yours Truly.

So I say to Bobby Anderson as such: "Bobby Anderson how very nice it is to meet you here. Are you coming or going?"

Bobby Anderson responds in a manner such as this, "I am both coming and going for I am coming from Teitle's Grocery and that is why I am carrying this bag containing several items what include Wonder Bread and a box of cereal what goes snap, crackle and pop and I am going to a place where such items are consumed, namely my apartment."

Now I must pause in my writing at this point to let you know that Bobby Anderson does not actually speak in the lingo of which I have become familiar as a result of reading Damon Runyon but it is my way of writing so Bobby Anderson sounds much different in my writing than in his speaking. The same is likewise for much of that which Nicholas says. But the meaning of what they say and what I write are the same, more or less.

Well I suggest to Bobby Anderson as follows, "Now is that not a go-in-see-dents for we are both headed in that very direction and we appreciate your invitation to visit with you in your apartment."

Well, it is clear that Bobby Anderson is more than a little confused since he does not remember inviting us to his apartment but since he is not one to argue over trivial matters, Bobby Anderson looks directly at me and states, "Right, you are invited but the last time you visited, after your departure, I could not help but notice my bedroom closet was a total mess. So you are invited to my apartment but not to my bedroom closet."

Well since that invitation is of little use, I state, "Well thank you very much for the invitation and all but I just now remember we have an apperntment for which we are both late so we must be on our way, is that not correct, Nicholas?"

Now Horseless Horace looks confused because I use his original name what is Nicholas but that is because, if I do not do so, Bobby Anderson is even more confused than ever and it takes little effort to confuse Bobby Anderson in the first place. So Horseless Horace agrees and as we approach Bobby Anderson's apartment house, we bid ado to Bobby Anderson who walks up the stairs to his apartment while we find our way to the alley and what do we find there but a closet. Well to tell the truth, what we find in the alley is not what is eggsactly a closet but a big Refrigidaire box what is empty and this makes a perfect outdoor and portable closet. So right there we are holding this meeting of OTS, what is otherwise known as Operation Top Secret, in the alley of Bobby Anderson's apartment house.

Well the Refrigidaire box is too small for the two of us, which from my point of view is more than a little fortunate, so I tell Horseless Horace, "You gotta watch the alley so nobody happens to come along for it would be very interrupting for Saint Closétus while he provides advice in a closet such as this, what is not actually a closet but a Refrigidaire box, but the main thing is that this is such a closet as what has no problem about persona non greater nor otherwise."

So Horseless Horace goes off to the corner of the building and takes his look-out position and Yours Truly opens the closet door what is actually one panel what is slit open on the side of the box and I walk inside but within a minute or so Horseless Horace comes knocking on the box to inform me that two guys just drive up in a 1952 Packard 250 Mayfair Hardtop and so this information has the effect of hastening our departure from this alley by jumping up and over a back gate. However, this is no major problem for we find a very satisfactory hiding place in a 1920 Model A Ford what is parked in back of Bobby Anderson's apartment house. We have no concern about anyone driving off in this auto because the hood is up on one side displaying a motor that had cracked in half from what looks like an engine fire.

While Horseless Horace and Yours Truly are seated on the rear floor of the 1920 Model A Ford, I relate the experience what takes place when Yours Truly was in the Refrigidaire closet, the amount of time being just long enough to receive a message or two from Saint Closétus and this is what I relate, "Saint Closétus suggests, no, he actually insists, we change our names infective immediately and from this moment on you are to be known as One Buck Upchuck and I am now known as Sammy the Sewer."

One Buck Upchuck, formerly known by a long list of names originating with Nicholas, agrees and states, "Saint Closétus is obviously a very wise saint for he comes up with names what are well connected to our most recent history."

After a nod or two of my head to indicate agreement that Saint Closétus is indeed a very wise saint, I state as such, "Saint Closétus is indeed a very clever saint who watches just about everything we do and although we cannot see him, I am quite certain he is right here with us in the back seat of this 1920 Model A Ford and he knows the importance of our mission to save the Catholic Church and the rest of the world from the Commies and other bad people."

Then I relate to One Buck Upchuck somewhat more of the message what Saint Closétus delivers and, in the eggsact woirds as the saint delivered, I state, "Although you have been detracted by side adventures, you must continue your investigation involving Big Boris, Gutsy Gus and the doll and what their activities have to do with Commies infilterating the Catholic Church."

But One Buck Upchuck interrupts and asks a question of a religious nature which is as follows, "If Saint Closétus is always watching just about everything we do, and if he is here in the back seat of this 1920 Model A ford, what are our two guardian angels doing at these times and is there enough room for all five of us in this tiny cramped back area of this 1920 Model A Ford?"

Although this religious question would be best addressed at a more convenient time, I put my head down and think of an answer that will quickly satisfy One Buck Upchuck so we can get back to more urgent things to talk about. But One Buck Upchuck continues his concern about the overcrowding problem by stating, "Remember the nun told us to sit on the left side of our desks so the good angel can sit next to us? And we should sit on the very edge of the left side so any bad angels what work with the devil have no room to sit and so they have to sit on the floor."

So I respond to this very serious question such as, "There is no problem about having enough room in the back of this 1920 Model A Ford for two reasons. One reason is that it is a well-known fact that angels can shrink themselves to such teeny tiny little things that one hundred and twenty angels can fit on the head of a pin and, in the back of this 1920 Model A Ford, there is much room for many pins. The other reason is that just a couple of days ago Saint Closétus tells me that all the angels are on summer vacation. So God sends the saints down here to be like substitute angels. So you see either way there is no problem with overcrowding in the back of this 1920 Model A Ford."

One Buck Upchuck is so satisfied with this answer that he asks another question on a different topic, "What about this bag of religious stuff what I am often holding in my hand and carrying here and there? I am ankshis to know about this bag of religious stuff for it is not light and indeed it seems to get quite heavy the more I carry it here and there."

Although One Buck Upchuck speaks about carrying that bag of religious looking stuff, it does not appear at present to be in his possession. So I ask as such, "The whereabouts of the bag of religious looking stuff is a mystery to me. Do you hide the bag in a safe place where it will go undisturbed?"

But before One Buck Upchuck has any chance to respond, a serious incident of a different nature takes presidents over any moving forward related to these discussions.

Chapter 14

The Model A Ford Incident

Dear John,

There is quite a bit to tell you about an incident or two or three or four and probably more, if you are counting. This one incident, or many incidents, depending on what one defines as an incident, involves the 1920 Model A Ford and what happens after and resulting from a decision by One Buck Upchuck and Yours Truly, Sammy the Sewer, to hide in the previously mentioned 1920 Model A Ford.

While still sitting on the floor of the 1920 Model A Ford, Yours Truly hears verses what keep getting louder as they seem to be approaching the vehicle which One Buck Upchuck and Yours Truly presently inhabit. But One Buck Upchuck continues to speak in a loud verse as I try unsuccessfully by hand motions to indicate that it is unwise to continue speaking in a loud verse. But One Buck Upchuck's loud verse stops when his mouth is covered with an earl rag what I find on the car floor. Without any ill content on my part, the rag, what is very smelly from the earl and gas fumes, finds its way into One Buck Upchuck's open mouth just as he is taking a very deep breath in and it gets stuck deep in his throat. One Buck Upchuck is gagging and looking like he will soon perspire but a quick pull of a thread what is dangling from his mouth dislodges the earl rag what then exits from his throat. But that does not completely solve the problem concerning noise because One Buck Upchuck starts coffing with intermitting choking. Since Yours Truly is once again a very helpful guy, with my fist I punch One Buck Upchuck on his back and this action causes him to stop choking but then he is about to be true to his name once again for he is dry heaving heavily. But dry heavy heaving is not such a problem as choking since One Buck Upchuck's dry heavy heaving is an activity what makes little or no noise, at least not sufficient noise to be audible outside the 1920 Model A Ford. This problem is soon resolved when I reach into my very own pocket and produce a piece of stale hamburger bun, one of many leftovers what I take away from a past visit to Randy's Restaurant. After One Buck Upchuck takes several nibbles from the stale hamburger bun, he soon settles down. But then he points to the left side of the Ford thus indicating that he now also hears verses. The verses are sounding much like two men and these could be the very two thugs who are driving in the 1952 Packard 250 Mayfair Hardtop. But a sneaky peek reveals that these men are unrecognizable and neither of these two sound like the 1952 Packard 250 Mayfair Hardtop thugs. One guy has a verse what is very gruff and the other guy's verse is sort of soft.

I lift my head just enough to see Sort of Softly shutting the hood on the burned out engine and the next sound is that of a truck getting louder as it is backing into the alley. It stops in front of the Ford and a chain is being applied to the front bumper. I am about to suggest we quickly exit the back of the 1920 Model A Ford but another sneaky little peak reveals the two thugs what drive the 1952 Packard

250 Mayfair Hardtop are standing at the front of the alley and they are showing interest in the activity just described.

Then the front door on the driver's side opens and Gruffy sits in front of the steering wheel. Yours Truly and One Buck Upchuck crouch down as low as possible on the back floor. Then the brake is released and the Ford starts moving.

One Buck Upchuck and Yours Truly look at each other but we don't even whisper one woird. Where the 1920 Model A Ford is heading is a complete mystery and since there is no way to look out the window without being seen by the driver, and possibly by the two 1952 Packard 250 Mayfair Hardtop driving thugs, the mystery remains a mystery for quite some time. The 1920 Model A Ford pulls out of the alley and turns left onto Maujer. As it passes Leonard the top of P.S. 18 is clearly visible. But what is also visible is the top front part of a 1952 Packard 250 Mayfair Hardtop what is now following very close. Then the Model A Ford pulled by a tow truck makes a right turn onto Lorimer and then another right onto what looks like Grand Street. At first, tops of apartment buildings pass and then after much of a ride tops of factories and warehouses come into view. Just about this time One Buck Upchuck indicates, by a hand motion, what is pointing to a part of his body what is best left unmentioned, that he has a need to use the baffroom. But then by his twisted face it becomes more than a simple need; it is becoming an urgent need.

Well, John, maybe you remember I previously recognize Nicholas's urgent need to be a problem. So Yours Truly looks around but there is obviously no baffroom in the 1920 Model A Ford and nothing else to offer as a substitute, not even a tin can on the back seat. But a tin can is not to be much of a help in any case because there is no room to move in any direction. So the next best thing to do is to help One Buck Upchuck forget about this need for there is no present solution other than maybe a detraction or two. But there is no way to create a detraction what makes the slightest noise since the motorless 1920 Model A Ford is very quietly rolling along and any noise will most certainly attract the attention of Gruffy.

So I do something what I practice somewhat more than often in school. See Yours Truly learns in school that practice makes poifect so I practice and again practice and keep practicing some things what are not eggsactly what a teacher wants practiced but it proves the pernt what is this, practice makes poifect. Well in fourth grade we have a real mean teacher what got the funniest face you ever see but then she makes it even funnier when she wrinkles her nose up and her mouth down. So that is eggsactly what I do to detract One Buck Upchuck's attention from his need to go to the baffroom. I tap One Buck Upchuck on the shoulder for the poipose of detracting his attention and when he twists his head around to see what the tapping is about, he smiles for I am wrinkling my nose up and wrinkling my mouth down. Although One Buck Upchuck smiles, all this effort does not seem to detract any attention away from what was previously mentioned. In fact, One Buck Upchuck makes a face what is almost as funny except for one or two things. In the first place this is not a funny face what is on poipose, and, in the second place, it is a face in pain and this pain comes from what appears to be an increasingly urgent need. But then One Buck Upchuck's need is also more than somewhat of an increasingly urgent concern given our present perdickamint.

Then with no action on my part, there comes a detraction of a different kind for I sniff a very familiar sniff and One

Buck Upchuck points to his nose and this indicates that he is sniffing what my nose is sniffing. What is it that the nose smells? As Jimmy Durante often says, "The nose knows." Well the nose knows Newtown Creek and that means we are heading a very long way from our neighborhood what is Williamsburg, Brooklyn. Since the ride what we are taking is occurring on a very hot summer day, the inside of the 1920 Model A Ford is getting very hot but the roof is tapping rain drops and I take a look between the front seats and see that the windshield is soon running with water and since the windshield is quite dirty to begin with, the rain is turning the dirt to mud and that means Gruffy cannot see where we are going. Gruffy turns a knob on the dashboard as if hoping somehow the windshield is about to clean the mud but nothing works when there is no motor to work it. Well, there is a good result what occurs from the rain and the windshield covered with mud and it is this, Gruffy first opens the side window and then pushes out the bottom of the front windshield. This activity sends much wet cooler air into the back seat and for a minute or two detracts One Buck Upchuck from his previous preoccupation.

Then the truck changes gears and starts climbing a pretty steep hill and we feel the gear change as a result the 1920 Model A Ford jerks forward resulting in my head clunking against the bottom of the back seat and likewise for the head belonging to One Buck Upchuck. Gruffy, the driver, who is not actually driving but steering the 1920 Model A Ford with a burned out motor turns his head to see what all the clunking is about but just then the truck makes a turn to the right and such a change is enuff to detract Gruffy who no longer appears concerned about clunking heads.

One Buck Upchuck is squirming more than somewhat as Yours Truly is doing the best that can be done in coming up with other detractions. But just then another detraction saves further efforts and this detraction is a bright flash of lightning followed very quickly by a crash of thunder.

As the ride continues the tops of any buildings vanish, only sky what is full of very dark stormy clouds is visible. The truck stops and the 1920 Model A Ford stops also but only after a slight collision into the rear of the truck. Both our heads clunk against the front seats but Gruffy is simultaneously clunking his head against the steering wheel and not paying much attention to other clunkings happening within the back seat of the 1920 Model A Ford.

After shaking his head, Gruffy opens the door and exits the Ford. Yours Truly and One Buck Upchuck peek our heads up for the poipose of discovering our whereabouts. There is a street sign what says Metropolitan Avenue and this surprises me more than somewhat because I suspect we have traveled a great distance but Metropolitan Avenue is not more than four blocks from Grand St. But this section of Metropolitan Avenue looks nothing like the avenue with the very same name what is in our neighborhood of Williamsburg. So I whisper to One Buck Upchuck as such, "Toto, I have a feeling we're not in Brooklyn anymore." Well, One Buck Upchuck responds to my statement in the following manner, "You must have clunked your head pretty hard because of the many names that you have recently known me as, Toto is not one of them."

There is another sign to which I pernt and One Buck Upchuck is also pernting to the eggsact same sign what reads *Ridgewood Auto Wreckers*. Now I know one very important thing about Ridgewood. It is not in Brooklyn.

Just then I see another car what looks very much like the 1920 Model A Ford in which we are presently hiding. The only difference is that the Model A Ford of which I speak is flatter than a pancake and is being dumped on top of several layers of cars what have also been crunched, flattened and pancaked. The car in which we are hiding is turned in such a way that it appears to be in line for the next crunching. Well this is not a very satisfactory proposition. So Yours Truly squirms over to the front, sits in Gruffy's seat and grabs the steering wheel.

Just then a crane with two big claws moves over this 1920 Model A Ford. The claws swing back and forth and knock against the roof. Just then a streak of lightning flashes and thunder crashes. The guy driving the crane jumps out of the cab and runs across the yard and into the office.

I release of the brake and the 1920 Model A Ford starts slowly and very quietly rolling downhill. I motion to One Buck Upchuck to squirm over to the other front seat but he does not do so. I look back into the rear but One Buck Upchuck is not to be seen at all in the 1920 Model A Ford. I look out the window to my right and then to my left but One Buck Upchuck is nowhere to be seen. I am indeed worried more than somewhat about this proposition.

Then One Buck Upchuck comes running out from behind a billboard while buttoning up his pants. I reach over, open the front door and pull the emergency brake as hard as is possible and the 1920 Model A Ford slows just enough for One Buck Upchuck to jump into the passenger seat. After a big bump, the 1920 Model A Ford enters onto Metropolitan Avenue.

Since it is a well-known fact that Brooklyn is downhill from Ridgewood, a ride along Metropolitan Avenue will head us in the right direction and away from the possibility of being crunched, flattened and pancaked. The 1920 Model A Ford is moving quite swiftly downhill and picking up more speed as it silently rolls along. Since the motor is not creating any noise, many citizens holding umbrellas are scattering in a variety of directions while others are jumping out of the way and some screaming to other citizens who are crossing Metropolitan Avenue at a very inopportune time. As we silently roll down Metropolitan Avenue, a glance in the rear view mirror indicates that many an index finger is pernting to the Ford and many a middle finger is pernting straight up.

Nicholas turns his head and looks back at the citizens perting middle fingers up and says, "Those people back there are pernting up to the clouds what are dark and dreary but indicating that the rain has stopped."

Although I believe the dark and dreary clouds are not what the middle fingers are indicating, there is no cash value to informing Nicholas about another reason for middle fingers to be pernting up.

For the safety of pedestrians crossing Metropolitan Avenue, Yours Truly opens the side window and squeezes the rubber ball on the bugle horn just outside the car window. Many a citizen's life is saved by a few squeezes of that bugle horn. By this time One Buck Upchuck is settled in the front passenger seat sitting up very straight and holding onto the dashboard and he is saying things like "Egads!" and "Holly, Holy Mackeral!" and finally he says something that may indeed help this situation. He begins as follows, "Hail Mary full of …" But One Buck Upchuck does not complete his prayer since he changes the subject and seeks help elsewhere. And this is because we are rapidly approaching a horse drawn wagon advertising blocks of ice for sale and that horse and wagon has come to a stop right in our lane. One Buck Upchuck starts shouting, "Stop! Holy sh… Shi…SHEEE! HOLY CHEEZE! STOP!" Well that is the very thing what Yours Truly is attempting to do for many blocks but no matter how often the brake pedal is pumped and no matter how hard I pull the emergency brake the 1920 Model A Ford does not stop and this situation is likely related to the wet slippery road and also to the smell of burning rubber what started shortly after the first bump. So neither the brake pedal nor the hand brake are of any help. With a fast turn of the steering wheel the 1920 Model A ford switches into the left lane, passes the stopped horse and wagon and switches back into the right lane just as a truck with a very loud horn passes in the opposite direction. The 1920 Model A ford is gaining speed and although it is good that we are moving faster and faster heading back toward Brooklyn and away from the chance of being crunched, flattened and pancaked, there is more than somewhat of an unpleasant situation directly in back for the rear view mirror indicates that a truck what looks very much like the truck what towed the 1920 Model A Ford to the *Ridgewood Auto Wreckers* is also moving very fast, even faster than the 1920 Model A Ford, and thus gaining and closing the gap. This rear view incident I do not mention to One Buck Upchuck who presently has more than one or two worries on his mind.

And then there is another more than somewhat unpleasant situation developing directly in front and this situation is one which cannot be sheltered from One Buck Upchuck. This is the situation as what follows. The traffic light at Flushing Avenue, a very busy crossroad, ahead has just turned red and cars are crossing Metropolitan Avenue in both directions at a very fast clip. However, this dangerous situation which we are rapidly approaching does not seem to concern One Buck Upchuck who is easily detracted as he pernts to the left side of the avenue and comments as such, "Look at that cemetery! I never see such a big cemetery right here in … in… Where are we?"

I do not offer an answer to One Buck Upchuck's question for although One Buck Upchuck appears to be amazed at the bigness of things, pernting out a cemetery on the left side of the Metropolitan Avenue and inquiring about our present location seems to be of little concern, considering the situation in which we presently find ourselves. Indeed One Buck Upchuck's indicating the nearness of a cemetery just as a traffic light in front just turned red is more than somewhat bad timing for two guys sitting in a 1920 Ford what is speeding at a very fast clip and unable to stop.

One Buck Upchuck turns his attention away from the cemetery and notices the dangerous situation in front. To cope with this situation One Buck Upchuck and Yours Truly have two very different solutions. One Buck Upchuck's solution is to finish his previously started Hail Mary and the other solution, and this, an action I choose, is to hold the steering wheel real tight and close my eyes and hope for the best.

Since my eyes are closed, I do not see any cars but my ears are wide open to many a horn blowing, many sounds of metal crunching against metal and many woirds shouted what I do not wish write here for they are such woirds what should neither be shouted nor scribed. Well I am not sure which of these two solutions contributed most to our living past this incident but, when I open my eyes, this 1920 Model A Ford continues rolling past Flushing Avenue and is making good time as it continues to roll down-hill.

The more than somewhat unpleasant problem, what was mentioned previously but not mentioned to One Buck Upchuck, that being the truck what looks very much like the vehicle what towed the 1920 Model A Ford to the *Ridgewood Auto Wreckers*, and what is previously pursuing and closing the gap, appears to be solved. The rear view mirror indicates that the truck is no longer in pursuit. But a closer look indicates that the truck appears to have stopped in the middle of the previous intersection and is now resting and rocking on top of another vehicle.

A slight turn to the left puts the 1920 Model A Ford onto Grand Street and we are back in Brooklyn but still a long roll to our neighborhood in Williamsburg. The downhill ride is over and the 1920 Model A Ford slows to a crawl and stops and rests right in the middle of the intersection between Grand St. and Bushwick Ave. Well there is nothing to do but to exit and to bid ado to the 1920 Model A Ford. Although many citizens in their cars are upset about our hasty departure from the 1920 Model A Ford now parked in the middle of the intersection, there is little to do about these disturbed citizens.

But there is one thing that is more than a little upsetting on our part for this is Mr. Pitsacola's neighborhood and just as Yours Truly and One Buck Upchuck are beginning to step onto Grand Street, a side door of a manshun opens and who steps out but Lucky Luigi followed by his two very big gorilla-looking sidekicks. They stop and are standing in the middle of the sidewalk directly across the street. The stranded 1920 Model A Ford catches their attention and this is good because One Buck Upchuck is so surprised to see Lucky Luigi and his two very big gorilla-looking sidekicks that he stops, extends his arm and pernts his finger at Lucky Luigi and his two very big gorilla-looking sidekicks. Yours Truly immediately grabs One Buck Upchucks arm and brings it down fast and somewhat furiously. As a result of my action, One Buck Upchuck lets out a scream. For three reasons this scream goes unnoticed by all citizens in this neighborhood. One reason is that a scream in almost any part of Brooklyn is not unusual and citizens do not pay much attention to that which is not out of the ordinary. The second reason is that Lucky Luigi is still looking at the disturbance in the intersection. The third reason is that the two very big gorilla-looking sidekicks are looking up Bushwick Avenue at the time and they do not notice One Buck Upchuck's extended arm and pernting finger. Their attention seems to be riveted on something taking place in the opposite direction and the object of their attention is a very attractive young blond with a long pony tail what is swaying and short shorts what are wiggling. After taking an extended gander, Yours Truly and One Buck Upchuck turn our attention back to Lucky Luigi and his two very big gorilla-looking sidekicks. But once again there is no need to be concerned about their noticing Yours Truly and One Buck Upchuck because two other men, who are also paying much attention to this blond with her swaying and wiggling, are walking and bumping into Lucky Luigi. This causes much concern for Lucky Luigi's two very big gorilla-looking sidekicks who demonstrate their concern by punching the two pedestrians with a result that both are lying stretched out flat on the sidewalk. At this time Yours Truly and One Buck Upchuck decide to exit the scene.

As we are walking across Humboldt Street, One Buck Upchuck makes a comment as follows, "I understand why you almost break my arm a block ago but there is no reason to believe that Lucky Luigi is recognizing us because we are now known as One Buck Upchuck and Sammy the Sewer but at our last meeting with Lucky Luigi our names are Two Cent Sam and Turnstile Tommy."

Yours Truly inquires, "You mean Lucky Luigi and his two very big gorilla-looking sidekicks do not recognize us because our names are different now as compared to when we last meet up with them?"

One Buck Upchuck answers with a most serious, "Yes! Of course!"

So just between you and me, John, what I say previously about my companion being seasonally smart in the summer, I take this compliment back. But then there is also the possibility that we are experiencing an early autumn. In any case we, One Buck Upchuck and Yours Truly, Sammy the Sewer, hoof it back to our own neighborhood where we must take up where we leave off before we are so rudely interrupted by the 1920 Model A Ford incident.

Chapter 15

Relics

Dear John,

This morning along about eleven bells One Buck Upchuck comes along and he is transporting the cloth bag with the religious stuff. He sits on the stoop and we get to conversating about this and that and one thing and another. Then Gutsy Gus opens the front door and we are very happy to see him because we are sitting on the stoop in hopes that Gutsy Gus exits the apartment house and thus gives us a chance to ask him a thing or two about this bag of bones and religious stuff what One Buck Upchuck is transporting around for a day or two.

So I turn to greet Gutsy Gus but he gets his two cents in first and greets us, "Hello Nicholas and Earnest. What are you two up to now?"

Nicholas informs Gutsy Gus as follows, "Those names what you just address us by are no longer our names. My name is One Buck Upchuck and my companion here sitting on the stoop is none other than Sammy the Sewer."

Gutsy Gus responds in such manner as, "Well it is very nice to meet you, One Buck Upchuck and Sammy the Sewer, but I must ask how you come by such attractive names?"

Since this is a long story about how we come by such attractive names and too long at that, I change the topic of the conversating by stating, "Gutsy Gus, we have come upon a cloth bag containing some bones and some stuff what look religious and that cloth bag, as you can see, is here resting on this stoop. We wish to show you the contents and we hope to know what you think about these bones and metal religious looking objects what are in this cloth bag."

Well Gutsy Gus suggests we not untie the string and open the cloth bag on the stoop for this is not a fitting place to open a bag what contains religious stuff. So Gutsy Gus makes the following suggestion, "Let us walk up to apartment 2B on the fourth floor where I live so we can look at the contents of this bag." And so Two Buck Upchuck and Yours Truly, Sammy the Sewer, rise from our seats on the stoop and walk up four flights of stairs to apartment 2B.

Since Gutsy Gus is on summer vacation from St. John's University and since his mother is out shopping or doing something else, and since Gutsy Gus's father is more of a rumor than a visible person, we have apartment 2B on the fourth floor to use for the poipose of demonstrating the contents of the bag what contains a big cross, some bones and lots of religious stuff. Thus we sit around the kitchen table and Two Buck Upchuck opens the bag and carefully lays out each religious piece and several bones and the assortment is so large that the items just about cover the entire kitchen table.

Well, as each item of the religious stuff is placed on the table, Gutsy Gus's eyes widen and when all the contents including some pieces of broken glass are finally distributed across the kitchen table, Gutsy Gus rises out of his chair and says something what sounds like, "Oh rest mirror balls!" He then announces as such, "What you have here is a collection of some very fine religious artifacts and I can see without much further investigation that quite a few of these are relics of saints."

I ask Gutsy Gus, "What is this you say about resting mirror balls? What is the meaning of what you say when you see this religious stuff?"

Gutsy Gus picks up a religious thing and says, "Oh res mirabilis. It means oh what a magical, miracle or wonderful thing it is. I think it is a very special thing to see these religious artifacts."

I am thinking to myself, "If Gutsy Gus is right about this religious stuff, then maybe we can work a magical miracle or two."

Then Gutsy Gus picks up a small cross what contains a small chunk of bone pressed inside what is covered with glass and he reads an inscription what is in Latin and he says, "This is a relic of St. August Tin for whom I am named." Then Gutsy Gus picks up a metal cup and says, "I can see an inscription on this cup." Then Gutsy Gus holds up the cup and squints his eyes and says something what sounds like, "*Vas vinum cenam sumo.*" And then he places the cup back on the table and sits back in his chair and whispers, "It is possible this is one of the cups used by one of the apostles at the Last Supper. It is not the Holy Grail but it may be pretty close."

Gutsy Gus picks up each of the pieces of the religious stuff and reads some inscriptions but he says it in Latin what I don't eggsactly comprehend all that good. Then he starts whispering stuff what does not sound like Latin. He looks at one relic and says something like, Vasilakalika, and another what sounds like Theodosiakiev. He goes on picking up pieces and reading things like Fyodor, Ushakov and Kuksha. I look at the ones that sound funny and the letters are all really strange. They do not look anything like American.

Then Gutsy Gus looks up and says, "Many people believe that relics like these have great power, more power than any weapon and some even believe they are far more valuable than gold and precious gems. Some believe relics may work miracles!" Then he picks up one of the round metal containers and quietly speaks like in a church whisper, "Here you can see this is what is called a reliquary. It looks very old."

At one and the same time One Buck Upchuck and Yours Truly ask, "What is a really quary?"

Gutsy Gus takes out a notebook, tears out a piece of paper, writes the woird and gives the paper to Yours Truly and that is how I know the right way to spell it.

"It is a reliquary which is a container for a relic and usually a reliquary is made of gold and most of these do look like they are made of gold."

Gutsy Gus is still holding one of the little bones and he reads an inscription carved on it and he says something that sounds like, "*Ex cubiculum Aug.*" He then explains as follows, "It means this is a piece of something St. August Tin used as a monk. This relic is very important to me because, although in these parts, namely Williamsburg, Brooklyn, I am not usually known by my birth name. I was named after St. August Tin and that is my birth name."

Nicholas asks, "You mean your real name is August Tin and it is neither August teen nor Gutsy Gus?"

"Yes, my real name is August Tin. When you say my name, you have to put a little wind in the gust."

Nicholas says, "Wind in the gust? OK, I get it but your mother puts no wind in your gust. She calls you more like August in the summer teen."

Gutsy Gus shakes his head and says, "My mother? That's…" He quits talking, shakes his head and points to a tiny piece of something inside a reliquary that looks like a bone and speaks as such, "This reliquary is probably gold and contains a relic, a piece of bone from a saint." Then he walks into the living room and returns with a magnifying glass which he holds up to the relic and says, "It says this is a relic of St. Anthony of Padua."

After Gutsy Gus looks through several more pieces of the religious stuff, he holds up the cross, brings it to the window and into the sunlight and says, "Look at this! You can see the rubies on the top and the bottom. They are shining so bright, they are reflected in every part of this kitchen. Some of the reliquaries were made a long time ago, probably hundreds of years ago." Gutsy Gus looks up and asks the question what I am expecting for many minutes, "Where did you get these?"

One Buck Upchuck starts, "A few days ago we are standing on the corner of …"

I interrupt before One Buck Upchuck spills the beans about our primary investigation what is something about what we do not wish to discuss with Gutsy Gus since he is a major suspect in our investigation of commies infilterating the Catholic Church. So I state the answer with a slight exaggeration as such, "Yes, it is just as One Buck Upchuck states. A few days ago we are standing on the corner of Leonard and Maujer when a fancy car, the make of which we are not able to identify, drives by real fast and the trunk pops open and this bag lands on the street and rolls into the sewer and the car keeps going real fast. So we go over and fish the bag out of the sewer and, when we open the content, you can see for yourself what we find when we fish this bag out of the sewer on the corner of Maujer and Leonard."

Then I turn and look at One Buck Upchuck and ask, "Is that not correct?"

To which One Buck Upchuck nods his head in agreement with what I just say but I can see his fingers are behind his back.

Gutsy Gus does not say one woird for a very long time as he picks up each piece of the religious stuff what are about twenty-five pieces. Then he speaks in a very low church-like whisper and says such as what follows, "You guys find something very important here and, although I am not totally certain about each and every piece, I am quite certain that what you find is a bag full of very important Christian relics."

I put my index finger to my head for this in a very big way helps my memory and I say, "I remember now the nun at St. Mary's tells us about relics what are like very old parts of a saint what are dead or something like that."

"That is correct but I think these are very special relics," Gutsy Gus says as he lifts a metal cross with a piece of wood in the middle and says something that sounds like, "Crux Crucis Verus! This says in Latin that this is the true cross and that means this is a piece of the cross upon which Christ died."

One Buck Upchuck opens his eyes wide and says with more enthusiasm than I ever see before. "Wow! What with that being the true cross and all, that means this cross with the wood inside is worth a lot of money!"

"It is not about money!" Gutsy Gus states emfamtically, almost shouting, "This is more important than money! There is a great deal of history here. If this is truly what it says, this may be part of the history of the Crusades to free the Holy Land back in the 12th to the 14th centuries. The Knights Templar had many relics and one was the relic of the true cross upon which Christ died but, according to history texts I have read, they lost that relic and many more in one of their crusades. Some of the leaders of the Knights Templar were tortured and killed by the order of King Philip IV. Actually in a way this does have something to do with money because by killing them the king solved some of his money problems. The Knights Templar loaned the King money and he paid them back by killing them."

One Buck Upchuck opens his eyes wide and says, "That is not a very nice way to pay back a friend what loans you money."

Then Gutsy Gus holds up another piece of metal and speaks as such, "Here! Take a look at this little box what contains a piece of cloth which is indeed a relic. Look at this reliquary. It's a leather case and when you open it, you can see on the left side it reads, 'VÉTEMENTS de Sainte Bernadette' and on the right side there is a picture of Saint Bernadette. That means the relic is a tiny piece of cloth from the habit of this saint. It's a second class relic. It is not as old as some of the other relics." Then Gutsy Gus picks up a small bone and reads a small paper what is stuck to the bone. Gutsy Gus says, "This is a bone from the body of Saint Ambrose of Milan. This is all a very big mystery because first class relics like part of a saint's body are not usually available to the public. First class relics are kept in monasteries. Second class relics are things a saint used or pieces of clothing worn by a saint and these are called ex indumentis which means from the clothing. A third class relic is usually a piece of cloth that has been touched to a first class relic. I wonder how these relics which are mostly first and second class relics got into a car trunk."

Well Gutsy Gus goes on quite a long time explaining what are first and second and third class relics and what he thinks and wonders about every one of these relics and then just about the time he gets into explaining more about first class and second class and some are from pieces of clothing what are called something like ex indumenta, I figure it is time to end our lesson for the day because my brain is getting quite full and I figure Gutsy Gus will just keep on going for a long time and maybe stop when he gets to explaining about a fiftieth class relic.

But before we part our ways, I ask an important question and it is as such, "Since these pieces of religious stuff, what are called relics, are not worth big money, what good are they?"

Gutsy Gus answers with one woird and it is this one woird what gives me a big idear. Gutsy Gus looks up from the relics and whispers, as loud as a whisper can be and still be a whisper, the one woird what he says is, "Power!"

Chapter 16

East River Fish

Dear John,

So Gutsy Gus says the religious stuff what we find and fish out of the sewer on the corner of 34th and the Americans are relics that have some kind of power and that there is many a person who desire to have such power and are ankshits more than somewhat to have relics such as these what we fish out of the sewer. When Gutsy Gus says, "Oh res mirabilis," he means these relics have the power to make religious magical miracles.

Dear John,

One Buck Upchuck and Yours Truly, Sammy the Sewer, are conducting a meeting of Operation Top Secret at the back table in Randy's Restaurant and we are very concerned about our investigation about the commies infilterating the Catholic Church but there seems to be no limit to the distractions what come along.

So One Buck Upchuck makes a very good suggestion and it is this what he suggests, "We need to hide the religious relics for now and go about the business what Saint Closétus tells us what is to investigate the commies infilterating the

Catholic Church and how all this may relate to Gutsy Gus, Big Boris, the doll, and maybe now Mr. Joey Pits."

"One Buck Upchuck," I say, "that is an excellent suggestion and tomorrow we will set out at twelve bells for our next expedition into solving the mystery what you have just mentioned.

One Buck Upchuck states, "I may also mention I have yet to behold the doll who you tell me is quite a good-looker."

I answer, "And maybe you will be fortunate to get a look at the doll who, believe me, is indeed a very good-looker."

Dear John,

Along about mid-afternoon today I am once again sitting on the stoop awaiting the arrival of One Buck Upchuck who arrives at eggsactly twelve bells. Without any hesitation I am up and off the stoop and One Buck Upchuck and Yours Truly, Sammy the Sewer, are off to Manhattan to continue our investigation of the Commies what are infilterating the Catholic Church and probably doing more than a few other things what are also very bad and evil to do. But just as we are heading up the stairs to the J train at the Lorimer Street station I look down on the newspaper stand and I read the headlines on the New York Daily Mirror what says, as best as I can remember, as follows, "Two reputed gangsters are fished out of the East River." But then right there, as big as a front page photo can get, are pictures of these two reputed gangsters. I tap One Buck Upchuck on the shoulder and point to the front page. One Buck Upchuck's eyes open wide and we both back down the stairs for the poipose of getting a better look at that front page photo and the headlines on the New York Daily Mirror.

One Buck Upchuck points to the picture of the reputed gangster on the left and says, "That is none other than the guy what we call Seabiscuit."

Yours Truly points to the picture of the guy on the right and I remark as follows, "That is none other than the guy what is Seabiscuit's driving companion in the Cadillac La Salle."

We read a bit of the first page before the newspaper stand proprietor tells us as follows, "You guys gotta buy that paper or skedaddle before I wop the two of youse with this here bat." And as he utters these woirds, what include more than one or two very nasty woirds. One even takes the name of the Lord in vain, what I do not here quote. Next the newspaper stand proprietor takes a baseball bat from under the boards and starts walking toward us.

Well immediately I notice this bat, which the newspaper stand proprietor is swinging, is one signed by a baseball player what goes by the handle Yogi Berra and since this is a New York Yankee player and I am a Brooklyn Dodger fan, I conclude this newspaper stand proprietor and Yours Truly have little in common and, since I do not wish to conversate concerning the better teams or anything else, I decide it is best that we part ways with this newspaper stand proprietor.

As I am walking up the stairs to the elevator station, my mind is in deep depth concerning the newspaper stand proprietor working in Brooklyn and yet not hiding the fact of being a New York Yankee fan. Now it is no small matter to be working in Brooklyn and being a Yankee fan. However, I am wishing the newspaper stand proprietor no harm.

But as we are about half way up the stairs, I hear a creaking sound from below. I turn and see the board, what is holding up the newspapers and magazines, sliding to one side and crashing to the sidewalk. The newspapers and magazines are scattering here and there on the sidewalk and some are in the gutter. The newspaper stand proprietor is looking down on the mess he makes and he is still holding the bat what is the very cause of his misfortune. That Yoggi Berra bat, what until recently is holding up the board upon which the merchandise is displayed, is best not moved from under that board.

But then One Buck Upchuck stops and pulls on my sleeve and makes the following suckgestion, "We should go back and help the newspaper stand proprietor pick up the stuff for he is an old guy and this is a very tough thing for him."

I offer a return counter-suggestion as such, "Since this newspaper stand proprietor is not a considerate person and since he says more than one or two very nasty woirds, one of which takes the name of the Lord in vain, and since he is working in Brooklyn when he is a Yankee fan, and since he swings that very bat with intention of smacking us, I do not think we should stop and help him pick up his merchandise. Besides the nun told us that people who are inconsiderate and speak nasty woirds and what are traitors are often punished here on earth and that is good for them for such a person deserves what comes to them, especially in the case here at hand, for this newspaper stand proprietor is the very cause of his own suffering."

One Buck Upchuck turns his head to look at the newspaper stand proprietor who is now on one knee and pushing up the board upon which his merchandise is previously displayed. Since One Buck Upchuck does not look all that convinced by my reasoning I add, "Besides, if this newspaper stand proprietor immediately offers his suffering up to God, either for his own sins or for the suffering souls in purgatory, he and all the suffering souls in purgatory are better off with his suffering than not. So we should let him suffer and that is the right thing for us to do."

To this One Buck Upchuck offers no counter argument

and thus we turn and ascend the stairs from which we just recently backed down but we do not speak a woird until after we put our subway tokens into the turnstile and walk out onto the station platform. Since the train comes and goes as we are observing the pictures on the front page of the New York Daily Mirror at the newspaper stand, we have more than enough time to discuss the possibility that this incident in the East River has more than somewhat to do with our own recent fishing incident on the corner of East 34th St. and the Americans.

Yours Truly, Sammy the Sewer, remembers something what is in the beginning of the newspaper article and I state that which I remember as follows, "The newspaper mentions that a witness sees two guys make a big splash in the East River and then two other guys drive away in a 1952 Packard 250 Mayfair Hardtop."

One Buck Upchuck looks at me and says, "I do not read so fast but, if what you say is what you read, then there is a possibility that this fishing incident in the East River does indeed have somewhat to do with our own recent fishing incident on the corner of East 34th St. and the Americans.

Dear John,

Well once in a while One Buck Upchuck asks a very good question but sometimes he asks one what is not so good a question. So when we are standing on the elevator station at Lorimer, he asks, "Should we go to their funerals?"

"Their funerals?" I ask back. "Why should we go to any funerals?"

"Well, we know these two guys what are fished out of the East River and wind up dead and all and maybe we should go and pay our respects. May they rest in peace and all.'

I stand still and shake my head and I say, "I do not think Seabiscuit and his driving companion are resting in peace since I read on the front page they are wanted for one or two murders of members of a rival gang in Red Hook. So I do not think we should go to their funerals and besides those two other guys what drive around in the 1952 Packard 250 Mayfair Hardtop may be paying their respects by making sure Seabiscuit and his driving companion are deep sixed and it is a far better thing that we do not meet up with these two guys."

One Buck Upchuck explains that he reads some of the front page what I miss reading and he says, "The person what we call Seabiscuit has a real name what is Joey Jarppardino and his driving companion is Larry Lucimarano and since these are Italian names, they are probably Catholics and maybe they went to the first nine Fridays and maybe then they got to heaven anyways because as the nuns told us, one Wednesday afternoon, that making the first nine Fridays is a guarantee you are saved. Besides, I always attend other people's funerals. Otherwise they are not likely to come to mine. So we should go to their funerals and show some respect to our fellow Catholics."

Well although his logic is somewhat difficult to understand, I get to thinking about what One Buck Upchuck suckgests and by the time the train gets us to 34th and the Avenue of the Americans, I can see some value to his suggestion of going to the funerals of these two dead guys. So when we get out of the subway and up onto the street, I actually buy a newspaper and I open up the front page and look all over and at the bottom it says the funerals of both Joey Jarppardino and Larry Lucimarano will take place in two days at the Church of the Most Precious Blood near Mulberry Street in Little Italy.

Dear John,

While sitting on the stoop, I am trying to compose my thoughts about our adventures earlier today, I am often interrupted by many a citizen who wishes to climb or declimb these very stoop steps because some of these citizens what live in this establishment have a need for the banister to help them with each and every step. This is because many of these citizens are heavier than a Ringling Brothers Elephant.

Be that as this weighty perdickamint may be, I am picking up where I leave off in the last letter. So One Buck Upchuck and Yours Truly, Sammy the Sewer, are standing on the corner of 34th and the Avenue of the Americans when an old friend happens along and it is none other than Officer Clancy. I understand this is not unusual for Officer Clancy to be seen in these whereabouts since this is his beat but nevertheless it is more than a little unexpected surprise to meet him at this moment. At first Officer Clancy walks right past us but then he turns around and says, "Hey, you kids, what are you doing here? This is no place for you two. Woird is out on the street that two guys who work for Carmine Decrepio are looking for you and they want something what they say you stole from Joey Jarpardino.

As innocently as I can put on, I ask, "Who is this Carmine Decrepio person who you say is looking for us?"

"You don't know? Carmine Decrepio is a major crime boss and he is more than a little upset about missing some important items what he claims you guys steal and he knows your names what are Whiskey Sour and The Handcuff Hunk."

Dear John,

Before I can get a woird in, One Buck Upchuck speaks and he says the following, "No, those are not our names.

My friend here is Sammy the Sewer and I am One Buck Upchuck."

At that very moment I am commencing to sniff something bad for I am taking a gander around this neck of the woods and I catch the shadow of a big thug standing in a doorway and what he does is even more than somewhat of a concern to Yours Truly for he turns away when I look at him and with great haste takes a powder. He is a very creepy looking guy who looks somewhat familiar. The next thing I see is this thug, what I previously mention, standing in the corner telephone booth and dialing a number which is not likely to be a lucky number for Yours Truly. So I suggest as follows, "Well it is such a lovely day in the month of June we should continue our walk along East 34th St. and enjoy the beauty of nature."

One Buck Upchuck adds, "And the beauty of these really big buildings."

Officer Clancy suggests as such, "Kids, whatever your names are, you better get on the subway and head back to Williamsburg because I have seen some of Carmine Decrepio's men walking up and down all around these whereabouts and they are probably looking for you. By the way, did you steal something from the Decrepio gang?"

One Buck Upchuck starts to say, "We do not steal anything but we find …"

Well, as fast as I can, I help finish One Buck Upchuck's sentence as, "We find it very funny that a crime boss thinks we steal something from him because we do not know him. As you can see we are just two kids visiting Manhattan like many a tourist does during a summer vacation."

"Not funny, kids, whatever your names are, not funny. Decrepio and his gang are looking for you. If they find you, well, it is not good."

So within about an hour One Buck Upchuck and Yours Truly, Sammy the Sewer, are sitting on the stoop and talking about this and that and one thing or another when we see a big 1952 Packard 250 Mayfair Hardtop turn the corner of Maujer and Leonard. Without saying one more woird and within about a few seconds, One Buck Upchuck and Yours Truly, Sammy the Sewer, are pounding on 2B on the fourth floor.

Chapter 17

Blanket on the Beach

Dear John,

I do not have time to finish what I am writing last night so I get up early this morning because what happens yesterday is of more than just somewhat important and includes some danger but as you can see from my writing, I survive but not without a close call or two. So I sleep on it because I want my head to be as clear as it can be for me to tell you of the events what pass yesterday.

Here is the beginning of the events what happen after One Buck Upchuck and Yours Truly, Sammy the Sewer, are pounding on 2B on the fourth floor. Well the door slowly opens just about a couple of inches and standing there in her bathrobe and with a cigarette dangling down off the right side of her mouth is Gutsy Guts's mother known in the vicinity here and about as Mrs. Manichy who responds to our knocking by saying in a very rough verse, "Stop the banging of the G ... d... door! Youse gonna wake up all them rats what live here and about. Whad ya want anyways?"

Since this is the very first conversation I ever have with Mrs. Manichy, I am taken aback somewhat by the way she pronunciates woirds but I am attempting to capture the flavor of her talking-ways as I write, as best I can, what her pronunciations sound like to me and it is immediately clear to me that Gutsy Gus does not learn the English language from his mother, known in the vicinity here and about as Mrs. Manichy. Also as you probably notice, I do not say the whole woirds but I write just the first two letters when Mrs. Manichy takes the name of the Lord in vain.

Well I am so taken back and more than somewhat disconcerted by the total picture and sound what I behold before me, I am more confused than a cat up a tree and so I just stand there speechless. But One Buck Upchuck asks the question that has not yet come to my vocals, "We beg your pardon, Mrs. Manichy, but we are looking for Gutsy Gus for we hope to conversate with him."

"He ain't here," snaps Mrs. Manichy, "and I don't have no clue where he's gone to. He don't tell me nothing no more. And stop calling him by that ugly name. His name is August teen." With that, the door slams shut. Just in the nick of time Yours Truly pulls One Buck Upchuck back from the door and saves his nose from being a bloody mess.

Well One Buck Upchuck and Yours Truly, Sammy the Sewer, are not about to descend the stairs, and exit upon Leonard where we may encounter two big thugs who drive the 1952 Packard 250 Mayfair Hardtop for we have no wish to make two more big splashes in the East River. So instead One Buck Upchuck and Yours Truly, Sammy the Sewer, ascend the stairs and open the door to the roof where we find two neighbors on a blanket what is laid out on tar beach. The one neighbor who lives across the street is none other than Mr. O'Reilly and the other neighbor is Katy Brown who works at Woolworth's Five and Dime on Metropolitan Ave. Well it seems One Buck Upchuck and Yours Truly, Sammy the Sewer, surprise Mr. O'Reilly and Katy Brown who are fast up off the blanket. Mr. O'Reilly is pulling up his pants and Katy with her left hand is pulling up her panties and with her right hand pulling down her skirt and in no time at all they are rushing by us like the wind in a storm and racing down the stairs.

Mr. O'Reilly and Katy Brown are in such a hurry they forget to pick up their blanket and take it with them. So One Buck Upchuck suckgests as follows, "We should call after Mr. O'Reilly and Katy Brown so they can come back and get their blanket what they leave as a result of their being in such a hurry."

I remind One Buck Upchuck by saying, "That is not a very good proposition for it may call attention to our whereabouts and there is no advantage to our informing those two thugs what drive the 1952 Packard 250 Mayfair Hardtop of our whereabouts. As for the blanket and what previously happens on that blanket, it is none of our business and that which is none of our business is none of our business."

One Buck Upchuck and Yours Truly, Sammy the Sewer, say nothing more about this suckgestion and also about what we observe because that is more than I wish to relate here. So we tip toe over to the edge of the building and peek over and down to the street where Mr. O'Reilly is scooting up Leonard in a very big hurry and Katy Brown is walking down Leonard also in more than somewhat of a hurry but the main thing and what is our actual business is that the 1952 Packard 250 Mayfair Hardtop is parked across the street and the two big thugs are busy walking around and stopping citizens and talking to them. All the citizens answer in the same way by shrugging their shoulders and shaking their heads as to say no.

Meanwhile Mr. O Reilly is walking very fast up and

across Leonard and is turning around to watch Katy Brown walking very fast down Leonard. Then because Mr. O'Reilly is not very careful about where he is walking, there is a very big crash of heads and a spill on the street what includes Mr. O'Reilly and one of the big thugs. Well, what follows does not go well for Mr. O'Reilly because the big thug gets up first and delivers a very forceful kick to Mr. O'Reilly's stomach and that leaves Mr. O'Reilly squirming on the sidewalk. When this thug reaches into his vest pocket and pulls out a black revolver, the other thug enters the picture and, after a short but meaningful conversation, the thug who happens to have a run in with Mr. O'Reilly returns the revolver to his pocket while the other thug delivers another swift kick to Mr. O'Reilly but this time the shoe lands below Mr. O'Reilly's stomach, where, as you can imagine, hurts a guy more than somewhat, and what immediately follows is a very loud scream what is so loud that upstairs windows fly open on almost every apartment along the entire street. Of course, when she hears the scream, Katy Brown turns around and proceeds to run back and across the street toward Mr. O'Reilly who continues to squirm while holding his hands onto that which is below his stomach and between his legs. In the meantime the two thugs waste no time in returning to the 1952 Packard 250 Mayfair Hardtop, and they start the engine and drive off fast but the 1952 Packard 250 Mayfair Hardtop swerves to the left and the front tire hits the curb and then knocks over a fire hydrant what gushes water up to the second floor of the apartment house just as Mrs. O'Reilly opens the window and is immediately drenched. The 1952 Packard 250 Mayfair Hardtop backs up and drives around Katy Brown who is standing in the middle of the street where she is nearly run over. Mrs. O'Reilly with a towel wrapped around her head, opens the door, runs down the steps and kneels on the ground trying to lift Mr. O'Reilly who continues to squirm while holding his hands onto that which is below his stomach.

Then Mrs. Manichy, still wearing her bathrobe, is running across the street toward Mr. O'Reilly who is lifted off the sidewalk and up the stoop with help from Mrs. O'Reilly and Mrs. Manichy. Meanwhile, Katy Brown is backing away from the scene. She turns and runs down Leonard.

Well after a while the water gushing from the fire hydrant is turned off by an employee of the emergency street department. Things calm down and return to normal on Leonard.

Just about the time everything is calming down and getting back to normal One Buck Upchuck and Yours Truly, Sammy the Sewer, walk down the stairs and onto the stoop what is very wet. So One Buck Upchuck lays out the blanket, what we previously find on tar beach. The blanket covers enough of the stoop for us to sit down. Well just then I see Gutsy Gus walking up Leonard and just about every person he meets stops him to have brief conversation. By the time Gutsy arrives where we are sitting on the stoop, there is no need to update him about the previous events for he is quite well informed. However, Gutsy Gus tells us something important and it is this what he says, "People are telling me about two thugs what are asking everybody they meet if they know the whereabouts of two kids who go by the names One Lucky Buck and Sammy Cesspool."

Chapter 18
A Revolting Perdickamint

Dear John,

Well John, as you can see, this summer is quite a bit more exciting and complexicated than what was ever planned by Yours Truly and it is only the end of July with a whole lot of August heading this way. Of course, you may suggest that we end this whole proposition by spilling the beans to my mom and dad about the thugs who are walking around for the poipose of killing One Buck Upchuck and Yours Truly. And then it is a very likely proposition that in situations such as these, moms and dads call cops and then every problem what has come up is solved. But that is not so easy. First of all from what we learn from Officer Clancy, the cops already know who the bad guys are and they are not about to do a thing about it. Second of all we can return the relics to Carmine Decrepio but then how do we do that without making two big splashes in the East River? Third of all what about Saint Closétus who tells us to investigate the Commies who are infilterating the Catholic Church? We know one thing for sure and that is Boris and the doll are Commies but we have not one bit of evidence that will convince anyone else. Besides we do not want to get Gutsy Gus in trouble if he does not belong in trouble. Last of all there is Lucky Luigi and his own brand of thugs who occasionally come to visit this neighborhood. So far they have not met up with us and we wish to keep it that way. But the main question is how do we get out of all these perdickamints? Somehow we have to get out pretty fast because school is starting in September and then we do not have time to deal with these little problems. Why? Because the really big problems start in September and those problems are the Wednesday afternoon religion instruction nuns!

Dear John,

As I am sitting on the stoop and writing this, two cops are across the street investigating something. Gutsy Gus is talking with the cops and then he crosses the street and sits down on the stoop next to where I am presently sitting. I ask Gutsy Gus, "What is the problem across the street that has the cops investigating?"

Gutsy Gus states, "When Mr. Joey Pits' comes home yesterday, he finds his apartment is robbed. There is no evidence of a break-in so this is quite a mystery since this is the sixth robbery in this neighborhood in recent days."

Dear John,

This morning One Buck Upchuck and Yours Truly, Sammy the Sewer, are sitting on the stoop in front of my apartment house and we are disgusting the very problems mentioned in my last letter and several more. One Buck Upchuck puts his head in his hands and says, "What a revolting perdickamint this is!"

I respond, "I admit we are in quite a pickle, actually more than one or two pickles, but things are never quite as bad as they are. There is always a good side to come out of every perdickamint if we only can think of one or two or maybe more."

One Buck Upchuck shakes his head and says, "This is more than a pickle or two or more. What we are in is a whole pickle barrel."

"Yes, it is true that we are in a whole pickle barrel. But we have power!"

"Huh? What power?"

"We have a whole bag full of relics and, from what we are told by Gutsy Gus, many citizens believe that relics have power. That is what we need to believe!"

"Wow! We do have a whole bag full of relics and that is a lot more powerful than a barrel full of pickles."

I personally am impressed by One Buck Upchuck's statement what compares a bag full of relics to a barrel full of pickles. This is another case of seasonal intelligence. I think summer is not yet over for One Buck Upchuck.

So our conversating continues when I say, "We have to have faith in the relics. If we do not believe in the power of the relics, they will not do us one bit of good."

One Buck Upchuck agrees, "Yes!" And he adds, "But we have to know how to use these relics what is a thing we do not know as of yet."

I suggest, "Maybe a relic is like a rabbit's foot. We just need to take one out and rub it."

One Buck Upchuck adds, "We should try that. I will go to my apartment and get a relic or two from the cloth bag what I hide in the bottom of my closet and return tonto!"

Now, I think *tonto* is not the woird One Buck Upchuck intends for Tonto is the name of the Lone Ranger's sidekick. Although his meaning is better expressed by the woird *pronto*, there is little cash value to my correcting this or almost any other of his woirds or deeds. So I smile, shake my head in support and say, "O.K. Go and get a relic or two and return tonto."

Dear John,

I wait for an hour, give or take a few minutes on either side but One Buck Upchuck does not return either pronto or Tonto. So I walk to his apartment and since I am persona not greater, I must communicate from outside. So I look for a small pebble to toss up at his bedroom window which is on the alley and on the second floor of the apartment house. But there are no pebbles so I find a small piece of a broken brick and toss this up to his window and it hits the mark but continues right through the glass much of which falls into the alley. At first I am standing in the alley with pieces of glass all around but very soon thereafter I am running out and away from the alley, down the street and once again I am sitting on the stoop quietly awaiting One Buck Upchuck to return tonto.

In about five minutes One Buck Upchuck is walking down Leonard with the large cloth bag in his arms. He says, "You will never guess what just happens."

"What?" I ask.

"A brick comes through my bedroom window and smashes the glass. Who do you think would do such a dastardly deed?"

"That is difficult to say because I can think of not one citizen in this city who would like to throw a brick through your window. But your biggest problem is that some citizen who we do not count as a friend knows the whereabouts of your bedroom and does indeed through a brick through your window."

A problem occurs just as I am saying the above woirds and it is that a small piece of glass falls out of my hair. This piece of glass, the size of a piece in a jigsaw puzzle, does not just drop quietly onto the stoop and stay there. It bounces on the step and bounces again on the step below and again bounces onto the sidewalk where it finally comes to rest after making more than somewhat of a commotion what with its tinkling and bouncing. The result is that there is no way to ignore this situation.

So before One Buck Upchuck mentions anything about the tinkling bouncing piece of glass, I say, "Did you see that?"

"I not only see it, I hear it too."

"That was a miracle what dropped out of heaven and a sign from Saint Closétus to let us know that he wants to talk to us and he needs to give us a message. We have to find a closet and get his advice right away."

Well that explanation does the trick by adding a real good distraction and also by changing the subject. So One Buck Upchuck and Yours Truly, Sammy the Sewer, search up and down the alleys but we find no empty Refrigidaire box or anything else what can act as a closet. But just as we are about to give up, along comes Bobby Anderson and he smiles and waves when he sees Yours Truly for he appears to be looking for some companionship. So I call from across the street, "Hi Bobby Anderson! What are you up to these fine summer days?"

Bobby Anderson crosses the street and states as follows, "These fine summer days are getting boring. Nothing exciting ever happens around here and I am up for some excitement before school starts in just a matter of a few weeks."

One Buck Upchuck says, "If what you are looking for is excitement, you come to the right place."

I add, "That's right! We are loaded with the stuff."

Bobby Anderson is all ears as we tell him just a little about our recent adventures with Lucky Luigi and other complexications. He is also most interested in the 1920 Model A Ford incident.

But then I wish to turn our conversating to more urgent concerns. I say to Bobby Anderson, "Do you remember the saint what appears to me in your very own closet?"

Bobby smiles, just a little crooked mouth smile, and says, "I do remember you saying that a saint appears to you when you are in my bedroom closet but that does not…"

I interrupt by pointing my finger up the street, and I ask, "Do you see that?"

Nicholas and Bobby Anderson turn around and look toward where my finger points. They look this way and then that way and then Nicholas says, "What is it that we are seeing."

I say, "Oh, You missed it but that is O.K."

Well with that little distraction I put a stop to that part of our conversating right there and then because it is a very wrong thing for Bobby Anderson to suckgest any doubt that the saint what appears to me in his bedroom closet is not a real and true appearance of a holy saint. What Bobby Anderson is beginning to say and what he is doing can lead to serious doubts of faith for Nicholas and that is just not right.

Nicholas continues the conversating but in a slightly different direction. He says, "Then there are the Commies what are infilterating the Catholic Church and we know about one of these Commies and his name is Big Boris and he drives the big beautiful black Fleetwood what brings a beautiful doll to our neighborhood.

Bobby Anderson opens his eyes wide and leans forward and asks, "Big Boris? Who drives a big beautiful black Fleetwood? I do not know what you are talking about? But the most important question is who is this beautiful doll who visits our neighborhood?"

Nicholas answers, "Actually, I do not know because I do not ever see this beautiful doll in person but I am taking Earnest's woird for it."

Bobby Anderson starts, "I can see there is more than one appearance that Earnest claims but he has not ..."

I interrupt by pointing up the street and I ask, "Do you see that? There it is again."

Nicholas and Bobby Anderson turn around and look toward where my finger points. They look this way and then that way and then Nicholas says, "What is it that we are seeing."

I say, "Oh! You missed it again but that is O.K. It is nothing important."

There is no problem now about the previous problem because Bobby Anderson asks? "I am very interested in knowing more about this beautiful doll."

So I build just a little on that story by saying, "A big beautiful black Fleetwood drives down Leonard Street and stops in front of the stoop where I am sitting. First, I see a very slim and beautiful ankle step out of the back door. Then the rest of the doll, who is wearing a fur coat in the summer, steps out. One thing I notice is that there is something shiny in her pocketbook."

Then out of nowhere I say something what surprises Yours Truly more than anyone else, "That shiny thing what is in her pocketbook is a pearl-handled pistol."

Bobby Anderson's eyes widen even more so and his mouth opens wide and he leans so far over he stumbles to keep from falling head first onto the sidewalk. That story sounds so good, what with the added detail about the pearl handled pistol, that I am convinced we have Bobby Anderson's attention and he will jern us in our adventures.

However, Bobby Anderson responds as such, "Well it sounds to me like you guys are having a more than somewhat exciting summer and as I listen to your adventures, I wish to be included in this excitement up to that pernt when you mention that the doll is a pistol packing momma. That convinces me to reconsider for I am not up for trading boredom for being dead."

One Buck Upchuck puts in his two cents, "I do not hear before about the doll packing the pearl-handled pistol. This is new what is news to me. In other words, this is new news."

One Buck Upchuck smiles at his witty use of language and Bobby shakes his head and smiles in agreement with such outstanding wit.

Well I ignore the two wits or nitwits and I add more facts about what Saint Closétus tells us about saving the Catholic Church from the commies what are infilterating. Then I include the fact that the doll hands me a roll of dollars and tells me to zip my lips and I use that story about the doll and include the pearl handle pistol as bait for we need a closet and Bobby's Anderson has just the right closet. But the pearl handle pistol backfires.

A few really important things I do not tell Bobby Anderson and there is little or no problem with One Buck Upchuck spilling any beans because he can be counted on to forget more than a few adventures in which we are deeply involved. But the main thing I keep secret and do not tell Bobby Anderson is that the relics what we find the sewer on 34th and the Avenue of the Americans have power.

Dear John,

Back to my story of the events taking place this morning. Bobby Anderson agrees to discuss the adventures further. So, as we head up the stairs to Bobby Anderson's apartment, I am considering the problem of keeping One Buck Upchuck out of range when Saint Closétus appears but now I need to consider a further complexication, and that is these two guys need to be kept out of range while Yours Truly holds a meeting in the closet. Then I get an idear.

We walk up to Bobby Anderson's apartment and enter through a hallway with the kitchen to the left. We take seats around the kitchen table but then I make a request as follows, "The walk around the neighborhood makes me quite thirsty and I bet everyone around this table would like a glass of water." With that I get up, step to the sink and turn on the faucet. I let the water run and splash noisily while I slowly search for three glasses. As planned, the running water sends an invite to both Bobby Anderson and One Buck Upchuck who rise from their seats and head to the bathroom. I look down the hall and Bobby Anderson wins the race. One Buck Upchuck is wiggling in the hallway and dancing to no music.

Just as Bobby Anderson returns from answering that invitation, Yours Truly is backing out of the kitchen closet after meeting with Saint Closétus. Bobby Anderson sits at the kitchen table and questions, "What are you doing in the kitchen closet? If it is peanut butter for which you search, I am sorry to tell you that I finish off the jar this very morning."

Before I answer Bobby Anderson's questioning and his inferencing, One Buck Upchuck is back from answering his invitation and sitting at the kitchen table. I speak as such, "Saint Closétus beckoned me to enter the kitchen closet and told me to tell…"

But just then Bobby Anderson's mom walks into the kitchen and states, "This meeting is adjourned and, Bobby, you have to pack because your Uncle Bob is driving over here right now and he is taking you to his boat what is docked in Canarsie."

Well with that information Bobby gets up and says, "Sorry guys. I will be having adventures of my own for the rest of the summer but not here. I'm off to the seashore"

Although Canarsie is not quite the seashore, there is no cash value in correcting Bobby Anderson's misunderstanding that Canarsi and seashore go together.

As One Buck Upchuck and Yours Truly exit Bobby Anderson's apartment and walk down the stairs, One Buck Upchuck states, "So that ends that, what turns out to be another revolting perdickamint."

"Well, not quite an ending and not quite a revolting perdickamint either." Then I continue, "When we are up in Bobby Anderson's apartment, Saint Closétus appears to me in the kitchen closet and tells me many things, the first is that we are to change our names."

"Again?"

"Yes again! But since many a bad citizen is searching for Horseless Horace and Medicine Mike or Sammy the Sewer and One Buck Upchuck or Hotdog Harry and Hasty Departure Dan or Two Cent Sam and Yours Truly, Turnstile Tommy and not one citizen is searching for two kids what go by the names Nicholas and Earnest, it is safe for now and Saint Closétus tells me we are to return to our original baptismal names and thus you are to be called Nicholas and I am none other than Earnest."

Nicholas says, "That is a very good idear what Saint Closétus tells you for I am happy to return to our own names for names are confusions and things complexicated enough without trying to remember who I am."

Nicholas asks another very good question. He asks, "What else does Saint Closétus tell you?"

But since I do not have a long answer, I suggest a fast answer as a delay tactic. So I say, "Tomorrow I will tell you the many things what Saint Closétus says but right now one thing he tells me is that you have to bring the cloth bag filled with the relics tomorrow morning at about eleven bells."

Dear John,

As I am sitting on the stoop I am thinking and reflectioning on what One Buck Upchuck calls a revolting perdickamint. I am also considering the bright side. As I take it, it is a good thing that I do not spill all the beans to Bobby Anderson about the relics and the power what they unleach. It is very good his mom cuts me off just in time before the big bean spill.

Chapter 19

Unleaching the Power

Dear John,

As I am walking to Teitle's Grocery this morning I see a grey 1950 DeSoto Custom hardtop, 4-Door Sedan at the Texaco gas station. Mr. Pitsacola who usually drives this car is nowhere to be seen. But there in plain sight I see trouble returns to the neighborhood and its name is Lucky Luigi and his two very big gorilla-looking sidekicks. The Texaco gas station attendant is pumping gas into the DeSoto as Lucky Luigi is walking around, stopping each citizen what walks by and asking a question. Although I cannot hear what is being said, since by now I am hiding under the vegetable stand outside of Teitle's Grocery, I can see citizens shrugging their shoulders and shaking their heads and that is sufficient evidence for me to conclude that it is a question what is being asked by Lucky Luigi.

Then one of Lucky Luigi's sidekicks opens the trunk and takes out a can what says *Evinrude Outboard Motor* on the side and the gas station attendant pumps gas into the *Evinrude* can. This information helps me relax more than somewhat for it is likely that Lucky Luigi is asking citizens about places to fish and not asking the whereabouts of two kids who go by the names Two Cent Sam and Turnstile Tommy. But anyway and just in case, I wait until the coast is clear which means the grey 1950 DeSoto Custom hardtop, 4-Door Sedan drives out of the Texaco gas station and up Grand Street.

Dear John,

So this afternoon along about two bells I am looking out the window and I see One Buck Upchuck, oops! I mean, Nicholas walking down Leonard holding onto the cloth bag filled with relics and now he is walking up the stoop and he sits down on the top step. I exit apartment 3B on the second floor and head one flight downstairs and as I open the front door, Nicholas looks back, holds the cloth bag up and says, "Earnest, I am hoping that by unleaching the power in these relics we will solve all the problems we face this summer."

I say, "Yes, autumn is fast approaching and summer will be over and we will soon be back to school and that is when some really big problems occur and for these problems we need to prepare and that means it is time to wrap up the problems with which we are presently dealing. So, Nicholas, today we will unleach the power in the relics."

Nicholas says, "But just how we are to do this remains a mystery."

I respond as such, "This is not such a big mystery because one time I hear about a genie who grants three wishes to a sailor named Al Ladden when he rubs a lamp what he finds on a beach. So all we need to do is just rub a relic and hope real hard that something good will happen."

After saying that, I sit next to Nicholas on the top step of the stoop, open the cloth bag and take out a tiny bone that is loose from a broken reliquarium. I say, "I will make a wish as I rub this relic between my fingers and see if the power is unleached." As I rub the relic, I speak as such, "I rub this relic and wish for something good to happen in the next five minutes. I wish that this something that is good will help us out of one or more of our perdicaments."

Nicholas and I sit on the stoop and wait and wait but nothing happens. Nothing at all! Not one person walks up the street. Not one car drives down the street. Nothing at all happens.

Finally Nicholas says, "That has to be at least five minutes and not one thing good happens. We better try some other way to unleach the power of this relic."

Noise up the street! Very loud noise and Nicholas says, "I hear noise like a big truck rattling. It is turning the corner. Maybe this noise means something good is going to happen just as we wish. Maybe this is a truck bringing us a lot of really great things."

As the noise approaches it is clearly that of a truck turning onto Leonard Street but it is not such a truck what brings anything one wishes. It is a truck what takes away things what one wishes to take away for this truck is garbage truck.

The truck pulls up and stops in front of the stoop where two big garbage cans await. A guy hanging onto the back of the truck jumps down and grabs the garbage can cover, tosses it onto the sidewalk and starts dragging the can to the truck but as he does so, he bumps into the other garbage can which tilts, crashes and empties much of its contents all over the sidewalk. The guy empties the first garbage can into the back of the truck and then lifts the other garbage can up and empties the remaining contents into the truck. With his foot he pushes some of the garbage what is all over the sidewalk into the gutter and jumps onto the back of the truck what moves down the street to the next apartment house where several garbage cans await.

So Nicholas and Yours Truly are sitting there on the stoop looking at the garbage scattered all over the gutter and some is still on the sidewalk. Nicholas says, "Well, you wish for something to happen and something happens but I do not see anything of any worth in the garbage before us, except maybe that half-eaten piece of that banana and then there is also that …"

"Shazam! That's what we need, a magic word. I gotta say a magic word when I rub the relic. Shazam is a very good magic word." So I pick up the relic, rub it and say, "Shazam!"

We wait but nothing happens. I am thinking and I say, "Abracadabra! Maybe that is the right magic word."

Nicholas says, "Abracadabra? I never hear of that word so I do not think it is a real magic word."

"Yes, it is a real magic word! That is a word what magicians say and I do see a magician on television once when we visit my Uncle and Ant who are so rich they have a television. The magician from Arabia said 'abracadabra' and a little rabbit turned into a full grown very beautiful lady in a red bathing suit."

"Here in Brooklyn, a rabbit is an animal very seldom seen. In fact I never see a rabbit except on Easter Sunday and that is a chocolate rabbit."

Just then a cat runs across the street and Nicholas who is not fast when it comes to thinking is indeed very fast when it comes to catching a cat which is a thing he does. Nicholas holds the cat what is squirming more than somewhat and says, "Quick rub the relic and say the magic word."

"Abracadabra! Cat turn into a full grown very beautiful lady in a red bathing suit. I repeat abracadabra."

The cat is squirming more than somewhat and scratches Nicholas on his arm and Nicholas yells, "Ouch! That hurt!"

But when the cat's claw is reaching up to scratch his face, Nicholas releases his hold on the cat who jumps to the sidewalk, runs across the street, up the stoop and just then the front door of the apartment house opens and the cat runs in and immediately out steps Mrs. Manichy in a house dress and that is a sight what is very far from a fully grown very beautiful lady in a bathing suit.

After this disappointing attempt to unleach the power of the relic, Nicholas suckgests, "*Hocus, poke us.* That's a real magic word."

Although *Hocus, poke us* is clearly not one word, there is no cash value or any other advantage to arguing the point, so I agree and say, "I will rub the relic, say that magic word, flip a coin and see if the coin lands so that I win the toss."

So I take a nickel out of my pocket and say, "Let's do heads or tails. You call it! Heads or tails?"

Nicholas says, "Tails!"

"OK then. You have tails. Watch me. I am rubbing the relic and saying, "*Hocus, poke us*! Heads I win. Tails you win. And now I will flip the coin and see if I win."

I toss the coin in the air and it hits the top step of the stoop, twirls around and the coin comes up tails and thus I say, "Well that did not work. *Hocus, poke us* is not the right word but let us try another word because I do believe we are onto something."

I can see Nicholas is already losing faith in the power of the relic so it is important for me to make sure something good happens when I rub the relic. So I say, "Let us not lose faith in the power of the relic. We just need to pick a different magic word."

Nicholas says, "OK! Let's try another magic word and there is one magic word what I hear can really do magic. It is an Italian word and that word is *Open says a me.*"

Once again I neglect to inform Nicholas that *Open says a me* is not one word. So I also let this opportunity pass for there is no cash value in disturbing our intention to unleach the power of the relic.

So I take the relic in my hand and rub it while I say, "Let this coin come up heads, *Open says a me.*" I toss the coin in the air and it hits the top step of the stoop, twirls around, falls on the step below and lands heads up. For this I am truly thankful but it is just one time and what I need is a convincing show of the magic that will work each time I flip the coin.

Nicholas states, "It is a good sign that the coin comes up heads after you say the magic word but that is only one time and that does not convince me of the power of the magic in the relic."

This remark by Nicholas concerns me more than somewhat for I have the feeling his faith is in danger and if he loses his faith in the magic of the religious relic, there is no telling what will come tumbling down next and I do not want to be responsible for causing Nicholas to lose his faith in religious magic. So it is very important for me to do my best to save his soul. So I take just a little precaustion and suggest to Nicholas, "If I win the toss ten times in a row, that means the relic along with the right word is a result of religious magic. Agreed?"

"Yes! I agree because if you win ten times in a row, that would be more than lucky."

"Good! I will toss the coin nine more times and each time I will rub it and speak the magic word and if I win ten times in a row, you will agree and believe that the relic has power."

So having said what I said, I make a slight change in what I say further, "Heads I win, tails you lose." Then I rub the relic, say, "Open says me" and I toss the coin in the air and it hits the top step of the stoop, twirls around and lands heads up. I say, "That's two times in a row and that's good. I win! Let's try the same thing again and see how many times I can win. Watch me again. I am rubbing the relic and saying, 'Open says a me.' Heads I win. Tails you lose. And now I will flip the coin and see if I win." The coin lands on the stoop, bounces up and down and comes up heads. I say, "OK, That's good. I win! Let's try the same thing again and see if I win seven more times. Watch me closely for I do not want you to think I cheat in any way. See I am rubbing the relic and I say, 'Open says a me. Heads I win. Tails you lose.' And now I flip the coin and see if I win."

The coin comes up tails and I say, "That's it! I win again!"

Nicholas looks at me with his head to the side and his mouth wrinkled more than somewhat and he says, "How come you win when the coin comes up tails?"

"Well, I respond, "Remember I say, "Heads I win and tails you lose." So when it comes up tails, you lose and that means I win. But let us not quibble about a minor detail. We should not depend on just a few tosses of the nickel. I will toss it six more times and say the magic words while I rub the relic."

So when I win every one of the next six tosses, I state as follows, "There we have more than ten tosses in a row and each time I win and that means the magic word unleaches the religious power of the relic."

Nicholas squints, scratches his head, wrinkles his mouth and moves his head to the side. But then he smiles and says, "OK! I get it." Then he squints, scratches his head and opens his eyes wide and says, "Right! That makes sense! Saying the magic words and rubbing the relic really works. You win more than ten times in a row."

Just then the front door opens and Gutsy Gus steps out onto the top landing of the stoop. He asks, "What are you two guys up to now?"

Nicholas states as follows, "We are working on unleaching the power of those relics what we showed you a while back. Earnest rubs this relic what he is holding in his hand and says 'Open says a me' and then he tosses the coin and he wins more than ten times in a row. In this way the power of the relic is unleached and the relic does religious magic."

Gutsy Gus puts his hand to his chin, sits on the top step of the stoop and says, "The coin may come up as a winner ten times in a row but that is either chance or luck but it is not religious magic."

I smile and say, "I agree and I believe you are correct, Gutsy Gus. It is not chance, it is not luck, and if it is not religious magic, it is indeed something else."

Gutsy Gus says, "The relics do not have power per say.

Nicholas asks, "Per say? Say what?"

Gutsy Gus explains, "Per say. That means they do not have power in themselves. It's Latin." Then Gutsy Gus spells it by saying each letter as p-e-r and s-e.

Gutsy Gus says, "You want to be careful about what you believe because if you believe the wrong thing, you may be committing heresy. Many people believe relics have power in themselves but that is a heresy. Relics can be links to the saints and when you pray to a saint and hold the relic of that saint, then the saint may intercede on your behalf. When a very good person dies and then other people pray for a miracle, and a miracle happens, that dead person is credited for the miracle. But neither the relic nor that dead person does the miracle. The miracle results when the dead person, who is in heaven and in very good standing with

God, intercedes and requests that God perform a miracle and when a miracle or two or three occur, then the Pope will beatify the dead person and then after a few more miracles the person may be canonized as a saint."

"You mean it is complexicated," says Nicholas.

Gutsy Gus lowers his eyebrows, frowns a little, then smiles and says, "Something like that. Actually it is both."

I ask, "So what is the best way to use these relics to unleach their power?"

Gutsy Gus says, "Some people believe that relics have a power to influence God to grant a request and that is why they are so desirable. But I have another question. What about the people who lost these relics? Do you know who they are? They are probably very concerned and want them back."

Nicholas starts to say, "We know the guy who lost these relics is …"

But Nicholas does not get to finish his sentence because it is more important for him to be jumping around the sidewalk on his left foot while yelling, "Ouch! That hurt. Wow! That really hurt!"

This jumping and yelling gives Yours Truly the opportunity to complete Nicholas's sentence and I say, "Yes, as Nicholas was just saying, we know the guy who lost these relics is probably very upset but we have no idear who this guy is." By this time Nicholas has calmed down and is sitting on the bottom step and rubbing the top of his shoe.

I say to Nicholas, "Is not that right, Nicholas? We do not know who this guy is who lost these relics."

Nicholas stops rubbing the top of his shoe for he seems to realize rubbing the top of one's shoe does little to ease the pain in one's foot.

Nicholas just shakes his head in agreement and starts to

Robert S. Pehrsson

remove the shoe on his right foot. After Nicholas removes his shoe and then his sock, Gutsy Gus stands up, says, "Whew! I think it is time for me to catch a breath of fresh air. I wish to take a walk."

But that does not happen as planned because, without our noticing, a cloud of dark smoke from the before mentioned black six-door Fleetwood arrives in front of the apartment house and a gust of summer breeze carries the smoke directly to the bottom of the stoop which causes Nicholas to cough, wheeze something terrible while he staggers on one shoe and then he hops around like a one footed blind man. Just as the driver's door of the Fleetwood opens, Nicholas's bare foot connects with the half eaten banana peel, and he goes flying feet first into the Fleetwood's front seat, hits the driver in the face with his bare foot and comes to rest upside down with his head on the running board and his feet on the lap belonging to none other than Big Boris.

Big Boris shoves Nicholas out of the Fleetwood, onto the sidewalk. Then Big Boris steps out of the Fleetwood, puts his right hand inside his suit jacket and pulls out a pearl handled pistol and points it at Nicholas.

Gutsy Gus immediately steps in front of Big Boris and says, "Nyet! Chto ty delayesh? What are you doing? Boris, put the gun away. This was an avarya, an accident. The kid did not mean to hit you in the face with his stinky gatky stupnya."

After some further disgustion, Big Boris says something what sounds like, "Dat pareen gloppy stupeed wit nahgah werry stupeed malchik wit stinky gatky stupnya."

Gutsy Gus answers, "Da! Nicholas is a little gloppy, not too smart, but I do not think he is stupid. But Boris you are correct about his foot. It is ugly and stinky."

"Nicholas? Nicholai? A Rusky malchick?"

178

"Nyet. He is not Russian. It is Nicholas, not Nicholai.

"Da! He ees ochen nekrasivo. How you say? Too ugly gloppy and stupeed malchik for to be Rusky!

So after some further disgustion much of which sounds a little like English and much like Russian, Big Borris does replace the pearl handled pistol back inside his suit jacket and sits back in the car but then he slides over to the passenger side and Gutsy Gus gets into the driver's seat, waves to Nicholas and to Yours Truly, and says, "Da svidaniya." With that Gutsy Gus starts the engine, turns the steering wheel and the six door black Fleetwood drives into the street and down Leonard, leaving a dark cloud of smoke what pours out of the tailpipe.

After Nicholas stops coughing, he gets up off the sidewalk, limps over to the stoop and sits on the bottom step where we spend a fair amount of time quietly reflectioning on the recent events and their complexications.

Chapter 20

Religious Magical Miracles

Dear John

Along about midafternoon I am sitting back on the stoop reading about guys and dolls when Nicholas comes walking down Leonard Street but unfortunately he is doing so with a slight limp.

I offer the following, "Nicholai! I notice you are a limping malchik today."

Nicholas looks at me directly in the eyes, squints, and frowns and finally, with a shake of his fist and an emphasis in his verse I never hear before, he says, "My name is Nicholas. I admit to many other names this summer but Nicholai is not one of them."

"So," I tease a little, "it seems to me that you are not all that excited about being kidnapped and sent to Russia where you are to be called Nicholai. Am I correct about this proposition?"

"Big Boris calls me *stupid* and this is a thing what works for me in school and it is quite OK for the teachers and nuns to think I am stupid because there is much advantage to that. But this summer I am not stupid and I am definitely not Nicholai."

I am quite taken back by the elegant way by which Nicholai, I mean Nicholas, defends himself and once again there is a show of some evidence that Nicholas has more of a brain during summer than during any other season of the year. Nicholas' intelligence is definitely seasonal.

"I agree that you are neither Nicolai nor stupid, at least not this summer. But I must agree with Big Boris about your foot. It is ugly and stinky."

Nicholas says, "My foot, whether it is ugly or stinky or both, is not important."

I respond, "I agree to the proposition that your ugly stinky foot is not important so long as you keep your shoes and socks on."

Nicholas makes a fist and shakes it at me but then he changes the subject and makes the following suggestion, "I think we need to seek advice from Saint Closétus because things around here are more than somewhat complexicated."

I shake my head up and down and I say, "Yes! For the poipose of doing so we need to immediately head off in two directions searching for a closet or some facsimile thereof."

Nicholas is halfway down the street when he turns and in a loud verse asks, "Some what? I do not know how to find any fact a silly there either off or on."

I shout back, "Facsimile thereof! This is a thing what radio announcers say when they want you to send in ten box tops of Cheerios to get a decoder ring."

Nicholas starts walking back, still with a slight limp, and says, "That makes no sense at all! We are not looking for boxes of any cereal or decoder rings. I am not the stupid one here. We are looking for a closet or something like a closet. So forget about your cereal or decoder ring or silly facts what of."

I wave to Nicholas and say, "Go ahead. Just keep looking

for a closet." I do not mention that a facsimile thereof may work in place of a closet for I have a better idear. So while Nicholas searches the neighborhood, I run up the stoop and enter the vestibule to await the return of Nicholas. While I am waiting, I am beginning to worry about Nicholas for he does not want anyone thinking he is stupid except for the teachers at P.S. 18 and the nuns at St. Mary's. This is a concern for it is not good for people to think Nicholas is stupid, even if maybe he is... just a little.

Dear John,

Well I wait for Nicholas to return but he does not do so. I believe his feelings are hurt because instead of looking for a closet I think he goes home.

Dear John,

There is another concern what comes to my mind and this is about the relics what needs to unleach their religious magic. We need some religious magic of the miracle kind and we need it fast. The methods described by Gutsy Gus take too much time for a religious magic miracle to work. It is now the middle of August and we have to solve all of the problems what we presently got into and we must get ready for the big problem what is to come in September. That big problem is school. But there are two schools. It's like double problems, the teachers at P.S. 18 and the bigger problem, the nuns at St. Mary's.

Dear John,

At about eleven bells this morning Nicholas is sitting on the stoop waiting for Yours Truly. I step out onto the top landing and Nicholas looks up and frowns.

I ask, "Nicholas, you are looking grim this morning

and I say that because there is a frown on your otherwise smiling face."

Nicholas responds, "My grim look this morning is on my face because I am thinking that, although you tell me about Saint Closétus who appears in a closet, I am wondering if Saint Closétus will ever appear to me for I am feeling just a little left out of this whole appearance thing. But even more than that, you keep telling me about this doll who also appears and comes out of the big beautiful six door black Fleetwood but I never yet get any opportunity to take a gander. So I am feeling more than a bit left out of the appearances of the doll too."

"Nicholas, you are quite correct in feeling left out and I will do my best to make things right so you do not feel left out in relation to these two appearances."

Dear John,

Evidence! Nicholas needs more evidence about appearances so he does not feel left out. I need to provide evidence.

I run upstairs to apartment 3B on the second floor and search through the drawer in the kitchen what contains everything nobody knows what to do with. I find something that may do the trick and I also cut a small piece of paper and some tape. Then I return to the vestibule where I await the return of Nicholas. While I wait, I am contemplating these propositions and considerating more than a few idears for about ten minutes, give or take a minute or two.

Then I see Nicholas returning to the stoop and he sits on the bottom step with his head way down. He turns and looks up at me when I open the front door and he says, "Yesterday I am feeling so bad about being left out that I spend no time looking for a closet. I just go home. So today

I start where I leave off but I can find no big Frigidaire box or anything like a closet anywhere in this neighborhood."

I smile and say, "It's OK! I find one just today when I head for the bathroom in my apartment 3B on the second floor. It is right there in my hall closet where Saint Closétus appears and states as follows, "The first and most important thing is that you must tell Nicholas that he is not stupid and indeed he even shows some signs of intelligence this summer."

Well, when Nicholas hears what Saint Closétus says about him not being all that stupid this summer, he lifts his head up, rises from the bottom step and with a slight limp walks up the stoop and sits on the top step and this is a thing I consider to be a good sign.

Nicholas asks, "What else does Saint Closétus tell you? Does he say anything else about me?"

Since I am not able to think up anything else Saint Closétus says, I answer, "No, but he does not just tell me things. This time he gives me something. Look here! For this is a relic what Saint Closétus puts in my very right hand what I hold out before you. As you can see this is a small key. In fact, it is a very small skeleton key and, as you can also see, there is a little piece of paper taped on it just like we see on all the other relics. Here, look and read what it says."

Nicholas looks at the tiny skeleton key and says, "Saint Closétus! This is a relic of the very saint what appears to us."

I personally do not quibble about who it is that Saint Closétus actually appears to because there is no cash value and little advantage to quibbling. So I say, "Right! Saint Closétus gives us this relic and says we can ask him to intercede on our behalf and he will ask God to do a religious magical miracle for us. He does this because he is in very good standing with God and because he knows all the good we are doing to investigate bad Commies what are infilterating the Catholic Church."

Nicholas asks, "Do you mean we do not need to go looking for a closet each time we need to contact Saint Closétus?"

"Yes! We do not need to find a closet. This relic is not like a party line. It is a direct person to person line. So for now on we can use this relic and, as Gutsy Gus tells us, relics are links to the saints and when we pray to a saint and hold the relic of that saint, then the saint intercedes on our behalf and God does a religious magical miracle or something like that."

Nicholas gently lifts the key, now known as the Saint Closétus relic, out of my hand and says, "You know this is only a second class relic and maybe not as powerful as a first class relic. Something from the body of Saint Closétus, you know a piece of his bone or something inside him, has more power."

Well I think over that for just a short time and then I say, "Oh! I forget to tell you something what Saint Closétus tells me and it is that this is a first class relic because it comes from inside him. See when he was getting torchard and martyred, the Romans ask him where he hides the key to the holy box. But Saint Closétus does not tell them and they can't find this very key because, before the Romans catch up with him, he swallows this key. That is why this is a first class relic. It comes from inside his body just like a bone or a kidney.

Nicholas shakes his head and says, "OK, Then! We should try this right now and see if this first class relic links us with a direct line to Saint Closétus. Ask Saint Closétus for a favor and let us see if he will intercede for us and if God will do a religious magical miracle."

I respond as follows, "OK! We should ask Saint Closétus to solve one problem at a time. We do not want to get him all confused with all these complexications what we have this summer."

Nicholas suggests, "So let us start off with the smallest of our problems, namely Lucky Luigi."

I say, "Good idear for he is a small problem but his two very big gorilla-looking sidekicks are not such small problems."

Nicholas clarifies, "I am not talking about Lucky Luigi's size. I am talking about the size of the Lucky Luigi problem what is a smaller problem than the several other problems what we presently got."

I shake my head and say, "I see Lucky Luigi this very morning along with his two very big gorilla-looking sidekicks. They do not notice me for two reasons, one of which is that they are at the Texaco gas station getting gas for the grey 1950 DeSoto Custom hardtop, 4-Door Sedan and they are also filling a can with gas for a boat with an outboard Evinrude motor and the other reason they do not notice me is that I slip under the vegetable stand outside of Teitle's Grocery and I am hiding there for quite a few minutes."

Nicholas adds, "Maybe Lucky Luigi is distracted by other matters like going fishing and maybe he is no longer interested in finding us."

I say, "But I hear from citizens here and about that from time to time Lucky Luigi is seen walking around in this very neighborhood and he is asking if any citizen knows the whereabouts of two guys who go by the names Two Cent Sam and Turnstile Tommy."

Nicholas says, "But maybe we do not need to waste a religious magical miracle on Lucky Luigi for it is now several weeks since we go by the names Two Cent Sam and Turnstile Tommy and he will not know who we are because we are now back to our own names."

I personally see no cash value in explaining that Lucky Luigi is very likely to recognize us whether we change our names or not. Autumn may be fast approaching for Nicholas. Maybe his intelligence is like rain in the summer. It comes and goes quickly.

Nicholas continues, "I see a movie about when the genie comes out of the lamp, you get only three wishes. So maybe we should save the religious magical miracles for problems what are bigger than Lucky Luigi."

But I suggest the following, "We should try to unleach the power of the relic as a test and that way, since it is only a test, it will not count as one of the three wishes because a test is not a real unleaching of the relic's power."

Nicholas says, "OK! If it is just a test, let us give it a try."

So I take the relic and rub it and say, "Open says a me."

Then I add the following just to make the whole religious magical miracle as strong as it can get, "Please, Saint Closétus, intercede for us and make our Lucky Luigi problem go away."

When I finish this prayer, Nicholas blesses himself and says, "Please grand us this religious magical miracle in the name of the Father and of the Son and of the Holy Ghost, Amen."

I say, "Nicholas, I am very impressed with the ending to the prayer. But now we need to wait because things do not happen right away in heaven. I mean Saint Closetus is just one of the many saints asking for help and there is a very long line. So let's just call it a day and see what happens."

Chapter 21

The Fast Acting Relic

Dear John,

Along about nine bells this morning as I am sitting on the stoop reading about guys and dolls, the front door opens and out steps Gutsy Gus who is holding a small soft-cover book in his right hand. Gutsy Gus sits down on the top step next to me and speaks as such, "Earnest, I am noticing very often when I step out here on the stoop, you are deeply grossed in this book what is scribed by this guy Damon Runyon and the book is all about guys and dolls."

I agree by saying, "What you say, Gutsy Gus, is totally the truth for this is the book and the only book what I ever read in my entire life. This book in fact teaches me not just to read but also how to write and even how to say things such as are said by guys and dolls what live in New York City."

Gutsy Gus hands me the small book what he carries with him and says, "Earnest, I think it is time for you to enlarge your library by adding a second book. In this way you are actually doubling the size of your library and this is quite an achievement. So I am giving this book to you on one the condition: that you read it."

This book is somewhat smaller than the one scribed by Damon Runyon. So I hold it up and read the name of the book's scriber and I say, "Mark Train?" So I say to Gutsy Gus, "OK, I will read this book and let you know just what I think about this guy's scribing."

Gutsy Gus says, "The name of this book is *Tom Sawyer, Detective* and you are correct about the writer's name, Mark Twain. I am giving you this book because I believe you will enjoy and even profit from reading a detective mystery. From what I can tell, you are more often than not trying to solve one or more mysteries yourself."

Dear John,

Well it is the next morning and I am sitting on the top step of the stoop reading about a guy or two what are just like me, looking to have adventures. A guy what goes by the name Huck Finn says he scribes the book but then this other guy, Mark Train, claims he is the writer. But then I find out that there is another guy who says he writes this book and he goes by the name Sam Clemons. So who really writes this book is the first mystery.

Dear John,

Once again I am worrying about Nicholas and his faith in appearances such as that of Saint Closétus. It is of great concern that, as a result of our summertime adventures, Nicholas may call things like apparitions and religious magical miracles into question and one question leads to another question and when all these questions start piling up, the answers are not always the right ones and may even lead a young Catholic boy to evil thoughts and even heresy.

I see it as a duty to conform Nicholas's faith so he does not lose it or believe in heresy or even convertate to a false religion. A religious magical miracle may do the trick but then miracles are not all that easy to come by. Then I remember a nun saying that God helps them what help themselves but I figger sometimes God needs a little boost especially when it comes to religious magical miracles what, as I say before, are hard to come by.

Maybe another relic what can work faster will do the trick. I remember an item or two what I see in the Saint Vincent DePaul Thrift Store. This relic can be worked fast and help with the boost. If it works, it can conform Nicholas's faith in religious magical miracles. So I am heading upstairs to apartment 3B on the second floor to check the funds available for a purchus as to what might do the trick.

Dear John,

So I check my funds and find enough money to purchus an item or two from the Saint Vincent DePaul Thrift Store. I walk up to Metropolitan Avenue and go into the Saint Vincent DePaul Thrift Store and I see the item what I am looking for. Actually two items what are in one box are still for sale. So with my 10 cents in hand I bring the box up to the counter. Now in most stores the sales person at a counter not only wants you to purchus the thing what you want to purchus but then tries to sell you more stuff what you don't want. But such is not the case in this Saint Vincent DePaul Thrift Store. When I put the item what is actually two items in one box, on the counter, there is a little old lady who asks "Sonny boy, what do you want with these two matching spoons?" Can you not see one of these two spoons is bent in the middle? It is way out of shape."

I answer "Yes mam, I see that one of these spoons is so mangled and out of shape that I think the price of 10 cents is way out of line. Indeed I believe these two spoons are actually worth about 5 cents and since my mother is very sick and needs a spoon for her medicine and since we have not a single spoon in our cardboard box we live in under the Brooklyn-Queens Expressway, I was hoping I could pay 5 cents for this box what is actually two items one of which is so badly bent out of shape it is likely unusable."

So the little old lady and I talk much about how bad conditions are what with living in a box under the Brooklyn-Queens Expressway, that tears start running down her face and then the little old lady says, "Sonny boy, I will put this item in a paper bag and you can take it to your home what is a box under the Brooklyn-Queens Expressway and I will ring up the sale for just one penny."

So I start taking out some change what is in my pocket but the little old lady says, "No, Sonny Boy, I am putting the penny in the cash register. You can just leave and bring this item, which is actually two items in one box, to your mother who is very sick and living in a box under the Brooklyn-Queens Expressway."

Dear John,

I am walking home from the thrift store and I am thinking that I am a little bit more like Huck Finn than I previously think. I confess I do work the old lady at the Saint Vincent de Paul Thrift Store but then she is not my relative. Well, I suppose that makes all the difference.

Dear John,

When I turn the corner and walk down Leonard Street, I see Nicholas sitting on the stoop waiting for me. His head is down and when he sees me, he shrugs his shoulders, then shakes his head and then raises his arms. This is a thing what I previously see Nicholas do on more than one occasion when he is flustrated. I come to know that the meaning of such actions indicates that Nicholas does not know what to do in a situation such as this. This indicates to me that I need to help Nicholas reduce his flustrations in a situation such as this.

So I walk up to Nicholas and say, "About an hour ago I am upstairs in apartment 3B on the second floor and I happen to open the hall closet door and there is Saint Closétus who is bending over and picking up stuff from the bottom of the closet. He looks like he is looking for something but I do not know what it is.

Nicholas looks up and asks, "What is Saint Closétus doing in your closet. He should be on that long line waiting to ask God for help in solving our Lucky Luigi problem."

Well that is a really good question what I have to think about for just a minute or two. So I take my time as I sit down on the stoop but then I say, "A saint is not like us because we have a body and a saint ain't got no body and that makes a big difference. A body can only be in one place at a time but a bodiless saint can be in two or more, maybe even up to ten places at one time. So Saint Closétus is waiting on line and he is also in my hall closet."

Nicholas shakes his head and says, "That makes sense. A body can only be in one place at a time but a saint can be in many places at the same time because he ain't got no body. I never think of that before."

"Right!" I say to Nicholas but I say to myself, "Me too! I never think of that before either." Then I continue my story and say, "But anyways when I open the closet door, Saint Closétus stands straight up real fast, bumps his head on the top shelf and turns around. Then he puts his hand on my head and says something what I hear Gutsy Gus say in Latin that sounds sort of like 'Ubi Oh ubi est meus sub ubi.' I do not know what that Ubi stuff is all about but then

Saint Closétus tells me, 'I am waiting in this closet for the poipose of giving you a most powerful relic but when you so suddenly open the door, you surprise me and so I drop a relic in the bottom of the closet floor. Here help me find it.' But just then Saint Closétus picks up something from the floor and tells me to close my eyes and open my hand and Saint Closétus puts this very thing in my hand and tells me to open my eyes. I look at the thing in my hand and it looks like a very ordinary spoon. But Saint Closétus says to me, 'This is not an ordinary spoon. It is a powerful second class relic and it works even faster than the other first class relic what is a key. I hereby give you this special spoon what arthurizes you to perform fast acting religious magical miracles to show that such religious magical miracles are real and true and should be believed.'"

Here, Nicholas, it is in my hand as you can plainly see. It looks like a very ordinary teaspoon but it is a real and true relic what got special fast acting power."

Nicholas says, "I want to see you perform a religious magical miracle to show me that such religious magical miracles are real and true and that I should believe."

I answer, "Well I do want to show you just how powerful and fast acting this relic is but I cannot do so right now and that is because I have something very important to do at the moment. If you return here on the stoop in about an hour, my very important thing to do will be done and then I will be happy to perform a religious magical miracle to show you that such religious magical miracles are real and true and should be believed."

Dear John,

When I tell a fact or two, I string it out and make the fact longer and that makes it more believable. You gotta build your facts to make them truthful and believable. A fast told fact ain't nearly as believable as a strung out fact.

But I regress! So after I bid ado to Nicholas, I run upstairs to apartment 3B on the second floor. I open the package what I get from the St. Vincent de Paul Thrift Store and take out the two spoons. First I hold the straight spoon up and then it drops on the floor. I bend and pick it up and that is when I switch spoons. I straighten out the bent spoon and hold it up and slowly let it bend back. I practice this for about an hour in front of a mirror until I cannot even see the switch. My hands are quicker than my eyes.

Dear John,

I am back downstairs on the stoop when Nicholas comes along and asks, "So is your very important thing, what you have to do, done?"

"Yes, I answer and now I can perform a religious magical miracle to show you that such religious magical miracles are real and truthful."

Nicholas says, "I believe what I see because seeing is believing."

So I show the spoon to Nicholas and I say, "Take this spoon what Saint Closétus gives me as a relic and examine it very closely to make sure it looks and feels just like a very ordinary and normal spoon."

Nicholas takes the spoon and turns it over and says, "Yes. I can see this is a very ordinary and normal spoon."

Then I put out my hand and Nicholas places the spoon in my hand but it drops on the sidewalk and I immediately pick it up and I hold it between my thumb and indexical finger and I say, "Now watch very closely because I am going to do a religious magical miracle, a small one, to show you that this relic of Saint Closétus does give us power and all the other relics also give us power."

So I lift the spoon and say this little prayer, "Saint Closétus help me show Nicholas that this spoon is a legitimate relic by performing a religious magical miracle." Then I add the magic words, "Open says a me." With that the spoon starts to move in my hand and the handle bends all by itself.

Nicholas's eyes open wide as he watches the spoon bend almost in half. Then Nicholas says, "That is indeed very convincing. I believe this is indeed a powerful relic because I see it makes a very good religious magical miracle."

But to further convince Nicholas that a religious magical miracle takes place, I say, "Watch and I will drop this spoon on the sidewalk and it will return to its rightful shape." And having said that I drop the spoon what is immediately and magically returned to its rightful shape with a little help from Yours Truly.

Nicholas says, "This indeed convinces me that this relic has power to bend itself but does it have enough power to help us with the Lucky Luigi situation?"

I ask, "Why do you ask such a question?"

Nicholas says, "It is because Gutsy Gus tells us about relics and how they come in classes. This spoon is a second class relic as described by Gutsy Gus but second class relics are not as powerful as a first class relic what is something what comes from inside a saint's body."

I respond by saying, "You forget what I say and that is that Saint Closétus informs me that although this is a second class relic, it is a very powerful second class relic. I say this for two reasons. One is that it comes directly from Saint Closétus and the other is that it can do a religious magical miracle right in front of us and, as you say, seeing is believing."

"Nicholas says, "Ok but we must use both this spoon, what is a legitimate second class relic, and also the key, what is a first class relic, at the same time and ask Saint Closétus to help us with the Lucky Luigi situation and do it faster."

I respond, "Yes, that is a very good idear indeed for it will almost double the power of our previous request to fix the Lucky Luigi situation."

Nicholas says, "Maybe the two relics together will help Saint Closétus move up in the line faster. But we must do eggsactly what we do the last time we ask Saint Closétus to intercede for us."

I confirmate Nicholas's suggestion when I say, "You are correct in that, by using two relics, one first class and one second class, at the same time, we almost double the power. I hope the two relics do the trick and help Saint Closétus move up faster in line."

So I take the key in my hand and Nicholas takes the spoon in his hand and we rub these relics and say the following prayer together, "Please, Saint Closétus, intercede for us and make our Lucky Luigi problem go away."

But just then a fire truck comes racing along Grand Street with the siren blasting and horn blowing. We begin to talk again but another fire truck blasts its horn on its way down Grand Street. We again begin to talk but another fire truck takes a short cut by coming up Leonard, going north, which is a problem since Leonard is a one way street going south. It is even more of a problem since a grey 1950 DeSoto Custom hardtop, 4-Door Sedan turns left from Grand and screeches around the corner and speeds down Leonard more than somewhat fast. The fire truck blasts its horn. The fire truck and the DeSoto almost meet head to head before the

DeSoto screeches to a halt and starts backing up so fast that it scrapes against three parked cars. The DeSoto backs up onto Grand, stops and pitches forward almost hitting some more cars. The fire truck drives up Leonard and turns right onto Grand. There is so much noise with one fire truck after another blasting sirens, we are not able to finish a sentence.

Nicholas shouts, "It is probably just a false alarm."

That may be the case for there is a fire box on many corners in this neighborhood and many are pulled just for the fun of it. But since there is no sense in trying to talk, I motion to Nicholas we should get up and find out where these fire engines are heading. I will let you know, John, when we return to the stoop.

Uh! OH! A big cloud of black smoke is rising above the apartment house across the street. This is no false alarm!

Chapter 22

A Long Long Time

Dear John,

This morning I am too busy to write about what is going on. So this afternoon I am picking up where I leave off when I tell you there are these big black puffs of smoke.

At first I think maybe it is the Fleetwood what always arrives with clouds of dark smoke but the puffs what we see this morning are much bigger and even darker than the puffs what come out of the Fleetwood. So if the smoke puffs are not coming from the Fleetwood, they must be coming from something else. Then I think maybe it is a fire in one of the apartment houses. So Nicholas and Yours Truly run up to Grand Street where we can see black smoke reaching up to some white clouds what then turn grey and soot falls out of them. It is a factory what is burning for many hours as flames and smoke keep bursting up into the sky. Then the sun is setting and it is getting dark and the firemen still cannot put out the fire.

Nicholas runs to his apartment to tell his mom and dad about the fire. So I am alone back here sitting on the stoop. I just now here a thundering crash. I'll be right back.

Dear John,

The thundering crash is the sound of the factory walls crashing to the ground. I also find out that the factory, what is now a smoldering rubble, is owned by none other than Mr. Pitsacola.

Dear John,

Well I am sitting on the stoop this morning at about ten bells reading about Tom Sawyer but my thinking is interrupted from time to time because I am contemplicating recent events when along comes Nicholas with something most unusual folded up in his right hand and that which is very unusual for Nicholas to be carrying is a newspaper. Nicholas takes three steps up the stoop and sits on the top step, unfolds the Brooklyn Daily Beagle and pernts to the headlines and then to the first paragraph what says, more or less as best as I can rememorize,

Factory Fire Arson, Four Arrested

Luigi Pitsacola is under arrest for arson related to the factory fire in Williamsburg. Pitsacola's son known as 'Lucky Luigi' is accused of setting the fire for the purpose of collecting insurance. Two other unidentical men are also under arrest. Witnesses say they poured gas around the factory building before Lucky Luigi struck a match and lit the fire.

In addition to arson Lucky Luigi Pitsacola is also charged with larceny. He is accused of robbing apartments in the

Williamsburg area and gaining access to the apartments with his father's keys. Luigi Pitsacola owns all the apartment buildings where robberies recently took place.

Nicholas pernts to the Brooklyn Daily Beagle and says as follows, "The relic of Saint Closétus worked! We asked for a religious magical miracle. Saint Closétus, intercedes for us and makes our Lucky Luigi problem go away."

"I'll say! The Lucky Luigi problem is going away for a long, long time."

Dear John,

Four revolting perdickamints what were mentioned in a preseeding letter are not totally solved. Allow me to remember you to these problems. The first problem what starts this whole thing off is that proposition in which the Commies are infilterating the Catholic Church. We are a long way off from solving that problem.

Then that Commie problem leads to the second problem, what is Seabiscuit and his traveling companion although that problem takes care of itself with two big splashes in the East River.

But that leads to the problem of the big bag of relics what we fish out of the sewer on the corner of 34 St. and the Avenue of the Americans. Carmine Decrepio sends his thugs to be looking for the big bag of relics and, if things go really bad, Nicholas and Yours Truly can be making two more big splashes in the East River. One good proposition is that we have the advantage because these thugs are looking for two guys what go by the handles Whiskey Sour and Handcuff Hunk. But this problem is a long way from being solved.

Since Lucky Luigi and his two gorillas are arrested for

arson and larceny, the Lucky Luigi problem is solved. Saint Closétus intercedes at our request. The key, what is a first class relic, done the trick with the help of the powerful second class relic, the spoon.

Chapter 23

The Water Problem

Dear John,

I wake up this morning after my dad is off to work and my mom is off to someplace else. Maybe she is shopping but then I think again. No. Today is the day she and her girlfriends go bowling. They go bowling in the morning for two reasons. One is that the bowling alley is cheaper in the morning and the other is one that they do not want anyone to know how many gutter balls they throw. I think the gutter ball reason is the more important of the two. Because it is so early in the morning they do not have any pin setters show up. That's because the guys what set the pins are up late every night and sleep late. So they take turns setting the pins themselves.

Well anyway after I wipe all the sleep out my eyes with a pillow case, I go into the kitchen to get a glass of water. So I turn on the faucet but nothing comes out. I figure the kitchen water is stuck. So I go into the bathroom and turn on the faucet but no water comes out of that one either.

Well this is a situation about which I am totally disturbed. So I go out to the street and I see this waterless problem is one what disturbs not just me but there is many a citizen, what live in my apartment house and several what live in the apartment house across the street, standing in line and they are carrying pots and pitchers. These citizens are taking turns filling their pots and pitchers with water what is pouring out from a fire hydrant.

Since I am not all that thirsty, I sit on the stoop and wait for the last citizens in line to fill their pots and then I just walk up to the fire hydrant, cup my hands, fill my handcup with water and drink. This I do several times until I am no longer thirsty.

But citizens are standing around and participating in what is known as a gripe session. But the griping increases more than somewhat after Mr. O'Reilly comes out of the apartment house, crosses the street, trips on the curb, staggers a little but then holds onto a lamp post what helps him stand still. Mr. O'Reilly makes the following gripe what sounds like the following, "The darn ploblem is with the darn lanblord who does not pay the darn water bill for seveneral darn months and now that he is in the darn klinker for larzony, we gotta rely on the darn fire hybrant for our darn water."

Now I admit Mr. O'Reilly does not say eggsactly what I write here since I substitute the word *darn* for many other more than somewhat nasty words what he says but these are such nasty words what I do not care to scribe here. But I continue listening to the gripe session and at the same time I am increasing my vocabulary with many more words and what include much more about the landlord and many more gripe words with added nasty words what I do not mention here. Mr. O'Reilly's verse gets louder and louder with each gripe along with many added words what I do not mention here. As the audience increases Mr. O'Reilly's verse also increases in loudness and his face increases in redness so much that he starts coughing and in between coughs he uses many a nasty vocabulary word what I do not scribe here.

Mr. O'Reilly builds and connects the waterless situation to every other situation what disturbs him and many disturbed citizens add more words about everything they can think of what gripes them. These seriously disturbed citizens, what are demonstirring their gripes, grows in number and the shouting grows in loudness, with many more nasty words what I do not scribe here but they do keep adding to my vocabulary. Then the citizens suddenly have other important matters to deal with and these other important matters are made somewhat more important at the moment a police patrol car arrives on the situation. Suddenly Leonard Street is no longer filled with disturbed citizens.

The patrol car stops. A cop gets out, opens the trunk, takes out a wrench and turns off the fire hydrant. Then the patrol car drives off. The demonstirring is over and done. Once again it is a quiet afternoon in the neighborhood. Everything is back to normal except for one thing, no water.

Dear John,

I forget to mention something unusual about this water situation. I am watching the events from my window and when the cops arrive, Mr. O'Reilly leaves but he does not go into his apartment house. Mrs. Manichy comes out and Mr. O'Reilly goes with her up to apartment 2B on the fourth floor. As they are walking up the stairs, I put a glass cup to my apartment door so I can hear. They are whispering but when they pass by the door, I can hear a few words. Something about the Catholic Church and some cardinal in New York City getting them some money.

Dear John,

Later this morning along about eleven bells I am sitting on the stoop reading this book what is scribed by these guys who say they write this book. The scribing is more than somewhat different from the scribing done by Damon Runyon. This Huck Finn guy talks in ways what the nuns do not approve like lots of double negatives and one thing I definitely learn from the nuns is never to use no double negatives.

Dear John,

After lunch, what includes a peanut butter and jelly sandwich with a glass of milk but still no water, Nicholas and Yours Truly are back sitting on the stoop and holding a meeting to discuss the problems what continue to exist. Nicholas makes a very good suggestion and it is as such, "Since the Lucky Luigi problem is solved when he is arrested for arsony and since we ask Saint Closétus to help us solve this very problem, there is good reason to believe that Saint Closétus is indeed a very helpful saint what with his first degree relic of the skeleton key and the second degree spoon. So we should ask for him to intercede again and help us solve the Camine Decrepio problem with a religious magical miracle."

Although I am not certain that Saint Closétus can actually help us out of that problem, Nicholas does offer a very good proposition and for that reason I run up the stairs to apartment 3B on the second floor and retrieve the skeleton key out of the kitchen drawer.

When I return to the stoop with the skeleton key what is a first degree relic, Nicholas is waiting and says, "We must do eggsactly what we do the last time we ask Saint Closétus to intercede for us because that religious magic done the trick." Then Nicholas looks at my hand and asks, "Where is the second degree spoon?"

So I run up stairs again but I cannot find the magic

spoon so I go into the kitchen and find a spoon what looks much like the magic spoon and that satisfies Nicholas.

So I take the key in my hand and Nicholas takes the spoon in his hand and we rub these relics and say together, "Please, Saint Closétus, intercede for us and make our Carmine Decrepio problem go away."

Nicholas finishes the prayer when he blesses himself and says, "Please grand us this religious magical miracle in the name of the Father and of the Son and of the Holy Ghost. Amen."

Dear John,

Along about three bells this very afternoon I am sitting on the stoop reading about Tom Sawyer who is invited to go to a city called Arkansas. Then the big beautiful black Fleetwood turns right on Grand Street and drives down Leonard Street and stops in front of the stoop on which I am sitting. The back door opens and out steps Gutsy Gus. When Gutsy Gus turns around, the doll grabs his hand and says something what I do not fully understand. I think whatever it is the doll says, she says it in Russian. Gutsy Gus holds her hand for about a second and just before the door closes he says what sounds like, "Da svidaniya."

Then Gutsy Gus starts walking up the stoop but, he is so busy watching the Fleetwood drive away, he almost steps on my hand. He stops in his tracks, looks down at me, and smiles and says, "So what do you think about Tom Sawyer?"

"The detective book is scribed in a very different way and is not what I am costumed to but so far I like it more than somewhat."

I look up at Gutsy Gus and I decide to show him that I like the way of talking what I read in this book. So I say, "I hain't never read before the way this guy scribes. Some of what he says surprises me so that my livers and lungs go falling into my legs. Sometimes what he says gives me the jim-jams!"

Gutsy Gus smiles, nods his head and starts to walk up the stoop and asks, "Is the water back on yet? It was off when I leave this morning."

I say, "No. The water is still off, but this morning there is much disgustion among many disturbed neighbors about that very subject and many more subjects and many a gripe is stated by citizens until the cops interrupt their disgustion."

Gutsy Gus shrugs his shoulders and is just about to open the front door when he stops real sudden and looks up the street. What with this sudden stopping and looking on the part of Gutsy Gus, I turn my head and see a grey 1950 DeSoto Custom hardtop, 4-Door Sedan drive down Leonard and parallel-park without tapping bumpers either on the car in front or on the one behind. The door opens and outsteps none other than the much disgusted landlord of recent memory, Mr. Pitsacola.

Chapter 24

Jumping to Confusions

Dear John,

Nicholas is walking down Leonard but he stops in his tracks when he sees a grey 1950 DeSoto Custom hardtop, 4-Door Sedan. Then Nicholas starts walking again and stops in front of the stoop upon which Yours Truly sits. Earnest asks, "Do I see what I see or is that some trick what the devil plays on me?"

"What you see, Nicholas, is what is there for you to see, namely Mr. Pitsacola's grey 1950 DeSoto Custom hardtop, 4-Door Sedan. In fact it is Mr. Pitsacola what drives up in that very DeSoto and walks into the apartment house across the street."

I say, "This, what we see, is not good for we believe Mr. Pitsacola is under arrest along with his son, Lucky Luigi, and his two very big gorilla-looking sidekicks.

Nicholas adds, "This is very bad news for it looks like Saint Closétus has disappointed us. His relic, what is supposed to help with religious magical miracles, is not working."

"But," I suggest, "although this gives me the jim-jams, more than somewhat, let us not jump to confusions."

"It is true!" Nicholas says, "We may be, just as you say, jumping to confusions but if the first class relic is not working religious magical miracles, then Saint Closétus does not have the power we think he has. That flustrates me and it is very disappointing indeed for we need to deal with our present summertime problems because school will be starting in two weeks and that is when we must prepare for even bigger problems."

I complete Nicholas's sentence, "Namely, nuns!"

Nicholas says, "You are sharp as a blade."

I add, "Right you are with Eversharp!"

We both start laughing at that and Nicholas laughs so hard he almost falls off the stoop. Little jokes like that can soften a guy in hard times.

Just then Mr. Pitsacola steps out of the apartment house, walks across the street and it looks like he is going to walk up the stoop but he turns and walks under the stoop to the cellar. Some citizens come out of their apartment buildings and are looking around. One citizen shouts to all the other citizens, "I hear Pitsacola is around here somewhere. Look! There is his 1950 DeSoto. We ain't got no water in these darn buildings. Where is that crooked landlord?"

Just then a truck, with *Brooklyn Water Department* painted on the side, pulls up in front and the driver goes under the stoop and then he comes out and says to the citizens what gather around, "Waters back on in this building. Pitsacola paid the water bills for all the apartment buildings and factories what he owns."

Nicholas whispers a contra bution to Pitsacola's last sentence, "Except for the water in the factory what he burns down."

Just then Mr. Pitsacola walks out from under the stoop and heads for his car but Mr. O'Reilly steps in front of him, crosses his arms, lowers his head and leans on the front door of the 1950 DeSoto. He says, "Luigi, you darn mother darn, why ain't you in jail where youse belong?"

In a loud verse Mr. Pitsacola answers in words what I remember such as, "I'm a notta in a jail cause I don't do nuthin what wrong. My son, Luigi, he done it all. He a very bad boy. I don know him no more. For now on Lucky Luigi is gotta be called Unlucky Luigi cause it stupid to burn down factory what I give him. So leave me alone causa I gotta all de water and other stuff what I gotta fix in all the places what I own. So donna botha me no more." Then Mr. Pitsacola lowers his head. His shoulders move up and down. He shakes his head from side to side. Then he takes a hanky out of his pocket and blows his nose.

Mr. O'Reilly slowly nods his head up and down and then steps away from the 1950 DeSoto.

Mr. Pitsacola gets in, starts the engine, steers the grey 1950 DeSoto Custom hardtop, 4-Door Sedan into the middle of Leonard and drives off. Then everything is back to normal when all the disturbed neighbors go home.

Dear John,

I am sitting on the top step of the stoop along about ten bells reading what Huck Finn scribes about his adventures with his friend Tom Sawyer when Nicholas walks up the steps, sits down next to me and shows me a copy of the Brooklyn Daily Eagle what he borrows from neighbors up the street. The headlines are something about Bishop Sheen and Cardinal Spellman who are fighting over spilt milk or something like that, what personally I do not give a fig about. But then Nicholas opens the newspaper to a middle section and I see a picture of a pack of Philip Morris and I read what it says, *"You'll be glad tomorrow, you smoked Philip Morris today!"*

But then Nicholas says, "No not that."

Then he puts his finger on a picture of the Church of the Most Blessed Blood and guys carrying two coffins of the diseased who are Joey Jarppardino and Larry Lucimarano, otherwise known to us as Seabiscuit and his traveling companion.

Nicholas says, "We missed their funeral and that is too bad. I wanted to go and say a prayer for them."

"Well, Nicholas," I say, "we just get so busy with so many problems we just forget about the problems what are in the past and Joey Jarppardino and Larry Lucimarano, otherwise known to us as Seabiscuit and his traveling companion, are definitely past."

Nicholas answers, "Seabiscuit and his traveling companion may be in the past but the problem what starts with them is not yet buried with them."

Sometimes Nicholas amazes me with what he says this summer. But then the seasons will soon be changing.

Dear John,

I find out today good news from Gutsy Gus when he says the following, "Although Mr. Pitsacola is no longer in jail for burning down the factory, Lucky Luigi is quite solidly behind bars and he is going to prison along with his two gorilla looking sidekicks."

I tell Nicholas what I learn from Gutsy Gus as follows, "Nicholas, we no longer need to worry about Unlucky Luigi and his two very big gorilla-looking sidekicks because they are up the river for 10 to 20. The trial goes fast because just about every citizen in the whole of Williamsburg sees Unlucky Luigi's two very big gorilla-looking sidekicks pouring gasoline from an Evinrude gas can all over the factory and then Unlucky Luigi strikes a match what starts the fire."

Nicholas says, "I do not think that is good enough because 10 to 20 is not all that far."

After I explain to Nicholas that the 10 to 20 of which I speak is years and not miles, he says, "Oh! That is right and it is a good thing too because in 10 to 20 years we will probably look all grown up and so different that Unlucky Luigi will never recognize us."

I am smiling when I suckgest, "We could always change our names again and then Unlucky Luigi will never know us."

Nicholas nods his head in agreement.

Chapter 25
Two Thugs and One Relic

Dear John,

Later today Nicholas and Yours Truly are sitting on the stoop reflectionating on recent events when a cloud of dark smoke preseeded by the big beautiful black Fleetwood rolls down Leonard. After the Cadillac double parks, the driver's door opens and out steps Gutsy Gus. He walks over to the stoop and sits down next to Nicholas on the top step. A cloud of dark smoke puffs up after Big Boris moves over to the driver's seat and switches the ignition on. Before he drives down Leonard Street Big Boris opens a window and in a loud verse says, "Do svidaniya Nicholai malchik stinky foot."

Nicholas shakes his fist but it is very fortunate for Nicholas that Big Boris does not see this gesture. Then Nicholas turns to Gutsy Gus and says, "I hear it said that Lucky Luigi, now known as Unlucky Luigi, will not be returning for a long time to the neighborhood for he is soon to be convicted of arsony."

Gutsy Gus lowers his eyebrows, frowns a little, then smiles and says, "Something like that. Actually it is both." Gutsy Gus smiles again and repeats, "Arsony! Actually it is both."

Dear John,

School is two weeks away and we still have problems to solve. One problem, about the Commies infilterating the Catholic Church, is not solved and then that problem brings up the mystery about Gutsy Gus, the doll and Big Boris. But at least the problem with Unlucky Luigi and Mr. Pitsacola is no longer a problem. We still have the Carmine Decrepio situation what also involves the relics what Nicholas will be bringing with him this morning.

Dear John,

Speak of the devil! Along about eleven bells this morning I am about to step out onto the stoop when I see parked right in front of this very apartment house a 1952 Packard 250 Mayfair Hardtop what looks eggsactly like the before-mentioned Packard what involves two thugs what are looking for Nicholas and Yours Truly. Well I know this is about the hour that Nicholas has agreed to be transporting the bag of relics to the stoop.

If the occupants of the Packard catch sight of Nicholas, there is no need for me to worry about Nicholas questioning his faith in religious magical miracles. Like they say "There are no atheists in foxholes and as I say there are no atheists splashing into the East River."

Since this situation calls for immediate action, I take the back door exit out of the cellar, up the steps, climb up and over two fences and come out of the alley at the end of the block and there I see Nicholas as he is crossing the street on his way to the stoop.

I peek out and see the two thugs walking around and asking questions of several neighborhood citizens. So I try to get Nicholas's attention with the loudest PiSSsst I can make in the direction of Nicholas. Nicholas is turning around making a circle in the middle of the street searching for the whereabouts of the PiSSsst but he fails to notice Yours Truly jumping up and down and waving my hands and continuing with PiSSsting as loud as I can.

But Nicholas's turning around and making a circle in the middle of the street is such activity what the two thugs notice. I peek out and see one of the two thugs pointing at Nicholas. Next the two thugs are off and running and heading right for Nicholas who is now standing still frozen in the middle of the street. Well there is no time for further Pisssting so I run out into the street and grab Nicholas's arm and we are both off and running back into the alley and I am jumping over a fence but when I look back, I see Nicholas has a problem and that problem is the bag of relics he is holding and this bag is more than somewhat heavy. Nicholas is jumping up grabbing the fence with one hand while holding onto the bag of relics with the other hand. He is not making much progress in climbing up the fence.

The two thugs are turning the corner from the alley into the back yard and gaining very quickly on Nicholas but this is no major achievement since Nicholas is frozen in his tracks and holding the bag of relics what is too heavy for the climb.

So I say to Nicholas, "Take out one of the reliquariums and throw it at the two thugs, then throw the bag over the fence and climb up and over as fast as you can."

Nicholas does eggsactly as I suggest and the two thugs are so busy picking up the pieces of the smashed reliquarium that Nicholas and Yours Truly are turning into an alley before two bullets ricochet off the brick wall.

Nicholas and Yours Truly are hiding in an unlocked bin in the darkest part of the cellar when we hear footsteps on the back stairs. They get louder and louder. Then one of the thugs says, "I don't see nuthin down here. What makes you think they come this way?"

The other verse answers, "I ain't soitin about where dem kids is at but at least we got one of dem relics and that means dese kids gots de udders what we better get or else we is in deep stuff with the boss. "

Now I admit I substitute the word *stuff* for another word what I do not care to quote here. I really want this scribing what I am doing to be clean and completely on the up and up and totally truthful.

Just then Nicholas starts breathing like he's heading up for a big sneeze. I am just putting my hand over his mouth but it's …

Chapter 26
Cellarbraking

Dear John,

Just in time! I cover Nicholas's mouth just in time. Last night I do not have time to finish the last sentence because I fall asleep.

When all that is going on down in that cellar, I get the jim-jams something awful so much so that my livers and kidneys and other stuff just about falls down into my legs. Well anyways, those two thugs take off with that relic what Nicholas tosses at them and they look mighty happy to at least have one souvenir even if it is busted up.

Dear John,

Later today Nicholas and Yours Truly are sitting on a stoop but this is a much smaller stoop in back of a store what is on Grand Street. This location is a precortion so that the two thugs do not find us so easily sitting on our usual stoop in front of my apartment house on Leonard. While reflectionating on the events of the previous couple of hours, Nicholas makes the following suggestion, "We need to ask Saint Closétus to help us out of this revolting perdickamint what with these two thugs looking for us and trying to get the rest of the relics. Do you have the relic of Saint Closétus on you?"

I answer, "I believe I do have the relic of Saint Closétus on me." So I start emptying my pockets onto the step. I pull out a bolt what does not fit a nut, a nut what does not fit a bolt, two small screwdrivers, two halves of a cigar, three matches, a half eaten peanut butter sandwich, one rabbit's foot and then finally from the very bottom of my pocket I pull out the tiny key what is the relic handed to me personally by Saint Closétus. "Here!" I say as I hand the sacred relic to Nicholas.

"Where is the spoon? Nicholas asks.

"I do not know where the spoon is but maybe the rabbit's foot will do the trick."

Nicholas takes the sacred relic and picks up the rabbit's foot and says, "We must do eggsactly what we do the last couple of times when we ask Saint Closétus to intercede for us because with this relic and the rabbit's foot we are doubling the power of the religious magical miracle what we ask for. At least I hope so."

So I take the relic and the rabbit's foot and say, "Please, Saint Closétus, intercede for us and make our problem with the two thugs go away."

Nicholas finishes the prayer when he blesses himself and says, "Please grant us this religious magical miracle in the name of the Father and of the Son and of the Holy Ghost, Amen."

Dear John,

Some of the citizens in Brooklyn are more dangerous than a barrel full of bullets. I know this because, just about every morning on his way down Leonard, Nicholas is in the habit of borrowing the morning edition of the Brooklyn

Daily Beagle from the front door of a neighbor and then, later in the day on his way up Leonard, he returns the newspaper from where he borrows it. Well as I am sitting on the stoop reading the detective book what Gutsy Gus gives me, Nicholas walks up the stoop and sits on the top step. He shows me the headline of the newspaper what I have just mentioned what says *Bullets Across Brooklyn*. Then beneath the headline there is a story about gangs rumbling in playgrounds. They fight to keep another gang out of their turf. Irish kids fight Italian kids, Puerto Rican and white kids fight and Irish Catholic kids and Protestant kids fight. They knock each other silly with chains and clubs. But last night one of the kids from the Tau-Taus gang had a gun and shot and killed three kids in the Jesters gang.

I say, "Nicholas, this is really stupid what these kids do."

Nicholas says, "It is really stupid. Fighting in a playground is not what a playground is for. These kids do not know how to play the right way what is fair and square in a playground. Instead of fighting they should be playing and being nice."

I think to myself when Nicholas says something like what he just says, he is not trying to be funny.

Then Nicholas continues, "They are just kids but grownups do not ever act in such stupid ways. They know a playground is for playing."

I just nod my head as if agreeing to what Nicholas says. What else can I do? The weather is changing and summer is fast coming to an end.

Dear John,

This morning I am taking a big bag of garbage down to the cellar and dumping it in a trash bin when I hear Nicholas outside calling out as such, "Earnest, where are you?"

I call out, "I am here in the cellar dumping garbage into the trash bin. Come down the steps under the stoop."

Nicholas, after about a minute or two, finds his way to the cellar and comes in skipping and stands still right in front of the trash bin. Then he takes two dance-like steps, puts his hand on the concrete floor, spins around, flips over on his back and spins a cartwheel. Then he lies on the floor and starts spinning around on his back.

I am concerned about Nicholas more than somewhat, so I ask, "What in tarnation are you doing with that crazy dance what you just do? You look overly exaggerated about something. What is this all about?"

As Nicholas is getting up off the floor, he is smiling more than somewhat and states, "I am cellarbraking because I have very good news. Thanks be to Saint Closétus, once again we have a religious magical miracle what just incurs. Come over here where the light bulb is bright and watch as I unfold this copy of the Brooklyn Daily Beagle. Now take a gander at what I am pernting to, what is the headline. It says, "Two Alfredolenti Mobsters Caught with Stolen Relic" and here is a photograph of the very two thugs what are after us yesterday."

I take a look at the Brooklyn Daily Beagle and sure enuff there are the two thugs what run after us yesterday. Then I read a little more under the headline. It says a Packard is stopped for passing a red light and the cop sees in the back seat some pieces of gold what look suspicious and it turns out to be a broken reliquary. The cop is even more suspicious because these two thugs definitely do not look like holy priests. So the cop makes a call in and more cop cars come and they find out that these guys what got the reliquary are mobsters what belong to the Alfredolenti Gang. Then they investigate and find that the relic is one of a lot more relics what were stolen many years ago from a church in Paris, France.

The Brooklyn Daily Beagle has a lot more to say but the main thing is that the two mobsters what are previously looking for us are no longer looking for us.

I say to Nicholas, "This is indeed very good news and we certainly owe this religious magical miracle to Saint Closétus. But I am confused more than somewhat because these two thugs, what got arrested and therefore are no longer looking for us, are mobsters what belong to the Alfredolenti Gang but Seabiscuit and his traveling companion are, or were, mobsters in the DeCrepio gang."

Nicholas asks a very good question, "Are we sure that Seabiscuit and his traveling companion are, or were, members of the DeCrepio gang?

I am impressed with that question. Summer is not completely over for Nicholas. So I answer, "Right! Maybe Seabiscuit and his traveling companion are, or were, mobsters of the Alfredolenti Gang."

Nicholas picks up the Brooklyn Daily Beagle and points to the very end of the story where it tells the address of the head of the Alfredolenti Gang. The address is in Red Hook, Brooklyn.

By this time all the garbage is in the trash bin so Nicholas and Yours Truly walk up the steps from under the stoop and sit down on the top step. Just then Gutsy Gus walks out of the apartment house across the street and beside him is Mr. Joey Pits, all dressed up in his Dapper-Dan zoot suit. Gutsy Gus is too busy looking at his pocket watch to notice Nicholas and Yours Truly but just then the big beautiful black Fleetwood drives down Leonard and stops in front of Gutsy Gus and Mr. Joey Pits. The back door on the left side opens and Mr. Joey Pits enters the Fleetwood. Gutsy Gus opens the front door on the driver's side and Big Boris slides over to the passenger side, opens the window and points his index finger at Nicholas and as the big beautiful black Fleetwood slowly moves down the street. As it passes the stoop, Big Boris opens the window, turns his head and in a loud verse says to Nicholas, "Da svidaniya, Nicholai malchik stinky foot." Then the big beautiful black Fleetwood turns at the first corner and is gone in a big black cloud of smoke.

Chapter 27

Natasha Natasha

Dear John,

This morning along about eleven bells I am sitting on the stoop reading about Tom Sawyer, Detective, when Nicholas comes along and says, "I do not sleep a wink all night because I got this very worried feeling that something real bad is going to happen today."

Well I just read some very good advice what Huck Finn gives in the detective book what I am reading and I say to Nicholas like the way I read it, "Worrying hain't no darn use for if you don't find out the facts of a thing, what's the sense in guessing out what hain't the facts and wasting your time on something not worth a darn anyways?"

Nicholas looks at me with one eye squinting almost shut and says, "Earnest, all summer you are talking strange like what they do in that *Guys and Dolls* book and I am getting use to your way of talking pretty much from the beginning but this talking what you just done is strangest yet and this way of talking will take some time for me to get all used to again."

I answer in the following way, "Well, don't get all up a stump about it. It's all tittle-tattle, like what I read in this here book, and this way of talking does me real good."

I can see Nicholas has had about enough of this tittle-tattle and he is about to head home when a great big puff of smoke comes rolling down Leonard.

Nicholas gets up from the stoop real fast and says, "I know this day something bad is going to happen and here it comes and its name is Big Boris."

But then the big puff of smoke stops in front of the apartment house two doors down the block.

I whisper to Nicholas, "This is indeed suspicious. Then I think of how Huck Finn would say what I mean to say. "Thunder!" I says, "What do ya make of all this? Ain't it suspicious like? Let's sneak over to the other side of the Fleetwood and investigate this what is going on."

Nicholas shakes his head and says, "No! I do not want to meet up with Big Boris. He calls me bad names and says I am a stupid malchik with stinky feet and stuff like that."

But I point to the driver in the car and say, "That driver looks more like Gutsy Gus than Big Boris."

So Nicholas and Yours Truly bend over, crouch down real low and do a Groucho Marx walk across the street. We are hiding on the other side of the Fleetwood right near the trunk when we hear a woman's verse saying something like, "Balshoy spaseba. Dank you mush, August tin."

By now Nicholas and Yours Truly are stooping real low at the back of the Fleetwood. On my knees I peek around the side of the Fleetwood. The driver's door opens and out steps Gutsy Gus who walks to the back of the Fleetwood and opens the back door.

An ankle in very high heels moves slowly out of the Fleetwood followed by a long thin leg covered with a dark nylon, the black seam straight as an arrow. I whisper to myself something what lots of time I hear my Dad say, "Nice gams!"

My hand grips the Fleetwood's back bumper to steady

myself. She is so beautiful, I must hold on tight to the bumper lest I fall flat onto the curb. She speaks in a very soft verse and it sounds something like, "August tin, you are krasi vay adya vooshka."

Gutsy Gus says, "Natasha, Natasha, you are vwery simpa tich nei, how you say? A very nice girl but you cannot... It is no good for ...

Natasha Natasha interrupts and says, "I know. Ya thes ma yoo. I understand.

Natasha Natasha walks up to the first step, turns and says, "August tin, Odin hour, one hour return, OK?" Then she walks up the stoop where Mr. Joey Pits, all duded up in his Dapper-Dan zoot suit, is standing on the top step. He holds the door open and follows Natasha Natasha as she steps through the doorway. Mr. Joey Pits shuts the door behind them.

There is much more to what I see and hear but I just I do not understand what I hear and I do not know how to write what I see. Quickly, I crawl on my knees to the other side of the Fleetwood and then my arms go out from under me and I fall flat out on the street. When I fall for a beautiful woman I really and truly fall. I just can't help it.

Well after taking a long look for himself, Nicholas creeps on all fours around the Fleetwood and finds Yours Truly just getting up off my knees. Then the Fleetwood motor turns on and surrounds us with a big cloud of black smoke. As the Fleetwood turns slowly away from the curb, Nicholas and Yours Truly do a Groucho Marx run across the street under the cover of a huge cloud of black smoke.

Dear John,

It is now about one hour later when Mr. Joey Pits opens the door of his apartment house across the street, a couple of doors down, and out steps Natasha Natasha just as beautiful as she is one hour ago. They stand talking for about five minutes and every once in a while Natasha Natasha glances down at her wristwatch and Mr. Joey Pits turns his head and looks up Leonard. The Fleetwood is late but that is no problem for me. I look real hard and squint to get a real good look at Natasha Natasha. When she turns around I can see the seams on the back of her nylons are straight as an arrow. The seams rise up from her high heeled shoes and disappear under her red skirt.

Nicholas is saying something but every one of my senses is distracted more than somewhat. My mind and much more of me is on the vision of Natasha Natasha. I am standing on the stoop, stretching my arms to grab onto the step above. I am doing my best so not to fall. Beautiful girls get me dizzy.

But then Nicholas speaks again and I hear him say, "I got this very worried feeling that something real bad is going to happen today."

"Nicholas," I say, "what could possibly go bad what with that beautiful Natasha Natasha standing there with Mr. Joey Pits?"

Nicholas says, "Well maybe there is the something bad right there and maybe its name is Mr. Joey Pits all duded up in his double-breasted Dapper-Dan zoot suit."

But very soon we find out that the something bad is not Mr. Joey Pits. Nicholas's feeling about something bad happening is indeed a correct feeling. Sometimes I should listen to Nicholas and this is one of those times because as Nicholas is going on about this and that and one thing and another and while Yours Truly is deep in thought and feelings about the vision of Natasha Natasha, we do not notice a black Packard slowly easing on down Leonard.

Although I do not at first notice the Packard, Mr. Joey

Pits turns his head, takes Natasha Natasha's arm, whispers in her ear, and they both turn around and step back into the apartment house. I can see Mr. Joey Pits looking out the glass window in the middle of the door. By the time I see the Packard, it is moving fast, pulling into a space directly in front of the stoop and screeching to a stop.

The two front doors open and two nicely dressed men step out of the Packard, walk across the sidewalk, stand very still directly in front of the stoop and look at Nicholas and Yours Truly. The nicely dressed man on the right opens his jacket, pulls it back with his left hand and with his right hand pulls a pistol out of a shoulder holster.

"We come for the relics. We know you two have them and you will give them to us one way or the other."

"Relics?" I ask. "What are relics? I do not have the slightest idear what you are talking about."

As a sort of a response the nicely dressed man on the left opens his jacket, pulls it back with his right hand and with his left hand pulls a pistol out of a shoulder holster.

To lighten the conversation I nod to the nicely dressed man on the left and ask, "Are you left handed? In spite of what the nuns tell us at St. Mary's that is nothing to be ashamed of. I read in the Brooklyn Diocese newspaper, what is called *The Tablet*, that it is not true that the left hand is Satan's hand."

The nicely dressed man, to whom I address my last remarks, speaks as follows, "Kid, if you do not shut your trap and hand over the relics, you will be visiting Satan very shortly."

Nicholas adds to the conversation, "What Earnest says is true and I do believe that sometimes nuns do not tell the whole truth about a thing. See when a kid is left handed, they try very hard to get him to write with his right hand."

I add as follows, "This is also true that nuns are not all that truthful about going blind by touching yourself in certain places what I do not mention here. I know this because Dennis Bowalski touches himself all the time in that very place."

Nicholas adds, "And Dennis Bowalski even does more than that for many years and he still sees real good."

I nod my head in agreement with what Nicholas. I say, "It is true that Dennis Bowalski does touch himself very often and for a very long time but his vision is not impaired in the slightest."

Nicholas adds support for this statement, "It is true Dennis Bowalski does not even wear glasses."

The nicely dressed man on the right begins to speak, "If you kids do not shut your…

But this man does not get to complete his sentence because he and his nicely dressed partner are suddenly face down flat on the ground.

Standing in back of the two nicely dressed men who are now flat on the sidewalk is Big Boris who is holding two pearl handle pistols with which he just recently brings down quite hard on the backs of the necks of the two nicely dressed men. Big Boris kicks their two pistols into the gutter and these are retrieved by none other than Mr. Joey Pits.

Nicholas looks down at the two nicely dressed men who are just regaining consciousness and adds a thought, actually a regret, "You two will need to send your nice suits to the cleaners."

Big Boris slowly puts his pearl handled pistols in two holsters, one on each side of his belt. Then he looks at Nicholas. He smiles and says, "Nicholai malchik stinky foot! More than suits go to cleankers."

After all our conversations run their course, Big Boris

looks at Nicholas and Yours Truly and says as follows, "Eto pilkho! It werry bad here for you. Para eettee. Vat I mean isht I vant you two malchik go into partment hoose. Avodna! Right avay. You malchiks Earnest and Stinky Foot say not word about what is here. Ponumayu? Unnerstand?"

Nicholas and Yours Truly nod our heads to show we agree but Big Boris fails to notice that my right hand is behind my back with my fingers crossed. Other than that, we do eggsactly as we are told.

We go up the stoop, into the apartment house and as we are climbing up the stairs, Nicholas says, "I hate it when Big Boris calls me Stinky Foot. A name like that could stick with a guy."

I do not say another word. I just keep my mouth shut as we climb the stairs to the roof and look down into the street. The Fleetwood is gone, the Packard is gone, the two nicely dressed men are gone and Mr. Joey Pits is standing in the doorway of his apartment house looking down Leonard and smiling. No trace of any problem. All is back to normal.

Chapter 28

Looking for Paris

Dear John,

This morning I am sitting on the stoop contemplicating the recent events and considerating more than a few idears about the mysterious goings on what happen yesterday when Gutsy Gus opens the front door, steps out onto the stoop and sits down next to Yours Truly on the top step.

Gutsy Gus asks, "How do you like the book I give you?"

"I think Tom Sawyer is having exciting adventures what I like very much but the topic of the conversation I wish to have with you is not about Tom Sawyer. It is about the events of yesterday and about those events I have questions and they are more than just a few."

Gutsy Gus answers with a question, "What were you doing when those two guys are pointing pistols at you?"

"At the time the two men are pointing pistols, we are just taking our good old time, talking about this and that and one thing or another and doing the best we can to keep their attention away from the black Fleetwood what is slowly driving down Leonard. But now I have a question or two which is as follows. Number one: yesterday you are driving the Fleetwood when all this comes down. Is that not right?

Gutsy Gus answers, "Yes. At that time I am driving the Fleetwood. Big Boris is in the passenger seat. We are a little late to pick up Natasha at the apartment house across the street and down a few doors."

I say, "Number two: How is it that the Fleetwood makes no noise and no smoke as it drives down Leonard?"

Gutsy Gus answers, "When we see those two guys standing in front of the stoop, we stop the Fleetwood at the corner and Boris pulls binoculars out of the glove compartment and he sees the two pistols pointing at you and Nicholas. So I give the Fleetwood some gas and then turn off the motor. The Fleetwood glides down Leonard making neither noise nor smoke. That's how we are able to sneak up on those guys. Boris gets out of the Fleetwood and whacks them in the back of their heads."

I say, "I have another couple of questions."

But Gutsy Gus cuts me off right there and then. He says, "Sorry, Earnest, you used up all your questions." With that Gutsy Gus gets up from the stoop and walks across the street to the apartment house a couple of doors down and walks up that stoop. There he meets Mr. Joey Pits and they both head inside and Mr. Joey Pits closes the door behind them.

At just about that same time, Mr. O'Reilly steps out of his apartment house, walks across the street and passes Nicholas and Yours Truly as he goes up the stoop to the front door. The front door opens and Mrs. Malichy meets Mr. O'Reilly and they both head inside and Mrs. Malichy closes the door behind them.

Dear John,

I am surprised that Gutsy Gus does not want to hear more of my questions because he is usually much more deceptive to my questionings. I have more than a few questions what are unanswered about the accurents of yesterday but this morning Gutsy Gus is secretive more than somewhat. So I sit back on the stoop and start reading about Tom Sawyer's problems on the Missippi. But then it is hard to think about Tom Sawyer's problems what with all the problems what we got right here in Brooklyn. But then I read something what Huck Finn says and I see we think a lot alike because he says something like, "I get the jim-jams and the fantods and my brain gets all caked up and it turns solid." That's eggsactly the way I am thinking at the present moment.

Well just as the Brooklyn problems are giving me the jim jams and getting all caked up and conflused in my brain, along comes Nicholas and he is carrying the big bag of relics, minus one what is previously counted for.

Without saying a word Nicholas walks up the stoop and clunks the big bag of relics on the top step and then speaks as such, "It is true that we wish to have an exciting summer but these relics are getting us into more troubles than what we wish for. These relics are doing us more bad than good. The only relic what we should keep is the relics what Saint Closétus gives us because those are the truest of all and we know they work religious magical miracles."

Well Nicholas's argument is hard to refoot so I must in spirit agree but I bring up a very good question which is, "Well just how do you propose to depose of these relics?"

Nicholas answers, "We can bring them back to East 34th St. and the Avenue of the Americans and dump them where they come from."

I am thinking this is not the right way to depose of the religious relics and just as some other more clever idears are heading my way, Gutsy Gus opens the door and steps out onto the stoop. He looks down and sees the bag what contains the relics and he says, "I see the bag of relics on the stoop here. What are you two up to?"

Nicholas says, "Here Gutsy Gus. This bag full of relics is a gift to you except for a key and spoon belonging to Saint Closétus what are the only relics what do the really good religious magical miracles."

Gutsy Gus says, "I have been asking around and doing some investigating. There is good reason to believe that some of these older relics were stolen from a secret hiding place. Some believe secret tunnels were dug near a tower and chapel in Paris. The buildings are no longer there but many still believe that the Knights Templar hid much of their wealth and sacred relics near or even under these places. The problem is that these building were built on a drained swamp and they may have disappeared very deep, swallowed up by the swampy ground. For many years people have searched for these treasures but no one found the hiding places."

I say, "But maybe someone did. Do you think all these relics came from these knights' hiding place?"

"No, not all of them. The newer ones may have been stolen from the Archdiocese of New York. I know the Auxiliary Bishop very well. He told me that some relics had been taken from a crypt in the Church of Saint Olga."

Just then Gutsy Gus's mother opens the window on the fourth floor and is shouting out the window to Gutsy Gus, "August Teen, where's the bread all ready? You back from the grocer without the bread? No, I see you ain't even gone yet. What's with you? Go get the bread from Teitelbaum the Grocer and while you're at it gets some baloney from Willy the Butcher."

Gutsy Gus waves to his mom and says, "OK, I'm on my way." Then he turns and says to Nicholas and Yours Truly,

"Keep those relics in a safe place. In fact, I strongly suggest you find a real secret place to hide them."

Nicholas says, "We can hide them back where they come from in Paris. Is that Paris place somewhere around here in Brooklyn?"

Autumn is fast approaching for Nicholas.

Chapter 29

Bad Feelings

Dear John,

This morning along about ten bells Nicholas and Yours Truly are conducting a meeting of Operation Top Secret at the back table in Randy's Restaurant and, while sucking down our two cents plains, we are conversating about this and that and one thing or another.

Nicholas states, "When I have a feeling that something bad is happening, it happens. I first have that bad feeling just before those two nicely dressed men show up and point pistols at us. Well, right now I have that same feeling. Something bad is happening right now but we just do not know what it is … yet."

Then Nicholas, shrinks down in his seat, scratches his head, shrugs his shoulders, and shakes all over. When Nicholas scratches, shrugs, shrinks and shakes, this is a sign that he is flustrated and does not know what to do in the present situation.

I am hoping to make Nicholas feel better. So I levitate Nicholas's flustration by stating in a very calm way, "Nicholas, not everything bad is happening to us. For example, it is a good thing that Randy is back from visiting his relatives in Italy but because he is there for more than a month, as a result he does not remember that we previously, on more than one or two occasions, depart rather hastily from his restaurant without clearing the bill."

Nicholas shakes his head and says, "That is a good thing that Randy is forgetful about our hasty departures without clearing the bill."

I confirmate Nicholas's last remark, "So we agree that good things happen even when you have feelings that something bad is happening."

Nicholas says, "Yes, I agree that some good things happen when I have the feeling that something bad is going to happen." Then Nicholas holds up the big bag of relics and says, "But we have to find a really secret place to hide this big bag of relics because I do not think it is a good idear for me to be carrying them around and to hide them under my bed is not the best place for them either."

"You are correct about that! We do need to find a better hiding place for the relics and do it soon."

"Yes we need to act fast," says Nicholas and with that he takes two sucks on his straw and the two cent plain gurgles its final gurgle. Then Nicholas stands up and makes the following suckgestion, "We should find this place what's called Paris and dump these relics back there."

I respond, "Paris is pretty far from here. I suggest we find some place a little closer."

Nicholas says, "Maybe Saint Closétus can help us find a hiding place what is closer than Paris. It is several days since we consult Saint Closétus and we need to ask for his advice and, even more than his advice, we need to ask him to perform a religious magical miracle so the mobsters stop trying to kill us and all."

I feel obligitated to help Nicholas avoid heresy errors

about religion and so I remind Nicholas, "Remember what Gutsy Gus tells us. Saint Closétus does not perform miracles but he intercedes for us and asks God to perform a miracle."

Nicholas adds, "But I do not particuly care who gets the religious magical miracle done, we just gotta get it done." Then Nicholas reaches into his pocket, pulls out the spoon and the key and says, "We got the power in these two relics, this spoon and this key, so let us take them and say the magic words eggsactly what we say before and we gotta do it now."

So I take the key and Nicholas takes the spoon. I say, "Please, Saint Closétus, intercede for us and make our problem with the mobsters go away."

Nicholas finishes the prayer when he blesses himself and says, "Please grant us this religious magical miracle in the name of the Father and of the Son and of the Holy Ghost, Amen."

Dear John,

I am back sitting on the stoop considering what takes place earlier this morning when Nicholas and Yours Truly ask Saint Closétus to help find a hiding place for the relics, somewhat closer to our neighborhood than Paris, and we also ask him to intercede to get a miracle done so we are not murdered by mobsters. After that, we get up from the table, walk to the cash register and pay for our two cents plains. Randy looks at us and squints as if he is trying to remember something but he does not remember what he is trying to remember and we do nothing to help him remember. So Randy just takes two pennies from each of us and keeps squinting.

When we go outside, we agree to meet back on the stoop this afternoon along about two bells. Then Nicholas takes the bag of relics and goes home for lunch.

Dear John,

Nicholas is right again. When he feels that something bad is happening, it happens.

This afternoon along about two bells Yours Truly is sitting on the stoop reading about Tom Sawyer and some di'monds what got hid in somebody's boot. Well time goes by and, before I know it, it is about three bells and still no Nicholas. Along about another half hour Yours Truly is getting mighty worried about Nicholas.

I try my best not to think of the worse so I am reading Tom Sawyer but that don't help one little bit because in his third chapter he is getting worried too and Huck Finn scribes like as follows, "Well, the time strung along and along, and that fellow never come! Why, it strung along till dawn begun to break, and still he never come. "Thunder!" I says, "What do you make out of this? Ain't it suspicious?"

Well reading that don't make me feel any better. Thunder! Ain't it suspicious indeed? So I get up and walk over to the apartment house where Nicholas lives and there is no sign of Nicholas anywhere. Thunder! Ain't that suspicious?

I am walking back and forth in front of Nicholas's apartment house when Earnest's neighbor, Mrs. Yablonskowits, opens her upstairs window and calls to me as such, "Earnest, I see you pacing up and down here. If you are looking for your friend, Nicholas, he is not here."

I ask, "Well do you know where Nicholas is? He was supposed to meet me on my stoop a couple of hours ago."

Mrs. Yablonskowitz says, "I do not know where he goes but it is just about two hours ago I am looking out this window when I see Nicholas walking down the street carrying a big brown bag. Then two nicely dressed men drive up in a black Packard and they get out and talk to Nicholas and then he climbs into the back seat of their car and they drive away. They seem really friendly, like really nice men, and it looks like Nicholas knows them. One of the men even helps Nicholas by taking the heavy brown bag and carrying it to the Packard and he puts it in the front seat."

Dear John,

It is now about three hours since I last see Nicholas and I am back sitting on the stoop. I am thinking as hard as I can about what to do without thinking about Nicholas making a splash in the East River or worse. As I am contemplicating really deep and trying to figure out what to do, then suddenly it all connects. I think I know what to do think and I know where Nicholas is.

I have no memory of how I get there but in no time at all I am knocking on the door of apartment 2B on the fourth floor. Mrs. Manichy, dressed in a red bathrobe and with rows of curlers in her hair and the usual cigarette hanging from her lips, opens the door and I say, "I have to see Gutsy Gus, I mean August teen, right away. I really need to talk to him."

Mrs. Manichy begins to close the door and says, "He ain't here. Go away."

Well just then I hear another door open in the apartment and Gutsy Gus himself comes to the door, grabs the door knob away from his mother, stands in the doorway and asks, "What's up?"

In a most calm verse I say, "Well it's nothing really. I just want to thank you for all the help you give us."

When I say that, Mrs. Manichy shrugs her shoulders, walks back into the apartment, opens a bedroom door, walks in and slams the door. But before the door slams. I get a glimpse of some guy sitting on a bed. He has no shirt on and, I think, maybe he has no pants on either. He looks very much like Mr. O'Reilly.

Gutsy Gus steps out into the hallway and says, "OK, what's this really all about."

I explain by whispering as such, "I think Nicholas is kidnapped by those two mobsters what point guns at us the other day. It's either those guys or some facsimile thereof. This is what happens. Nicholas is supposed to meet me on the stoop about three hours ago but he never shows up. So I go to his apartment house and Mrs. Yablonskowitz says she sees Nicholas walking down the street carrying a big heavy brown bag. Then two nicely dressed men drive up in a black Packard and they get out and talk to Nicholas and then he gets in the back seat of their car and they drive away. I think I know where they…"

Gutsy Gus puts his hand up to stop me from saying anything else. Then he shakes his head and says, "Wait downstairs on the stoop. I am coming down very soon but first I have to make a phone call."

Well I am back sitting on the stoop but not for long. In almost no time at all Gutsy Gus opens the front door and says, "You are going to tell me something when I stop you. What is it?"

"I think I know where Nicholas is. It's the Alfredolenti Mobsters and they are here in Brooklyn, in Red Hook."

Gutsy Gus says, "I know a couple of the addresses where the Alfredolenti Mobsters hang out in Red Hook." Just then a big cloud of smoke rolls very fast down Leonard and the Fleetwood screeches to a stop in front of the apartment house. Gutsy Gus continues, "You stay here. I'll try to find Nicholas. If he is in Red Hook, Boris and I will find him and get him home." Then Gutsy Gus gets in the Fleetwood which drives away fast.

So I sit back down on the stoop. This kidnapping worries me more than somewhat but then I think about what Huck

Finn says and what I tell Nicholas. So I turn to the place on the stoop where Nicholas mostly sits and I say as if I'm talking to Nicholas, "Worrying hain't no darn use for if you don't find out the facts of a thing, what's the sense in guessing out what hain't the facts and wasting your time on something not worth a darn anyways?" But then I just sit on the top step and think. No, I hain't just thinkin. I just cannot help myself. I don't know the facts. I don't know what is happening to Nicholas. I am very worried!

Chapter 30
Stinky Foot and All

Dear John,

It is about two hours since I write that last letter and much is happening in that time. The first thing is that about one hour ago, a big black cloud of smoke rolls slowly down Leonard and this slowness of the Fleetwood adds much to my worries. It reminds me of a funeral. But then the Fleetwood stops and backs up into a parking space in front of the stoop. The back door opens and out steps Nicholas.

I am so glad to see Nicholas that I jump down from the top step, run across the sidewalk and give Nicholas a big hug. I say, "Nicholas, I am so glad to see you alive and not chopped up into little pieces."

Nicholas removes my arms from around his neck, takes a step back and says, "Calm down. Let us not get overly exaggerated about my return. There is still a problem and it is that we do not have the big bag of relics. I think I know the whereabouts of the hiding place for them but the hiding place is in Red Hook."

"Do not worry about the relics," I say. "The main thing is that you are not feeding the fish in the East River."

Nicholas says, "The most important thing is that I still

have the two most important relics what Saint Closétus gives us and they are right here in my pocket."

By this time Gutsy Gus is out of the car and is sitting on the top step of the stoop. As the Fleetwood starts to pull out of the parking space, Big Boris leans out the driver's window and in a loud verse says, "Goodbye Nicolai malchik stinky foot."

Nicholas turns and waves back and says, "Goodbye, Big Boris and thanks for all your help."

I am surprised more than somewhat by Nicholas's wave and friendly goodbye to Big Boris. I say, "Now Nicholas and Gutsy Gus I have a strong feeling that you have quite a story to tell me and I am very happy to hear such a story."

Gutsy Gus says, "Sit down, Earnest, and we will fill you in on the events what recently take place in Red Hook. Nicholas, the story starts with you, so begin."

Nicholas leans back on the stoop and says as follows, "It all starts when I am walking home for lunch. As I am getting close to my apartment house, the two nicely dressed guys, what we meet a couple of days ago, step out of their Packard and one of the nicely dressed men takes the big bag of relics off me and the other one asks, "Where's the other bag?"

"Other bag? What other bag? I do not know of no other bag."

"Then one of the nicely dressed men offers me a ride. I thank him for the offer but I inform him that I am indeed very close to my apartment house and a ride is not necessary. But they are more persuading the next time and tell me to get into the back seat of the Packard or else and the or else is very persuading because of the two pistols in their holsters under their jackets. One guy takes the big bag of relics and puts it in the front seat. So I sit still in the back seat, mainly because one guy has his pistol pointing at me and he keeps asking me about the whereabouts of some other bag."

He keeps asking, "Where is the other bag?"

I tell him, "I see three bags at the corner of East 34th St. and the Avenue of the Americans. Two of the bags are full of hundred dollar bills and then there is this bag what we fish out of the sewer."

He says, "The other bag where is it?"

"What other bag?" I tell him again about the money bags but that does not interest him.

He says, "The other bag what contains the other half of the relics. That bag! Where is it?"

"I do not know nothing about some other bag what contains relics. I only got this one big bag of relics what is presently on the front seat of this Packard."

Then Nicholas whispers, "Of course I do not tell him about the two relics what are in my pocket."

Gutsy Gus asks, "What relics are in your pocket?"

Nicholas is reaching into his pocket but I interrupt and say, "Nicholas, keep those in your pocket for now just in case a bad guy or two is watching from a roof or a window or somewhere. We do not want any bad guys to know about those two relics."

Nicholas removes his hand from his pocket minus the spoon and the key. He looks at the roofs of all the buildings around and says, "You are right about that. We gotta be real careful especially because those are the best relics what we got."

So I suggest, "Nicholas continue your story about being kidnapped and all."

Nicholas shakes his head and says, "Then the Packard drives to a warehouse some place near a lot of water and some big ships. They tell me to get out of the Packard and they take me inside the warehouse because they want to introduce me to their boss. The place is filled with all kinds of stuff I see in churches. I see big statues and crosses and lots stained glass and paintings of saints and lots of church furniture. So I am walking up a stairs on my way to meet the boss when I hear a loud truck drive up real fast and it crashes right through the wall and stops in the middle of the warehouse. Then a whole bunch of guys are jumping out of the truck and they all start shooting with rifles and some have Tommy guns. There is a whole lot of bullets bouncing off walls and it is very noisy. Then some guys are lying on the ground alive or otherwise. The guy who is taking me upstairs to meet his boss is suddenly rolling and tumbling down the stairs. I think he is otherwise."

Nicholas glances down and shrugs his shoulders and then continues as such, "So anyways I run up the rest of the stairs as fast as I can and I see this big fat guy who is probably the boss. He does not see me and, what with all the guns shooting and making much noise, he does not hear me. I hide behind the door and watch the boss who is holding the big bag of relics and he turns and then the big bag of relics is gone. He hides the relics in a secret place in his office. Then I hear guys running up the stairs and lots of shooting getting closer so I run across the upstairs office and climb into a box what says Cargo. When I get into the box and close the lid, the box starts moving and is fast sliding down a ramp or something. It's all dark in the box but I can tell I am moving downhill pretty fast. Then the Cargo box hits something and suddenly stops. I can still hear lots of shooting but it is pretty far away so I figger the best place for me is right there in that Cargo box. Then after a few minutes all the shooting stops but I am not about to take any chances so I stay right there, quiet as a church mouse in that Cargo box."

Nicholas stops talking. Then he says, "You take it from there, Gutsy Gus. I am all talked out."

Gutsy Gus says, "OK. I'll take it from there. When Boris and I drive close to the warehouse, we see a couple of cars leaving the area with tires screeching. Then everything is real quiet but there are about twelve bodies all over the place. Some are crawling around and bleeding and others, as Nicholas says, are otherwise. We get out of the Fleetwood and start looking around. Boris and I are looking everywhere for Nicholas but we are not able to find him."

Gutsy Gus smiles at Boris and says, "Boris has had some run-ins with some of these mob guys and he recognizes a couple of the ones what are otherwise. I immediately recognize two of the dead guys because they are the very ones we remove from our neighborhood after they are pointing pistols at you two. Then I turn over a big fat guy and my suspicion is correct for that fat guy is none other than Fredo Alfredolenti himself, the boss of the Brooklyn crime family. Boris tells me he sees some other dead guys who are, or were, members of the Decrepio crime family in Manhattan. So it looks like there was a war between these two crime families. I do not know exactly what the war is about but when I go into the warehouse, I see all the religious objects. So then I step over a couple of bodies and walk upstairs to the office. I can see the whole place is filled with religious objects but the very best ones are in the office and there are several very important relics. Well, as we are looking around trying to find Nicholas either alive or otherwise, we hear in the distance police sirens and they are getting closer. So I run down stairs and Boris and I run back to the Fleetwood and get in and Boris starts up the motor. Boris, why don't you take it from there?"

Boris asks, "What? I should tack vat from vere?"

Gutsy Gus explains, "I mean you can tell the rest of the story."

Boris nods his head and says, "OK! I tack vat from vere."

Then Boris explains, "I is insistant that vee not leave til vee find Nicolai malchik stinky foot. One time avound to drive the warehouse. One time avound to look for stinky foot. Then I looks in rear mirror, pulls out pistol from undershirt and points it to the back of the Fleetwood. I shouts, 'You, in back seat, hands up or to shoot.'

Then I turns avound all the vays, lowers pistol and say, 'Nicolai malchik stinky foot right here in back seat!'"

Gutsy Gus adds, "So I turn around and there you are, stinky foot and all."

Boris says, "I so wery glad I see Nicholai I says, 'Nicolai, I so happy see you, maybe I not call you stinky foot no more.'"

Gutsy Gus says, "So we are all safe in the Fleetwood and we head back here before the cops get to the scene of the mob war. It is best not to be hanging around after a situation such as this."

Nicholas adds, "Then we all have a very pleasant ride back home and I do not mind it one bit when Big Boris calls me 'stinky foot'."

Chapter 31
Bad News

Dear John,

Late this morning at almost twelve bells I am sitting by myself in the back booth of Randy's Restaurant while gurgling my way to the bottom of a two cent plain. I am waiting for Nicholas who is a little late but that is no problem with what he goes through yesterday. Then I see this kid come in and at first I think it is Nicholas but instead it is Bobby Anderson who I am very glad to see. He notices me sitting in the back booth mainly because he cannot miss my happy-to-see-you waving hands. After Bobby Anderson gets himself an ice cream cone with a double scoop of tutti fruitti, he comes to the back booth and sits across the table.

I ask, "Bobby Anderson, you must be in a high rolling financial state what with you spending so much bread on a tutti fruitti double scoop ice cream cone. How is it that you come into such a large amount of do-re-me?"

Bobby Anderson answers, "I earn some money from helping my Uncle Bob on his boat. But I earn even more money from a nice old guy what calls himself Captain Canarsie. He lives on a boat what is named *Queen of the Bay*. When I am on the *Queen of the Bay*, I have to wear a sailor's cap and say things like, 'Aye, Captain' and then I have to salute him."

Captain Canarsie hates the way things smell and he thinks it is the *Queen of the Bay* what smells bad, so he pays me to help clean up his boat. It does get really smelly but that is mostly because the *Queen of the Bay* is tied up to the Canarsie Pier. He keeps thinking the smell on the boat can get clean but it got almost nothing to do with the *Queen of the Bay*. The smell got a lot more to do with the tide in Jamaica Bay. So I clean the *Queen of the Bay* about an hour before the tide is coming in and then at high tide it smells pretty good but then when the tide goes out, I get to cleaning again. So I make a little bit of cash about every twelve hours. It all adds up to a tutti fruitti double scoop ice cream cone."

"That sounds pretty exciting what with you being a sailor and all. Are you done with all the exciting vacations what you have this summer?"

Bobby Anderson closes one eye and tilts his head and answers my question, sort of, as such, "Earnest, I am back. Yes, I have some exciting times this summer and I am sorry if you are having a very boring summer by having to stay here in this neighborhood but I am doing my best to have a very good time now that I am back specially since I get really bad news today."

"Bad news? What is the bad news of which you speak?"

Bobby lowers his head and whispers, "Well this is the last week of summer and that's pretty bad news."

I shake my head in agreiving with Bobby Anderson and I say, "That is indeed something I do not want to even think about."

Then Bobby Anderson looks up at me with the most sorrowful of eyes I ever see in my whole life and he says,

"It's even worser than that. The really bad news is that I'm not going back to P.S. 18 next week. P.S. 18 is a pretty nice school, mostly."

First I say, "P.S. 18 has its good moments and some not so bad teachers, even a couple of nice ones, but …" Then I stop and with my mouth wide open and in a totally seriously sad way I say, "Uh oh! You are not going to St. Mary's! Are you?"

Bobby Anderson lowers his head and says, "It is true. I am going to St. Mary's where I get the nuns, not just on Wednesday afternoons for religious destruction, but the nuns are there to torture me and other kids every day of the week."

I say, "This is one of those revolting perdickamints what should never happen to a nice kid like you, Bobby Anderson."

Bobby Anderson is licking the tuti fruitti off the cone as a way of detracting himself from thinking about the torture he is sure to reciprocate from the nuns.

So I try to cheer him up by saying, "I have been hanging out with Nicholas much this summer and we are counting down the days until what we consider is a major perdickamint but that what we are unhappy about is nothing compared to the perdickamint what you are about to suffer. We are only dreading the nuns on Wednesday afternoons at religious destruction. Although we have a problem or two this summer, what worries us mostly is the nuns on Wednesday afternoons"

Just about then in walks Nicholas and he sees Bobby Anderson and Yours Truly in the back booth mainly because we are both waving to him, not in a happy to see you way but in a come over here bad news way. So Nicholas comes over, pulls a chair over to the end of the table and sits himself down. He looks at the two of us and says, "Something is dreadful wrong. I can see it in your two ugly mugs."

Bobby Anderson lowers his head and speaks, "I am being sentenced to years of torture for I am transferring from P.S. 18 to St. Mary's school with the full-time torturing nuns."

Nicholas looks about as sad anyone can be for another guy and he looks at me and says, "We think we got problems! Well don't Bobby Anderson's problems put our problems onto a lower rung on the problem ladder?"

"It is true what you say, Nicholas" But then I turn and look at Bobby Anderson and say, "There just is not anything I can think of or do to levitate your spirits, Bobby Anderson, mainly because I just cannot imagine anything much worser than spending five days a week, pratickly for the rest of your life, getting tortured by nuns."

Nicholas asks, "Why this sudden change? Do you not like P.S. 18 where most of the teachers are pretty OK?"

I add, "Although it is true some of the teachers are a little bit mean and scream sometimes but at least they never take a kid into the clothing closet and wup him with a yardstick like they do to me from time to time on Wednesday afternoons during religious destruction."

Bobby Anderson explains, "I am on the waiting list for a long time but when all the rich families move out to Queens and even farther away, the list opens up and there I am at the top of the list."

Although I do not intend to rub it in, especially into a very sore spot, I say, "My mom got me put on that list too but I do not worry one bit because every time she calls, the nun tells her I am at the bottom of a very long list."

Chapter 32

Two Relics Work Better Than One

Dear John,

That afternoon Nicholas and Yours Truly are sitting on the stoop considering the bad news what Bobby Anderson delivers earlier today. Nicholas and Yours Truly are feeling pretty sad for Bobby Anderson but glad for us since we are not in Bobby Anderson's shoes.

I remind Nicholas when I say, "Last year we have the orneriest, low-downest teacher in the whole woirld. Mrs. Cornwall never ever smiles and she does not teach. She spends all her time correcting. But most of the other teachers are really nice teachers at P.S. 18. I cannot say the same for any nun at St. Mary's."

Nicholas looks up and says, "Well we just cannot get all detracted by Bobby Anderson's problem because we still got one or two of our own problems what need to be cleared up real quick."

"You are correct about that, Nicholas. It is too easy to get detracted by somebody else's problems and forget about the one or two what are unfinished for us before school starts next week. Now let us considerate about where we stand on the list of our problems. First of all we do not have the relics what we fished out of the sewer on East 34ᵗʰ St. and the Avenue of the Americans. In addition, one of the nicely dressed men, let the cat out of the bag about there being another bag of relics somewhere. Then there is the biggest mystery of all and I am talking about the commies what are infilterating the Catholic Church."

Nicholas says, "I think we may be wrong about the doll and Big Boris. They are up to something but I am not sure they are commies and I think Gutsy Gus is …"

Just then the front door opens and out steps Gutsy Gus who says, "Do I just hear someone mention my name? What are you two guys up to now?"

I say, "You are correct in that your name is just mentioned. Nicholas is just saying he thinks you are very helpful in finding him and bringing him home."

Gutsy Gus says to Nicholas, "Now it is time for Nicholas to help me and some of my friends. Nicholas, I need your help in finding the big bag of relics what you see Alfredolenti hide. Those relics are stolen and we need to get them and return them to their rightful owners."

Nicholas says, "I do not know if the relics are still there because yesterday that is what the Decrepio gang is looking for all over the place."

"Yes," says Gutsy Gus, "but they do not break any of the relics and I do not think they know where Alfredolenti hides the big bag of relics. So wherever Alfredolenti hides them, they are most likely still there and I …"

Nicholas interrupts and says, "No! Not you! We need to find them and return the relics to their rightful owners."

I add my two cents, "That's right! We need to find them so let's get going!"

Nicholas says, "I think I know where Alfredolenti hides the big bag of relics but I am not going there unless Earnest comes too."

Well, just by coinseedents a cloud of dark smoke comes rolling down Leonard and the Fleetwood stops in front of the stoop. Big Boris rolls down the window and says what sounds like, "August tin, allow droog! Voydiye!" He opens the door and says, "In! In! Mny nopa. Go!"

Gutsy Gus explains, "Ya ponimayo. I know! We have to go but these two guys are coming with us. Nicholas thinks he knows where Alfredolenti hid the big bag of relics but he won't come unless Earnest comes with us."

Big Boris scratches his head and asks a question, "Ti spyatil?"

Gutsy Gus answers, "No I am not crazy. We have to go now. Bistra! Fast!"

Then Gutsy Gus opens the back door of the Fleetwood and Nicholas and Yours Truly hop in. Nicholas is sitting on the left side, in back of the driver's seat, and Yours Truly is sitting on the right side. This seating arrangement should have been planned better because it is easy for Big Boris to turn and look at Yours Truly. But first he looks in the rearview mirror and says, "Zdorovo hallow droog, Nicolai malchik stinky foot!" Then he turns his head around and looks at me and says, "We meet before? Vazmozhna? Maybe? Nyet? Da? Da! I know we meet before. I remember face. Where we meet before?"

I answer, "No. We do not meet before."

Nicolas helps, "You do not see Earnest before. He never ever goes to 35th Street in New York City."

Big Boris smiles, shakes his head up and down and says, "Da! Yah! I do remember! I chase you and you run not so fast. When perzon is nosey, perzon got to be fast run. You are nosey but slow run."

Then Big Boris laughs at his joke and starts the motor which leaves several neighbors coughing in a black cloud. When we drive to Lorimer Street, Big Boris turns right.

Gutsy Gus yells, "Nyet! Boris. Turn povyernitye nalyevo. Turn left. We are going to the warehouse in Red Hook."

Big Boris says, "Nyet. Napravo! Turn right! Vwe do not go Reed Hok. Vwe go napravo. First iditye pryamo go to straight to offeez in Manhotan."

Gutsy Gus asks, "Why are we going to the office?"

Big Boris answers, "Cause Anah say we go dere now. Das why I drive get you. Later go Reed Hock."

After several turns the Fleetwood drives over Newtown Creek via the Pulaski Bridge and then into the Queens Midtown Tunnel and we soon arrive at the alley on East 35th Street. Big Boris parks the Fleetwood next to the building. Big Boris and Gutsy Gus get out and walk to the side door. Big Boris walks back to the Fleetwood, shakes his finger and says, "You, Nicolai Stinky Foot vhit your malchik droog, who I never see me before, vwait here."

Big Boris and Gutsy Gus walk up to the side entrance. Big Boris puts his finger on the bell and in about ten seconds, give or take, the door opens. It's just a glimpse but the door is opened by Natasha Natasha.

After the door closes tight, I say to Nicholas, "I see many movies where somebody says, 'Stay in the car,' but what does that person do?"

Nicholas puts his finger up to his temple as a sign that he is thinking. Then he says, "I know! That person, who is told to stay in the car, does not stay in the car!"

"Right and that is when something really exciting happens. Well are we in for excitement or not?"

Nicholas answers by opening the door and he stands looking around to make sure the coast is clear. I follow and we are standing in the alley. Nicholas walks over and puts his hand on the doorknob of the alley door. He turns and whispers, "It is locked tight."

"OK but the front door of this building is probably not locked. So let's go. We need to investigate these mysteries goings on. "

Nicholas says, "Right! This is Operation Top Secret back in action!"

So Nicholas and Yours Truly run around to the front of the building and sure enough the door is unlocked. We open it and walk into a beautiful huge lobby with a glass chandelier and a beautiful winding staircase toward the back. There are four offices with heavy wood doors. Each has a small window on the top and big doorknobs that shine like gold under the windows. One office that interests us most is the one on the left. A sign on the door says, "ARCHDIOCESE of New York", and under that sign I see Auxiliary Bishop Melinshikov and under that name is "Office of the Population of the Faith."

Then through the glass door I see a nun sitting at the desk. She is turning over papers and writing on some.

I move aside and let Nicholas take a peek. He whispers, "Look at all those papers that nun is correcting. She probably has a lot of kids in her class."

I look more closely at what the nun is doing. She is pulling a handle down on her adding machine and then writing numbers on a paper. Then she circles one number. The kid probably got that arithmetic problem wrong.

Then Nicholas points to a door in back of the nun and whispers, "Look at that!"

I look! First I see Natasha Natasha. She is standing in the doorway. She is wearing a dark grey dress and a babushka is wrapped around her head. But she is still beautiful. To keep myself from falling, I am holding onto the office door and my left hand is sliding onto the doorknob and then my right hand hits hard against the door at the same time my left hand hits and turns the doorknob. The door begins to open. Nicholas and Yours Truly do not stand around waiting for an invitation to enter. Instead we duck down and do the Groucho Marx run out of the building and in no time we are sitting in the back seat of the Fleetwood.

About two seconds later the building's side door opens and Big Boris and Gutsy Gus step out into the alley. A hand reaches out from behind the door and taps Gutsy Gus on the shoulder. He turns around and two arms go around his neck and it looks like Gutsy Gus is receiving a big hug.

Big Boris is sitting in the driver's seat and he looks up into the rear view mirror and then he turns around and says, "You, Nicolai malchik stinky foot, vhit your malchik droog, who I never see me beforem turn places in back seat."

It is true! Nicholas is sitting on the right side and Yours Truly is sitting on the left side, in back of the driver's seat.

Nicholas responds to Big Boris as such, "Yes we change seats because I get …"

Nicholas does not get the opportunity to finish his explanation because suddenly he has a pain in his left leg and he is yelling, "Ouch!"

So I complete the sentence for him by saying, "Yes we stay right here in the car because you tell us to stay here which, of course, we do just as you say. We do stay right here in the car but I get bored with just sitting still and looking at the same brick wall on the right of the building. So Nicholas agrees to change seats so I can have a better view. Then I look out the window at the building on the left side of the alley and see a more interesting brick wall. See you can see for yourself that brick wall on the left side across the alley is a better view."

By now Nicholas recovers from the pain in his leg and supports my proposition, "Yes, Earnest likes that brick wall across the alley and I really like the brick wall on this side."

By now Gutsy Gus is scratching his head and Big Boris is shaking his head and laughing.

Well not all that long after that event, we are driving south on the East River Drive, into the Brooklyn-Battery Tunnel and back in Brooklyn.

Big Boris announces, "Reed Hock, vwe back in Reed Hock."

After a few turns the Fleetwood drives up to a warehouse with a large metal garage door in front. Big Boris parks the Fleetwood on the side of the warehouse near a small door.

Big Boris turns around and shakes his finger and says, "You, Nicholai Stinky Foot vhit your malchik droog, who I never see me before, vwait here. Theez time I mean it. Vwait here."

Big Boris walks up to a door on the side of the warehouse. He pulls on the door but it does not open. So he walks back to the Fleetwood, opens the trunk, shuts the trunk and walks back to that door.

While Gutsy Gus is walking around and looking here and there and up and down to make sure the coast is clear, Nicholas and Yours Truly are staying put. We sit there real quiet and I get to thinking about Tom Sawyer when he scribes about time slowing down and stood still. Time strung along and along.

Then I say out loud, "Thunder! What do ya make out of this? Ain't it suspicious?"

Nicholas says, "Thunder? There is not a cloud in the sky. How come you hear thunder?"

I says, "Forget it. This proposition of just sitting here quiet is giving me the jim jams and I am getting all caked up and conflused in my brain."

Then Nicholas, shrinks down in his seat, scratches his head, shrugs his shoulders, and shakes all over. I see this kind of thing before. Whenever Nicholas scratches, shrugs, shrinks and shakes, this is a sign that he is flustrated and does not know what to do in the present situation.

Nicholas turns to me and says, "I got this very worried feeling again that something real bad is going to happen. You know when I get this feeling something bad is going to happen, it happens. I think something bad is happening right now but I just do not know what it is … yet."

This bad feeling, what Nicholas has, worries me more than somewhat because it is a sign of losing faith what I very much want to make stronger. So I ask, "Do you have one of the relics what Saint Closétus gives us?"

Nicholas digs down deep into his pocket and pulls out the small key.

I ask, "What about the spoon? You know two relics work better than one."

Nicholas goes digging again and pulls out the other relic, the spoon.

I say, "Let us pray."

Nicholas says, "We must do eggsactly what we do all the other times when we ask Saint Closétus to intercede for us because he does religious magic miracles what do the trick."

So I take the key in my hand and say, "Please, Saint Closétus, intercede for us and make whatever Nicholas is feeling bad about go away."

Nicholas is holding the spoon and finishes the prayer when he blesses himself and says, "Please grant us this religious magical miracle in the name of the Father and of the Son and of the Holy Ghost, Amen."

Just then the car door opens and Gutsy Gus says, "OK,

guys, come on out. Boris and I can't find the big bag relics. We need your help."

We get out and walk to the door and I notice that the lock is smashed, some pieces on the ground and some still in the door. We go inside and Nicholas points and says, "This way! We have to walk up these stairs to the boss's office. I think that's where Alfredolenti hid the big bag of relics."

So we walk up the squeaky stairs. I step over a reddish orange puddle of dried blood splattered across the stairs. The blood is not totally dry. It is still slippery. Big Boris, walking behind me, does not step over the splattered blood. He slips and falls to one knee.

The boss's office is totally a mess. A desk is upside down. A book case is on its side with a door hanging off. Six drawers of a filing cabinet are on the floor with its papers all over the place. Splintered glass crunches with each step. The one thing that looks totally undisturbed is a large cross leaning in a corner of the room. Nicholas walks over to the cross, reaches his hand behind it and taps on its back. Nothing happens. He squeezes himself against the wall and looks toward the back of the cross. Then he taps on the back again and this time a board falls to the ground. Nicholas twists his hand around and pulls a big brown bag out from behind the cross. Gutsy Gus takes the bag from Nicholas, places it on the floor and unties the cord. The bag opens wide and three small relics fall onto the floor. Gutsy Gus replaces the relics, ties the cord, grabs the big bag of relics and we start climbing down the squeaking stairs. Big Boris is holding tight to the railing and limping as he places his foot carefully down onto each step.

Just then the big garage door rattles and starts sliding open.

Chapter 33

A Bumpy Ride

Dear John,

A black Packard slowly moves forward into the warehouse followed by a blue Chrysler. We reach the bottom of the stairs and Gutsy Gus opens the side door. We run outside but, by the time we reach the Fleetwood, Big Boris is no longer with us. He is just coming out of the doorway, limping more than somewhat and trying as hard as anyone can to make it to the Fleetwood before he is noticed. But he is noticed and this is signaled by a gunshot. A bullet sparks off the side of the metal door. Big Boris grabs his arm, trips and begins to fall. But in no time flat Nicholas is standing on his right and Yours Truly is on his left and we each grab an arm and help him limp fast to the Fleetwood. Gutsy Gus opens the back door and Big Boris crawls in and Nicholas and Yours Truly follow. Three men are running and firing their pistols and bullets are pinging and bouncing off the Fleetwood. Some bullets strike the side window but they don't make it through. The bullets just hang there in the glass. When the three men are about five feet in back of us, Gutsy Gus starts the engine and a huge cloud of smoke catches the men off guard. They suddenly stop in their tracks, hands up to their eyes, coughing loud. Then they turn around and run back toward the warehouse. One of the men is running and rubbing his eyes but it is not a good idear to run and rub at the same time because he is flat on his back after slamming into the side of the warehouse.

The Fleetwood is slowly moving down the street and making turns this way and that way. In the meantime, Nicholas and Yours Truly help Big Boris sit up. His arm is bleeding.

Big Boris says, "Vwe got get out here fast but thees Fleetwood too heavy, not move fast. But, August tin, you got relics, right?"

Gutsy Gus says, "The relics are right here in the big bag on the passenger seat. Do not worry about them." Then Gutsy Gus leans over and opens the glove compartment and takes out a cloth and says, "Earnest, use this cloth to wrap Boris's arm so it stops bleeding."

Nicholas moves up and takes the cloth and hands it to Yours Truly. Big Boris holds one end of the cloth and Yours Truly starts to wrap tight but then there is this bullet sticking out of his arm. Big Boris looks at the bullet, smiles and pulls it out. He does not even flinch. Then we wrap his arm tight and in about a minute the bleeding stops.

Then Nicholas is looking out the back window and he says, "Uh Oh! The Packard is coming up fast."

The Packard pulls up very fast on the left side of the Fleetwood. The window rolls down and a man is yelling and pointing a pistol at Gutsy Gus.

Boris shouts, "Slam brakes!"

When Gutsy Gus slams the brakes, Nicholas is soon upside down in the front seat and Big Boris is holding Yours Truly back from joining Nicholas. The Fleetwood is now in back of the Packard. Gutsy Gus steps on the gas and the

Fleetwood hits the back of the Packard which turns just a little to the right and then Gutsy Gus hits hard against the corner of the Packard which spins out of control and lands sideways in a ditch.

Boris looks at me, smiles and says, "I teach August tin he drive like that."

Nicholas crawls over the front seat but before he is able to get back he looks out the back window, points and says, "There's a very big Chrysler in back and it's coming up fast. Gutsy Gus looks in the rearview mirror and says, "That's a Firepower Chrysler with a V8 engine. We can't win a race against that one."

Big Boris says, "August tin, you know what to do when it gets closer. Is there a sudden turn ahead?"

"Yes, I'll stay off the Brooklyn-Queens Expressway and take Hamilton. I'll make a fast turn left onto Van Brunt Street."

The Chrysler is right in back. It hits the back bumper and the Fleetwood takes a skip in the road.

Big Boris says, "They try to spin us like we do to Packard."

Gutsy Gus keeps turning the steering wheel first to the left and then to the right to keep the Chrysler from hitting the Fleetwood but that does not work. The Chrysler smashes into the rear bumper again and then again. Big Boris is holding Nicholas and Yours Truly tight so we don't wind up on Gutsy Gus's lap. At the end of Hamilton Avenue in front of us I can see large shipping containers and beyond that the East River.

Just as we come to the end of Hamilton Avenue, Gutsy Gus shouts, "Hold onto whatever you can! We are going to get a big bump out of this."

Gutsy Gus slams on the brakes and the Chrysler slams

hard against the Fleetwood. Then Gutsy Gus slams his foot on the gas pedal and at the same time reaches over and pulls up a handle on the dashboard. A huge cloud of black smoke pours out of the back of the Fleetwood as Gutsy Gus turns the steering wheel fast to the left. The Fleetwood turns onto Van Brunt Street. The Chrysler fails to make the turn, keeps going straight, bounces as it crosses Summit Street and smashes straight into a large shipping container. The Fleetwood slows, stops and slowly backs up.

Big Boris asks, "What you do? Why Stop? Why you go back? August tin, go!"

Gutsy Gus says, "I am curious. I want to take a look. I saw who was in the Chrysler. Loan me your pistol for just a minute or two."

The Fleetwood backs up and stops. Gutsy Gus opens the door, gets out and walks up to the crushed Chrysler. He looks inside, looks back at the Fleetwood, shakes his head, reaches through the front window and pulls out some keys. Gutsy Gus walks to the back of the Chrysler, opens the trunk and pulls out a big brown bag.

Chapter 34

The Population Office

Dear John,

Last night after a more than somewhat exciting day, I write some things about the goings on but I am too sleepy to tell the rest of the story. So here it goes.

After Gutsy Gus pulls the big bag out of the trunk, he walks calmly back to the Fleetwood, places the big bag on the passenger seat, walks around the front of the car and gets in.

Gutsy Gus turns around, hands the pistol back to Big Boris and asks, "How's that arm? The bleeding stop?"

Big Boris answers, "Bullet stick out of arm but Doctor Earnest fix it all."

Nicholas asks, "What about me? I helped."

Big Boris laughs and says, "Him doctor. You stinky foot."

Nicholas says, "You know, a name like that could stick with a guy."

Sirens are shrieking in the distance and they are getting louder. Two police cars with lights flashing and sirens screaming speed down Van Brunt Street coming right at us but they suddenly turn right and stop in the container terminal.

Nicholas asks, "Don't you think we should get out of here fast?"

Big Boris answers, "Nyet! August tin do correct thing. He move too fast and politsiya look and come and they invwestigate. We nyet want politsiya. August tin do right. I teach him right way to do when politsiya coming. Not to fuss." Big Boris grins and says, "No fast fuss."

The Fleetwood starts up and a very small cloud of black smoke puffs up and quickly vanishes. Gutsy Gus says, "Big Boris, we have to get more smoke. I used up most of it in that last turn."

Well one good turn leads to another good turn and we are soon driving through the Brooklyn-Battery Tunnel, on to the FDR Drive and, before you know it, we are back in the alley next to the office what is called the Population of the Faith.

Gutsy Gus walks around the front of the Fleetwood, opens the back door and offers a hand to Big Boris who struggles to get up but falls back when he tries to stand up. Big Boris says, "My leg eez nyet goodt. May broke eet on stair when slip on blood."

Gutsy Gus says, "OK. Boris, you stay here and I will get some help."

Nicholas offers, "We can help him. We got him into the Fleetwood."

I think to myself this is a good way to get inside and see if these are Commies infilterating the Catholic Church and the Population Office. So I say, "Good idear, Stinky Foot, I mean Nicholas. We can help get him inside."

Gutsy Gus agrees, "OK, let's see if we can get him out of the Fleetwood and standing on one leg. Just wait a minute and I'll ring the bell so someone can open the door."

Gutsy Gus walks over to the door but before he even

touches the bell, the door swings open. Four girls come rushing out and open the Fleetwood's back door. They all start talking to Big Boris in Russian so fast that I have no idear what they are all saying but then they lift Big Boris out of the Fleetwood and these four girls actually carry him into the Population Office.

Gutsy Gus reaches inside the car, lifts the two big bags off the front seat, and says, "I'll be right back and then I'll drive you two home. Wait here in the car."

Well, John, you know very well what we do when someone says, "Wait here in the car." We do not wait here. As soon as Gutsy Gus turns away, Nicholas and Yours Truly shake our heads and start moving. Nicholas is out of the Fleetwood first and he is so fast that when Gutsy Gus closes the door, Nicholas has his hand on the doorknob and holds the door from slamming shut.

Nicholas holds the doorknob and I place my hand behind the door and slowly open it. I peak in. No one is in the hallway. Nicholas whispers, "The door to where the nun corrects homework is locked. The stairs? Up or down? What do you think?"

I whisper back, "The stairs up. Be real quiet."

Slowly and very carefully we take each step until we come to a landing with a door and behind that door we hear verses, lots of talking but it is all Russian.

I kneel on one knee and peek through a keyhole. People are walking around and waving their arms excitedly. Several girls are standing behind a large table. Natasha Natasha, Gutsy Gus and the doll are standing together and talking in Russian.

Nicholas taps my shoulder. I stand and step back. Nicholas kneels and peeks but then he gets up fast and points to the stairs going up.

We run up the stairs to the next landing and hide in a shadow along the wall. The door below opens and a priest wearing a purple belt walks out and down the stairs. He is carrying a big bag. The door closes behind him.

Nicholas whispers, "He has the relics. Let's follow him."

I shake my head in agreement. So we carefully and quietly, but as fast as we can, step down the two flights of stairs and stop at the door to the alley. The door to where the nun sits is open slightly. I put my hand on the door and push gently. The door opens. The room is empty so we open the door wide and walk in. Another door on the side of the office is closed but I can hear someone talking but only one verse with pauses in between. It sounds like a telephone call. Then the verse gets louder, what always happens when a phone conversation is ending.

Nicholas walks over to the desk and looks at the pile of papers. He whispers, "These pages are filled with numbers what have dollar signs in front. These kids get pretty tough homework."

Footsteps on the stairs. Verses getting louder. The door into the other room starts opening. Nicholas and Yours Truly look at each other and Nicholas begins to shake, shrug, and shrink to the floor and then crawls under the desk. Without shaking or shrugging I shrink to the floor and follow Nicholas under the desk. Both doors open and the priest, Gutsy Gus, Natasha Natasha and the doll meet in the middle of the Population Office.

Natasha Natasha speaks and says, "Alexandria, vwe all know there eez a pwoblem. Do you tell us what pwoblem eez?"

The doll who is now called Alexandria answers, "We must ask our Bishop for advice."

Natasha Natasha asks, "Your Eminence, vwat you want me and girls do to help?"

I am thinking to myself a priest is not called Your Eminence but then I remember the sign on the population door also had the name of some Bishop. The priest is wearing a purple belt. He must be the Bishop!

So the Bishop says, "Tell the girls to stay calm and we will continue to protect them. They have nothing to worry about. You go tell them now. OK?"

After Natasha Natasha heads upstairs, Gutsy Gus starts to speak, "Your Eminence…"

The Bishop stops him and says, "No, I want you to call me father. To you I am Father. Uh, … call me Father Melinshikov."

Gutsy Gus says, "Yes Father, I will but I do not understand when everyone else calls you …"

The doll stops him and says, "Yes, Bishop Melinshikov feels a zertain lyoo beet, how you say, love you almost, well ya! Yes, he love you like father for son."

Bishop Melinshikov says, "Yes that is exactly the way I feel. So, August tin, do call me father. Yes, I mean, Father Melinshikov."

Gutsy Gus answers, "Yes, Father Melinshikov, that is what I will call you. Thank you for feeling like I am your son."

Just then there is a knock on the side door and also a bell rings. Gutsy Gus opens the door and a man carrying a small case walks in and introduces himself, "I am Doctor Vokolov and come to see Boris with leg hurt pwoblem."

Gutsy Gus says, "Good! I'll take you to see Boris. This way. He's upstairs."

"Upstairs with hurt leg pwoblem? How?"

"Yes, we have very strong helpers here. They carried him up so he can be comfortable in his own bed."

I can hear Doctor Vokolov and Gutsy Gus walking upstairs. Bishop Melinshikov and the doll, who is now called Alexandria, stay in the room. Alexandria speaks, "Augie, you do love August tin like a son, do you not?"

Bishop Melinshikov and Alexandria laugh just slightly, more like a giggle. When they start walking out of the room, a piece of paper with some writing on it drops on the carpet in front of the desk. A hand comes down almost immediately and picks up the paper. I can hear it being folded.

Nicholas and Yours Truly look at each other and Nicholas points up. I shake my head and mouth OK. Nicholas crawls out from under the desk and peeks over the top. He whispers, "The coast is clear. Let's go."

We start walking toward the door in the hallway but then we hear verses at the top of the stairs. So we turn around and open the door to the big beautiful lobby. No one is there. We run out the front door, around to the alley, open the door of the Fleetwood and scramble into the back seat. About a second later the side door in the alley opens and Gutsy Gus steps out, walks to the Fleetwood. He opens the door and says, "Sorry guys. That took a lot longer than I thought. I hope you didn't get too bored."

Nicholas starts to say, "We were not bored because we had some things to …"

Nicholas does not get to finish his sentence because he is busy rubbing his leg and yelling, "Ouch! Ouch!"

So I say, "Oh, Nicholas, you hit your leg on the door handle. That's too bad." Then I finish what Nicholas was saying, "We were not bored because we had some things to talk about and many things to think about. So we just sit here and talk and think until you come back."

"That's good. Actually, I got so involved with stuff, I almost forgot about you two sitting all this time in the Fleetwood."

So Gutsy Gus starts up the motor and in a short time we are back on Leonard Street where Gutsy Gus backs into a parking space large enough for the Fleetwood. To find a large enough parking space is unusual but there is something else unusual. During the ride Nicholas and Yours Truly are yapping and talking about this and that and one thing or another but it is strange because Gutsy Gus is unusually quiet. He does not say one word during the whole ride.

Nicholas and Yours Truly get out and take our usual seats on the stoop. Gutsy Gus also gets out but, without saying a word, he walks up the stoop and enters the apartment house.

"Nicholas," I say, I think something is worrying Gutsy Gus."

"Yes, he is very quiet and he looks like he has a worry or two." But then I stop and say to Nicholas, "I think I may know what worries Gutsy Gus. Do you remember that piece of paper what falls on the carpet in the Population Office?"

Nicholas shakes his head and says, "I saw it but the Bishop picked it up so fast I do not get a chance to see what it says."

I say, "Yes. It was fast. The piece of paper was on the floor only for a second but just long enough for me to read the words what said, "Deliver $10,000 to x on map at 2 p.m. tomorrow or you will be exposed."

Chapter 35

Tomorrow is Today

Dear John,

This morning along about eight bells I am looking out the window while munching on a bowel of Rice Krispies what go snap, crackle and pop on the radio but not in my cereal bowl when I see Nicholas come running down Leonard. He stops in front of the stoop. He looks up at the window and starts jumping up and down when he sees me. Then he motions with his hand to come down. Well I am still in my PJs but I know Nicholas has something really important to tell me or he better have something really really important to tell me to make me come out at this early hour of the day.

Well, as fast as I can, I change into my clothes and I am downstairs sitting next to Nicholas on the stoop. I look at Nicholas who is sitting and bouncing up and down with excitement. He says, "Sometime in the middle of the night I wake up from a dream where I am in the Population Office and I remember looking at the arithmetic homework what the nun is correcting on her desk and I see a long column of numbers with dollar signs in front. There are addition signs and minus signs on a lot of the numbers. At the bottom of all numbers is one number what is circled. It is the number ten thousand dollars.

I say, "And that is exactly the same number what is on that note Bishop Melinshikov drops on the carpet."

Nicholas says, "Right! Earnest! That ain't just no goinseedents! Or is it? Thunder! What do ya make out of this? Ain't it suspicious?"

I say, "This is definitely the kind of thing for Operation Top Secret because we gotta investigate this. Remember the note says the ten thousand dollars gotta be at someplace marked x tomorrow. But tomorrow is today."

Nicholas asks, "Doesn't the note also say if the ten thousand dollars are not at x someplace, something or somebody is gonna explode?"

I answer, "It says something like that. No, I think the word is *exposed*. Somebody or something is gonna be exposed but I do not know what that means."

Nicholas says, "We just can't go around asking people what expose means. I got an idear! Let's ask Saint Closétus. If he does not know, he can ask God because he knows everything."

"Right! But it takes a long time to get an answer what with that long line and all. Of course we need a closet first but I do not see any closet in the nearby viscenity."

Nicholas suggests, "I know! I remember seeing a Refrigidaire empty box in the alley two doors down."

Well then, I say, let us proceed to this Refrigidaire box and see if we can conjurate Saint Closétus."

Well unfortunately it is that time of the day and that day of the week when the garbage truck comes along and picks up the garbage. And so it is that two doors down, the garbage truck is backing out of the alley and a large cardboard box is being crushed in the back part of the garbage truck.

Nicholas says, "Maybe there is another Refrigidaire box up the street. If we run maybe we can beat the garbage truck."

"No, I am not in the mood to do such but I do agree we need to conjurate Saint Closétus and ask his advice about the present circumstance what I must admit, we do not understand because we do not know what the word *expose* means in a situation such as described in the note what Bishop Melinshikov drops on the carpet in the Population Office."

Nicholas says, "Yes, we do not know what the word *expose* means in the situation as you describe but we do know what ten thousand dollars means."

I say to Nicholas, "That is a powerful amount of do-re-mi and I don't mean maybe. I have an idear. I am on my way up to Apartment 3B on the second floor where I can find a closet so I can conjurate Saint Closétus and ask for his advice. Sorry. You cannot come up cause you are still person not greater."

Nicholas says, "I know that and likewise to you. But we need advice from Saint Closétus. Oh! Do not forget to ask him what *expose* means in a proposition such as this."

So I run upstairs to Apartment 3B on the second floor and the first thing I do is to find my little school dictionary and I search for the word *expose*. I find it and it says, expose means *to deprive of shelter*. So what do I do? I look up the word deprive and I find that it means to remove. So expose means to remove a shelter. Why would anybody pay ten thousand dollars to remove a shelter?

When I return to the stoop, Earnest is sitting with a map of New York City open.

I ask, "What are you doing with that map?"

Earnest says, "I am looking all over this map of New York City.

I ask, "Where did you get that?"

Nicholas answers, "Instead of just sitting here on the stoop and doing nothing, I make myself useful when I run up to the Texaco gas station on Grand Street and get this map what they give out for free."

I ask, "What are you looking for on that map?"

Nicholas answers, "The note what drops on the carpet in the Population Office and what you read says, "'Deliver $10,000 to x on map at 2 p.m. tomorrow or you will be exposed.' So I am looking for x on the map."

I respond, "So you think there is an x on that map what shows where the $10,000 will be delivered?" Of course in my asking such a question I am really asking a question about the summer ending and autumn's fast approach.

"Yes! If we can find the x on this map, we can know where the $10,000 are to be delivered. But more important is what will happen if the $10,000 is not delivered to x and we already know what will happen. Someone and maybe Bishop Melinshikov will be exposed. But that is still a mystery. So what does Saint Closétus tell you when you ask his advice and also what it means to be exposed?"

I sit on the stoop next to Nicholas and explain the meaning of the word exposed as such, "Nicholas, Saint Closétus tells me the meaning of exposed but it is still a little confusing. He says expose means to remove a shelter."

Nicholas says, "I get it. A bomb shelter. You know like Bert the Turtle in the movie what they show in school. We gotta duck and cover when a monkey has a stick of dynamite hanging from a tree. So when we are in school we have to duck under our desks and cover our heads when the Commies drop an Atomic bomb."

"And what does Bert the Turtle have to do with understanding the word shelter?"

Nicholas explains, "Well, the movie shows what the commies are doing what with making big mushrooms and then monkeys fall out of the sky and landing in trees so we have to run to a shelter so the Russian Commies and monkeys what are falling from the mushroom don't fall on us."

"And Bert the Turtle?"

"Right we have to crawl into the shelter what is made from turtle shells."

I ask, "So what does shelter from falling monkey have to do with $10,000?"

Nicholas responds, "Well I do not rightly know but it all adds up to $10,000 one way or another."

After Nicholas's explanations of the word *expose*, I do not pursue any further discussion about the meaning of the word *expose*.

But I do suggest as such, "Nicholas, I think that map of New York City what you get from the Texaco gas station does not have the x on it. I think the map what has the x on it is another map."

Nicholas says, "Well we need to find that other map. I'll go back to the Texaco gas station and look for a map what has x on it."

I say, "Well, Nicholas, I cannot argue against that. You go right ahead to that Texaco gas station and look for a map what has the x on it and I will go up to Apartment 3B on the second floor and finish my bowl of Rice Krispies what do not go snap, crackle and pop."

Chapter 36

Mr. Manichy Arrives on the Stoop

Dear John,

A clock moves and time moves but they do not always keep the same time. Time moves slower sometimes and time moves faster other times but a clock just keeps tick-tick-tocking. Today time moves so fast that it is 2:15 before I know it and I realize that $10,000 is either exposed or not exposed. Since there is nothing to be done about that exposing and the $10,000 and how they fit together, I just sit on the stoop reading exciting adventures of *Tom Sawyer, Detective.*

Then about half an hour into Tom Sawyer, a man comes walking down the street and at first I do not recognize him but I think I see him one time before. If I am remembering right, the man is Mr. Manichy who is quite a stranger in this neck of the woods. I do notice something strange and unusual about him and that is that he has a great big grin on his ugly mug. After almost stepping on me, without saying a word, like maybe excuse me or some facsimile thereof, Mr. Manichy walks up the stoop, opens the door and is double hoofing it up the stairs.

Just about that time Nicholas comes walking down Leonard and he takes a seat next to me on the stoop and says, "I look through many maps in the Texaco gas station. I search for an x all over New York City and even New Jersey but I give up when I look over every inch of Connecticut. Not one map has an x on it and now it is past 2 pm so I guess whatever was gonna get exposed is a done deal."

Well I start telling Nicholas about the strange appearance of Mr. Manichy when another strange event takes place and that is Mr. O'Reilly who walks, actually staggers a little less than usual, down the street and steps up the stoop causing Nicholas to shift to the left and enters the apartment house.

Well in about ten minutes later, give or take a minute or two, there is a loud scream coming from the roof of this apartment house. Well naturally Nicholas and Yours Truly are curious about such a scream coming from the roof so we get up off the stoop and stand on the sidewalk and we look up at the roof. There is Mr. Manichy leaning over the edge of the roof but he does not look as if he likes looking over the edge of the roof because he is screaming and yelling, "Stop, you dirty darn." Well he does not actually say darn but what he is saying is not what I wish to relate here. But then after Mr. Manichy yells stop you dirty darn and some other words I do not relate here, Mr. Manichy comes over the ledge and down off the roof, tumbling through the air, and goes thud on the stoop. After that thud on the stoop, Mr. Manichy is lying upside down on the third and fourth and fifth steps and not moving one bit.

Nicholas and Yours Truly are surprised more than somewhat by Mr. Manichy's sudden arrival on the stoop.

I look up at the roof and I see someone looking over and down at Mr. Manichy.

Nicholas says, "It is a good thing we get up from the stoop when we hear the scream because Mr. Manichy is now occupying our places on the stoop."

I remark, "Yes but the worst thing is that when we get up, I do not remove my book from the stoop and now I see Tom Sawyer nowhere."

Nicholas sympathizes, "Yes, I know you really like *Tom Sawyer, Detective*, but now it looks like you may not get to read the rest of the book for I think Tom Sawyer is not only missing but ....."

Just then our conversation about the missing Tom Sawyer is interrupted when the front door opens and Mrs. Manichy comes running down the right side of the stoop and she screams, "Oh, Reginald, Oh, my God." And she is looking more than somewhat sad for she is screaming, "Oh, my God, my God! You are dead!"

Personally I think she means Mr. Manichy is the one who is dead. But the main thing is that while she is kneeling next to Mr. Manichy she is turning him over. Now he is on his back and his eyes are open wide and he is looking up at the roof but he is not commenting about that or anything else. Then Mrs. Manichy reaches into a pocket in his jacket and pulls out a thick envelope. Then she gets up and takes a step up the stoop. Then she turns around and kneels down and rolls Mr. Manichy over again and reaches into his back pocket and pulls out his wallet. Mrs. Manichy then stands up, runs up the steps and slams the front door in back of her.

Although Nicholas and Yours Truly are standing on the sidewalk right in front of the stoop, Mrs. Manichy does not pay any attention to us. It is like she does not even see us watching her and everything she is doing.

After about a minute Mr. O'Reilly comes running out of the cellar, climbs up the steps from under the stoop and stops in front of Mr. Manichy. He kneels down and turns Mr. Manichy over. Mr. Manichy's eyes are again staring up at the roof. Then Mr. O'Reilly puts his hand into Mr.

Manichy's pocket. He removes his empty hand and tries another pocket. After coming up empty handed from every pocket, Mr. O'Reilly stands up and looks around. By this time Nicholas and Yours Truly are on the other side of the street where we are walking backwards for a couple of minutes and since Mr. O'Reilly is standing up and looking around, we are now walking forward.

Mr. O'Reilly shouts to us, "Hey, you kids, do you see anybody take anything out of this guy's pockets?"

I answer and say, "We are just now at this moment walking this way up Leonard so we just get here. So we do not see anybody doing anything."

Nicholas offers, "Right! We just get here by walking frontwards like what we are now doing on this side of the street. We do not see Mrs. Manichy take anything from Mr. Manichy's pockets."

Nicholas says that before I have any opportunity to step on his foot. I attempt to change the conversation by asking, "It looks like someone trips on the stoop and falls down. You want us to help him up?"

Mr. O'Reilly says, "No, kids. This guy is not ever getting up on his own, never, not even with help. Then he says, "Wait a second now. What did you say about Mrs. Manichy?"

Nicholas answers, "I say nothing about Mrs. Manichy. We never sees Mrs. Manichy or what she does."

By this time people are leaning out of their windows and asking, "What's all the commotion about?" or "What happened?" and things like that. Mr. O'Reilly ignores questions. He quickly backs away, turns and runs very fast across the street, and up the steps into his apartment house.

Nicholas asks, "Why do you think Mr. O'Reilly is in such a hurry?"

"I do not know because I never before see him running

so fast and so straight. Mr. O'Reilly usually has trouble more than somewhat just putting one foot in front of the other. But maybe Mr. O'Reilly does not wish to discuss this incident with the police since I hear a siren in the distance."

In a couple of minutes sirens, what start in the distance, are soon getting louder. A police car turns onto Leonard and pulls up in front of the stoop.

Nicholas and Yours Truly are still standing across the street and I suggest to Nicholas as follows: "I think things for us this summer are complexicated enough and it would not be good for us to spend time conversating with police officers because we know from our recent experience with Officer Clancy that it is best to avoid such conversatings.

Nicholas says, "Mrs. Manichy did seem upset that her husband took our place on the stoop. But Mr. O'Reilly was even more upset when, whatever he was looking for, he did not find."

I say, "We should think about Gutsy Gus and how sad he is when he finds out about his father being upside down on the stoop and dead and all."

Nicholas says, "Thunder! These are suspicious goings on what with Gutsy Gus's mother no longer being around to greet the police officers."

I say, "Yes, these goings on are indeed suspicious and it means this is a job for Operation Top Secret but as for explaining what we see before, during and after Mr. Manichy's fall from the roof, I am not for it."

Nicholas suggests, "This is a time to consult Saint Closétus directly."

"Yes, I agree and it is a time for us to make ourselves scarce before the police officer, who is now looking down at Mr. Manichy, turns his attention elsewhere."

So Nicholas and Yours Truly turn around and walk

to the corner, hop two fences and wind up in back of the apartment house where I live. We walk to a door leading to stairs and these stairs lead down to the cellar. I turn the doorknob but it does not turn. I say to Nicholas, "The door is locked."

But suddenly that very same door opens fast and slams wide and Mrs. Manichy comes up out of the cellar. She is carrying two suitcases and she is very much in a big hurry. Indeed she is in so much of a hurry that she knocks Nicholas flat on his back when one of her suitcases collides with his knees.

In addition to knocking Nicholas flat on his back as she passes by, Mrs. Manichy says "Get the darn out of my way." Now Mrs. Manichy does not actually say darn but what she says is a word what I wish not to scribe here.

Well Nicholas gets up off the ground and brushes the dirt and spider webs off the back of his pants. Mrs. Malachy walks very fast to the back fence where she stops, throws one suitcase over the fence which is followed by the second suitcase. Then Mrs. Manichy kneels and places her two hands on the fence and pulls the wires apart and opens a hole what is previously cut into the fence. I never even know the fence is cut but Mrs. Manichy knows exactly where the fence is cut. She crawls through the opening, stands up, grabs the two suitcases and walks very fast between two buildings on the other side of the block.

Well Nicholas and Yours Truly do not know what to make of such activity but Nicholas suggests, "Maybe Mrs. Manichy is also not interested in conversating with the cops."

"I agree, Nicholas, I think Mrs. Manichy is not interested in conversating with anybody."

Chapter 37
Not Bad News

Dear John,

Much happens after Mr. Manichy lands upside-down on the stoop. After Mrs. Manichy opens the door to the cellar, I grab the doorknob and keep the door from locking. Then Nicholas and Yours Truly walk down the steps, cross the cellar and head up to apartment 3B on the second floor. As we are walking up the stairs we hear two cops open the front door. This causes Nicholas and Yours Truly to move very fast up to the second floor and I have the key ready and we enter apartment 3B on the second floor just before we hear the cops climbing up to the roof.

Although Nicholas is persona non greater, no one else is in the apartment so we go in and I open the two living room windows and so we can hang our heads out and watch the activity down on the street.

First an ambulance shows up. Two men in white coats get out, look at Mr. Manichy, kneel down, and put their hands on his throat. Then one of the men takes his hand and closes Mr. Manichy's eyes. They talk to the cops who are walking around and taking pictures. Then the ambulance drives away leaving poor Mr. Manichy still, very still, upside-down on the stoop but he looks better with his eyes closed.

Then in about ten minutes a black car what looks like a big station wagon without windows in back rolls down the street and double parks. It has a sign what says Kings County Morgue on the side. Two men take a big black bag out of the black station wagon. They spread it open and lift Mr. Manichy into the bag.

Nicholas says, "Look! Look! There is Tom Sawyer still on the stoop. He was under Mr. Manichy but … Uh Oh! One of the cops picks up Tom Sawyer."

I look down from the window but I do not see any sign of Tom Sawyer. But I do see a lot of blood on the stoop. Then Mr. Manichy gets put in the back of the station wagon.

Nicholas looks up and says, "Mr. Manichy is probably more comfortable in the back of the station wagon than upside down on the stoop."

When Nicholas says that, I just nod my head and I do not say anything about whether Mr. Manichy is comfortable or not.

Then after the black station wagon drives off down the street, the cops stand around for a while and then they leave. Then Mr. Pitsacola drives up in his grey 1950 DeSoto Custom hardtop, 4-Door Sedan, and parallel parks without tapping bumpers either on the car in front or the one behind. I am always impressed when I witness parallel parking such as accomplished by Mr. Pitsacola. Mr. Pitsacola steps out of the DeSoto and walks over to the stoop, looks down at the steps and shakes his head. Then he walks to the back of the DeSoto, and opens the trunk. He then takes out a bucket and a mop. He opens a faucet on the side of the building, fills the bucket with water and then Mr. Pitsacola empties the bucket onto the stoop. Then he takes the mop and moves it around on three of the stoop's steps. Then again he fills the bucket with water and splashes it all over the steps. When he finishes splashing and mopping, he goes back to the DeSoto and puts the bucket and mop in the trunk. He soon drives away.

Nicholas and Yours Truly are hanging our heads out the window and we look at each other and Nicholas says, "It looks like the coast is clear."

I suggest, "We better get out of here before anyone comes home and finds you, persona not greater, in this apartment. That would mean big trouble."

So in a short time Nicholas and Yours Truly are standing on the stoop. We are standing because most of the stoop is still wet and some is pink wet. So we are standing and sometimes walking around.

Nicholas walks over to the side of the stoop near the steps to the cellar and bends down. Then he says, "Look what I find tossed here on the steps."

I look at what Nicholas is holding. It is Tom Sawyer, Detective, with just one tiny spot of blood and when that is wiped off, Tom Sawyer is as good as new.

Well as I am paging through Tom Sawyer, who, to my surprise, comes walking along but Gutsy Gus.

Gutsy Gus walks up to the stoop, looks at it and asks, "Why is the stoop all wet and what are these pink streaks?"

That is when I realize that Gutsy Gus does not know what has been going on for the last couple of hours. Nicholas starts to answer, "We have quite a bit of excitement happening today and your father is …"

As Nicholas starts to explain Gutsy Gus is looking at the wet stoop and he points to some pink streaks what Mr. Pitsacola fails to mop up. Gutsy Gus interrupts Nicholas and asks, "What happens here? This looks like blood. Did someone have a nose bleed? Then he turns to Nicholas and asks, "My father? You said something about my father?"

Gutsy Gus is still looking at the pink streak on the steps when Nicholas begins to explain again, "Yes! We have quite a bit of excitement happening today and your father is ..."

But Nicholas does not get to finish his sentence because he is hopping around on one foot and yelling, "Ouch! Ouch!"

"Oh Nicholas," I say with much sympathy in my verse, "you stubbed your toe."

Then I take up Nicholas's sentence and say, "Yes, indeed as Nicholas says we do have quite a bit of excitement happening today and your father is…"

Gutsy Gus interrupts me and says, "My father? Who do you think my father is?"

"Well your father is Mr. Manichy," I answer.

Nicholas says, "Or was."

Gutsy Gus says, "No, Reginald Manichy is not my father and of that I am very glad."

I ask, "Well isn't Mrs. Manichy your mother?"

"No! Mildred Manichy is not my mother. And of that I am also very glad."

"So maybe the bad news we have to tell you is not all that bad news."

"What is this bad news which you have to tell me?"

"Well you better sit down first. Uh! Over here on this dry part of the stoop."

Gutsy Gus sits on the right side of the stoop and Nicholas and Yours Truly stand on the sidewalk in front of the stoop and I say, "Well we do not know exactly what causes it to happen but about two hours ago Mr. Manichy comes tumbling down off the roof and lands on this very stoop where you see these pink streaks. Mr. Manichy lands right here and takes the place where we are just recently sitting. This pink streak what you see here is all that is left of him on the stoop."

Gutsy Gus asks, "Why is it that he did not land on you or Nicholas? Were you sitting on the stoop at the time?"

Nicholas answers, "Yes at the time just previous to Mr. Manichy taking our place we are sitting on the stoop but when we hear Mr. Manichy up on the roof and he is screaming, we get up off the stoop and are standing right here looking up when we see Mr. Manichy come tumbling down and go splat on the stoop."

"Nicholas," I say, "splat is probably not the best word to describe this tragic event. I think thud is a better word."

Nicholas says, "I would say both thud and splat describe what I hear and see better than either one of the two words alone. I see Mr. Manichy go splat and I hear Mr. Malichy go thud. I see a splat and I hear a thud simontinatously. So both words describe better than either one what I see and hear."

I secretly admire Nicholas's brief discussion about the best words one should use in a situation such as this. Summer is not yet over for Nicholas.

Then my attention turns to Gutsy Gus who has his head down and his shoulders are moving up and down like he is shivering from grief. So I sympathetically say, "Is it that you are shivering because you are so sad and if that is the case I am sorry for..."

Gutsy Gus looks up at me. His shoulders are indeed moving up and down and his eyes are getting wet but he is neither shivering nor crying. He is shaking his head back and forth and sort of chuckling and almost smiling. Gutsy Gus stands up and puts his hand up to his mouth and covers it trying as best as he can to hide his mouth what is smiling.

Then Gutsy Gus says, "I guess I should go upstairs to the apartment and see how Mildred is doing."

Nicholas says, "I do not think your mother, I mean, Mrs. Manichy is upstairs because we see her leaving with two suitcases and she is in much of a hurry."

I confirmate what Nicholas says, "Yes, that is correct what Nicholas speaks. We witness her exit us. We are in the back of this apartment house and she comes out of the back door of the cellar with two suitcases and she crawls through a hole in the fence and that is the last we see of her."

Gutsy Gus is not laughing now but he is smiling just a little. He asks, "Does she come down here after Reginald Manichy goes splat and thud on the stoop?"

"Yes, she comes out the front door right after the splat and thud and she looks in Mr. Manichy's pockets and takes a thick envelope out of his jacket pocket."

Nicholas adds, "And she takes his wallet out of his pants and later Mr. O'Reilly is looking for something in the very same pockets but he does not find anything."

Gutsy Gus shakes his head up and down and asks, "Mr. O'Reilly? Where did he come from?"

Well since it is too late to keep a secret about these recent goings-on, I say, "I think I see Mr. O'Reilly first up on the roof when Mr. Manichy comes tumbling down but I am not sure. But at that time someone else is on the roof and it looks like Mr. O'Reilly. Later Mr. O'Reilly comes up from under the stoop and goes right over to Mr. Manichy and starts looking for something in his pockets.

Nicholas adds, "But he comes up empty handed."

Gutsy Gus says, "That all makes sense." Then he pauses and asks, "Do you tell the cops about what you see Mildred and Mr. O'Reilly doing?"

We both shake our heads and Nicholas says, "No. We no longer enjoy conversating with cops."

"Good!" says Gutsy Gus, "I am going to run upstairs and make a phone call."

Dear John,

Since the stoop, where Mr. Manichy takes my place is still a little wet with pink streaks, and since Nicholas has a need, what he often does, to go to the bathroom, and since Nicholas is persona not greater in my apartment, and since he is back in his own apartment taking care of that need what I already mention, and since, after Gutsy Gus makes his phone call, he comes out of the apartment house and runs down Leonard in the same direction what Mr. O'Reilly takes when I last see him, and since I am quite curiositied about where Mr. O'Reilly goes previously and where Gutsy Gus is now going, I decide to take a little walk around the neighborhood. Well after I walk down Leonard and cross a few streets, I soon find myself at Broadway at the bottom of the stairs what go up to the Lorimer Street train station.

I am standing at the bottom of the stairs for some time because there is cop standing on the first step and he is saying, "Sorry, folks. This station is temporally closed.

A small crowd is gathering around the bottom of the stairs. One old lady complains, "This whole thing is very annoying. I have to get to work or I will be late."

The cop says, "Sorry, lady. There has been an accident. Just as a train is pulling into the station someone falls onto the tracks."

Chapter 38
Gory Details

Dear John,

Since there is little to do and no place to go, Yours Truly turns around and heads back up Leonard where I find the stoop is now completely dry and inviting me to take a seat. I am sitting here on the stoop for just about five minutes when Gutsy Gus comes walking up Leonard and sits down next to Yours Truly.

I ask, "Gutsy Gus, I hear there is quite a bit of excitement down at the Lorimer Street train station. Do you know of any news regarding excitement at that train station?"

Gutsy Gus answers, "Yes I do. I see the whole thing. Would you like to know what happens?"

I answer, "I would most certainly like to know what happens."

Gutsy Gus leans back and says as such, "Well, Uh, Mmmm! It was an accident. Somebody falls in front of the train as it comes into the station."

I say, "Now, Gutsy Gus, what you are giving me is a bunch of mumble jumble what just gives me the jimmy jammies. I am reading enough of Tom Sawyer to know when someone is pulling my leg and, with every word you just speaks, my leg is about a foot longer. So stop your pulling my leg and don't let me go on limpin all the way up to apartment 3B on the second floor. You hear?"

"Well OK, Tom," says Gutsy Gus, "I just think maybe you are too young to hear the gory details of what actually happens."

"Too young? Are you kidding? What Nicholas and I are going through this summer of 1952 would make any kid my age, a lot older than you any day. In fact, this summer brings with it so many complexications that I am now double your age. How old are you, Gutsy Gus? Maybe Eighteen? That makes me at 36 years old and that's old enough to hear the gory details."

Gutsy Gus looks at me hard and long while wrinkling his brow and then says, "OK, I will tell you." Then he stops like he's thinking it over whether he should go on and tell me the gory details or not. So he decides to spill the beans and says, "It was no accident. It was more like a murder."

"I already guessed that but what I want to know is who got murdered and what rapscallion done did the murdering?"

Gutsy Gus smiles and says, "I think you are overdosing on Tom Sawyer."

I say, "Well that don't matter enough at all! Wasn't you expectorating I know how to express myself like that smart, scholarship guy, Tom Sawyer? But what does matter is who it is what got murdered and who done the deed. I'm thinkin it was one of them rapscallions what done it because there was them what smooched around about the corpse formerly known as Mr. Manichy who t'aint your father after all.

Gutsy Gus looks at me and smiles.

I continue, "Well, Gutsy Gus, I wanna hear you tell me about it cause I know you can paint it up mighty fine and have the glory of being the one what knows a lot more about this and many a thing more than just about anybody else does in this whole world of Brooklyn."

Gutsy Gus puts up his hand and says, "Enough of this trittle trattle. If you promise to return to Earnest-speak, I will tell you what I know of the incident on the Lorimer Street train station."

I shake my head in agreement but Gutsy Gus says, "Take your hands out from behind your back so I can see that no fingers are crossed and uncross your legs."

"Gladly," I say as I uncross my fingers and uncross my legs but then I try to cross my eyes. Then Gutsy Gus looks at my eyes and points to them and shakes his head.

"OK, Earnest, this is what I see with my very own eyes. I run as fast as I can toward Broadway because I am pretty sure that Mildred and Mr. O'Reilly are both heading in that direction. And sure enough when I get to the bottom of the stairs, I see Mr. O'Reilly at the top. I take the steps two at a time and by the time I get to the top, Mr. O'Reilly is walking out onto the station platform. About half way down the platform I see Mildred Manichy standing between two suitcases. I place a token into the turnstile and walk out onto the platform. I stand still as I watch Mr. O'Reilly slowly walk up to Mildred. Her back is to him but then I see a streak of sunlight bounce off a mirror she is holding. Mr. O'Reilly walks very slowly up in back of her and then I see another streak of sunlight but this one is bouncing off a pistol in Mr. O'Reilly's right hand. The train is approaching the station. Mildred bends down and picks up the suitcase on her left side and swings it up and around. It hits Mr. O'Reilly in his right arm. The train is now rattling into the station. Mr. O'Reilly spins around and loses his balance. He lifts his gun, fires a shot. The bullet sparks off an exit sign. Mr. O'Reilly falls off the platform right in front of the train.

"Holy mackerel! What does Mrs. Manichy do then?"

"Mildred picks up her suitcases and walks down the stairs on the opposite side of the train platform."

"I turn around and run down the stairs on my side of the platform and, when I get down to Broadway, I see Mildred getting into a yellow cab."

I ask, "Why did she not hail a cab in the first place?"

"I guess she got lucky this time. She probably tried to hail a cab before but you know they don't come around here very often and when they do, they do not usually stop to pick up passengers. There have been too many robberies in this part of Brooklyn."

I add, "Right. That makes sense. That is why, even though she gets quite a head start on Mr. O'Reilly, she is on the platform when he gets there. So where do you think she is going in the cab?"

"I am pretty sure she is heading to Idlewild Airport and taking the first plane to ..." Then Gutsy Gus stops and puts his hand to his chin. Then almost under his breath, he whispers, "Leningrad."

"Leningrad?"

"You did not hear me say that!"

"I not only heard you say that but you are wrong. I know planes do not fly from Idlewild to Leningrad. Idlewild Airport is one of my adventures last summer. I remember the places they fly and the Soviet Union is not one."

"She will most likely fly to East Germany and cross over to Communist West Berlin and then get a flight to Leningrad."

"So Mildred is a Commie?"

"We suspected Mildred and Reginald for quite a while and that is why I was placed in their home. It was a good way to watch their activities."

"Who would place a nice kid like you in the home of Commies?"

Then Gutsy Gus shakes his head and says, "They thought I was about sixteen but I'm actually much older than I look. I have been working with a Catholic organization whose purpose is to rescue young people, mostly girls, from the Soviet Union."

I ask, "What if they found out you are a spy what with you being all alone and all."

"I was never alone. Mr. Joey Pitschalnikov watches everything from his window. He is my uncle and he is here to keep me safe."

"Mr. Joey Pits is your uncle! Uh… What about Natasha Natasha?"

"His daughter. Natasha Pitschalnikov is his daughter. We just recently got her out of the Soviet Union."

I say, "I cannot help but notice Mr. Joey Pits is always paying compliments to girls but they do not seem to appreciate these compliments."

Gutsy Gus chuckles and says, "I know! He was using a book to learn conversational English, British English actually, but it was not exactly the right phrase book. The book he was using to learn English was written for Russian sailors. I gave him another book with more appropriate greetings in American English."

"Another question then. Do you really go to St. John's University?"

"Yes, I have a scholarship supported by a fund set up by Bishop Melinshikov. I am a student of philosophy and theology."

I say, "I have one more question."

"Well, ask it and I'll tell you if I can answer it or not."

"Who is that beautiful doll who drives around with Boris?"

"My mother."

I say, "Wow, your mother? I am sorry for calling her a beautiful doll because I am speaking of your mother but I must confess your mother is really a most beautiful... uh... lady.

Gutsy Gus nods his head and smiles, "I know. She is very beautiful."

"I have another question and it is this; is your mother Russian and are you ..."

Gutsy Gus interrupts and says, "Yes. My mother is Russian and I am Russian too but we are not Communists. We are here to do what we can to help people, especially young women, escape from behind the Iron Curtain and to stop the spread of atheistic Communism."

I say, "So Senator McCarthy is right about all the Commies infilterating the government and the movies."

Gutsy Gus lowers his eyebrows and says, "Senator McCarthy with his blacklist is doing more harm than good. I do not trust him and I hope somebody someday will be brave enough to expose the harm he is doing."

I shake my head and say, "I want to have an adventure or two this summer but this whole summer and all the events are far more complexicated than I ever think they will be."

"I can agree with you. Things are quite, as you say, complexicated this summer." Then Gutsy Gus puts up his hand and says, "You know what? I am telling you too much. So you better know how to keep a secret or else."

"What? If I do not keep all these secrets, Big Boris is gonna cut out my tongue?"

"That sounds like something my mother would say.

When she lived in Russia, she had to deal with the KGB and they did things like that and even worse."

"OK! I promise not to speak one word about what you are saying to anyone, not even to Nicholas. But how about one more question what has me wondering for a long time?"

"Well, maybe just one more question but I may not be able to answer it."

"OK! How come you live in apartment 2B on the fourth floor? It should be 4B on the fourth floor. Right?"

"Reginald Manichy arranged that. I think he changed the numbers to confuse people who might be after him for one reason or another. The confusion would give him a chance to get out of the apartment. He was doing a lot that made many people want to kill him and, of course, one of them did."

Gutsy Gus smiles and says, "You and Nicholas have had quite a summer but next week school begins."

Then I say, "I do not want to think about that! So let us go back and finish talking about what happens today at the Lorimer Street station. What happens next? Do you stay around to see or what?"

"OK, getting back to the incident on the Lorimer Street station, I do not wait around to answer any questions because, like you, I never enjoy conversating with cops."

"OK and what about that brown envelope what Mrs. Manichy takes off Mr. Manichy's upside down body on the stoop?"

"I do not think I should discuss that with you. That is pretty confidential and besides I do not know myself all the facts. I really do not know what it is all about. It has something to do with Bishop Melinshikov."

I add by asking, "Does it have something to do with ten-thousand dollars?"

Gutsy Gus stands up and opens his mouth so wide that if my father did that, his teeth will fall out. Then he says, "What do you know about ten-thousand dollars?"

I say, "You tell me yours and I'll tell you mine."

Gutsy Gus says, "You may be right. That brown envelope probably does contain ten-thousand dollars. It has something to do with paying somebody to keep quiet about something. And now I think that somebody who got paid is or was Reginald Manichy."

"Blackmail?" I ask.

"Yes. And Mr. O'Reilly was in on it."

"And do you think Mrs. Manichy was in on it too?" I ask.

"I do not know if she was in on it but she somehow got wind of it."

I add, "She got more than wind. She got ten-thousand dollars."

Chapter 39

Another Revolting Perdickamint

Dear John,

    As you can imagine, I do not tell Nicholas about that conversation what Gutsy Gus and Yours Truly had yesterday. Besides it is Friday and on Monday school starts.

Dear John,

    I am thinking that, since summer is over, I should tell Nicholas the truth about Saint Closétus. But I do not know what good it does to tell or what good it does not to tell.

Dear John,

    This morning along about eleven bells I am walking to Teitle's Grocery to buy a loaf of Wonder Bread and to pick a dill pickle from out of the pickle barrel. As I am passing the apartment house where Nicholas lives, I hear Nicholas calling to me from his upstairs window. He says, "Earnest, I got something really important to tell you and it is real bad news. So meet me in about half an hour at Randy's Restaurant. Believe me, it's real bad news."

    I say, "So tell me now. I cannot wait to hear the really bad news. What is it?"

Just then I see Nicholas's mother in back of Nicholas and he shakes his head and closes the window.

Dear John,

So it is half an hour later and I am sitting at a table in back of Randy's Restaurant when Bobby Anderson walks in. He goes up to the counter and orders a two-cent plain and then he sees me at the back table. He walks to the back and sits on the bench on the other side of the table.

Bobby Anderson looks sad and I mean more than somewhat sad. He looks at me and then he says, "One more day of freedom. One more day to torture."

I say, "I feel very sorry for you. I just can't see any way of helping you fix that big problem what is coming your way on Monday morning."

"I got big nun problems. Really big nun problems!"

I say, "I know! Yesterday I am passing St. Mary's and I see the nun what is the principal walking in the school yard. She is one really big sister."

Bobby Anderson says, "They do not call most nuns Sister. Not this big one! They call her Mother Superior. Her name is Mother Mary Celestine. She is one big mother of a nun problem."

I say, "Nicholas has some bad news to tell me but I do not know what it is. About an hour ago he tells me he will meet me here and tell me what it is."

Just then the door opens and Nicholas enters Randy's Restaurant. He walks past the counter and sits on the bench next to Bobby Anderson. Nicholas stretches his arms out and places his head between his arms on the table.

I ask, "Nicholas, what is it that makes you look so very unhappy?"

Nicholas lifts his head. His eyes are moist. He folds his

arms about him and speaks, "I am indeed unhappy, more than somewhat unhappy!"

I ask, "The cause for this unhappiness is?"

Nicholas lowers his head to the table and answers, "My mother got me transferred to St. Mary's."

I say, "Oh! That is indeed a cause for unhappiness and indeed more than somewhat unhappiness."

Bobby Anderson's mouth is open wide. But then he closes it and a very sneaky smile appears on his face. Bobby Anderson says, "I know this is more than somewhat sad for you but I am feeling…

Nicholas interrupts, "Sad? Sad? This is more than sad. This is tragic! My life is ruined! I begged my mother not to do this to me but she did it anyway. I thought my mother loved me but now I know she hates me."

At a time as sad and indeed as tragic as this proposition, it is often better to say nothing and that is what I say. I just look at Nicholas and then at Bobby Anderson. I shake my head to show my total sorrowfulness. That such tragedies could fall on two of my best friends is indeed a great concern. But then I am also feeling somewhat relieved that I myself am not in such a tragic proposition.

Finally I do speak as such, "This is one of those revolting perdickamints what should never happen to a nice kid like you, Nicholas. I know you are sad and I am also sad for two reasons, well actually three. I am sad that you, Nicholas, and you, Bobby Anderson, are condemned to spend most of your lives imprisoned and tortured by nuns. You are two reasons for my unhappiness. The third reason is that P.S. 18 will not be the same for me now that you two reasons for my sadness are no longer there."

So the three of us just sit in Randy's Restaurant and we are so sad and doing our best not to bust out crying. I am thinking what with Nicholas transferring to St. Mary's, the guy's gotta have some hope. What without me looking after him, Nicholas needs all the help he can get. Well at least I do feel a little good can come out of the summer vacation. I mean at least Nicholas can get lots of spiritual help from Saint Closétus.

Chapter 40

The Haircut

Dear John,

It is Sunday night and tomorrow is the first day of school and I am home all by myself. My mom and dad are doing church stuff. My dad is attending a meeting of the Knights of Columbus and my mom is at a meeting of the Legion of Mary. So I look out the window on the alley and I see the Kelly's apartment. They got a television. They are watching a guy what crosses his arms mostly and goes by the handle Ed Sullivan. Then acrobats come on and I see Mrs. Kelly gets up and changes the station. A movie what's got these kids called Our Gang is on. So I pull a chair to the window and I look real close. I cannot hear anything but I can see the kids are real funny. One kid, named Alfalfa, got a big tall pointy hair standing up on top of his head. It's from when a cow licked his hair. It's real funny looking. I watch for about ten minutes but then Mr. Kelly gets up and pulls down the shade.

I walk around the apartment looking for something to keep my mind off the terrible things what are gonna happen to my two friends tomorrow at St. Mary's. But then I am not exactly wild about my tomorrow either. After a very exciting summer I gotta sit still in a classroom and that is not an easy thing to do for an adventurous guy like Yours Truly.

I am walking around trying to find something exciting to do. Then I walk into the bathroom and look in the mirror. Now this is a thing what I have little opportunity to do during this very busy summer. So tonight when I look in the mirror, I see my hair is so long I can't see my ears. The hair on top of my head is standing straight up and it looks like about twenty cows give it a licking. I really need a haircut. But it's Sunday night and all the barber shops are closed and my mom and dad are doing that holy stuff at church. But it is never a good thing when my mom or dad cut my hair anyway.

I do want to make a good impression tomorrow and a haircut is just the ticket. Besides I do not want the teacher to put me on the girl's line. So I decide to do a little hair cutting for myself.

Dear John,

I finish! I give myself a haircut. First I get out the scissors and a comb and I cut the sides so I can see my ears again. But the hair in the back of my head is so long it is not only covering my shirt collar, it is long enough for me to tie it into a ponytail. So I take the scissors and cut my hair across the back of my head. Then I look in the mirror and turn my head first this way and then that way. My hair is shorter but now it looks like somebody put a bowl on top of my head and cut around the rim. It looks like what I just see on the Kelly's television, an Alfalfa haircut. But it's worse than an Alfalfa cut because only one cow licked his hair. I can see why he never gets Darla to like him. An Alfalfa haircut just does not look good on Yours Truly!

So out comes the scissors again and I cut up the two

sides and up the back. That looks better! But now the top is too long and sticking up all over. So I pull up my hair with the comb and cut. The comb slips. The scissors slip. I have a crew cut in the middle of my head. Well I fix that by cutting some more hair off the top of my head. Well now my hair is sticking up in some places and down in other places. I look a little like Buckwheat and that is definitely not good. I keep cutting here and there and there and there. I look in the mirror and I make a big decision. I put on a hat.

Dear John,

It is Monday morning, the first day of school. I finish off a bowl of Snap Crackle what don't go Pop and I am off to the fifth grade at P.S. 18. I will write again this afternoon and I will tell you about all the events what will be taking place today.

Chapter 41

First Day of School

Dear John,

The events what take place today are not good. After I wake up this morning, the first thing I do is to go into the bathroom. I look in the mirror. Uh oh! My hair cut looks even worse than it did last night. I am bald in some places and cow licked everywhere else. I put on a hat.

I walk into the schoolyard five minutes before the nine o'clock bell. I figger I am off to a good start, what with being on time and all. I meet some of the kids I never see all summer long. But no Nicholas and no Bobby Anderson! The bell rings and we all stand still and that's kind of fun, like playing statues. When the bell rings again, we all walk to our lines. My line is the fifth grade class and a teacher who I never see before is standing holding a sign with big letters, FIFTH GRADE! Big letters, big sign, very big teacher! Ugly too. Last year we have an ugly teacher but at least we have a real pretty student teacher.

I stand in line and then we walk up to the classroom, all the way up on the fourth floor. The teacher tells us to line up in the hallway and then she unfolds a paper with a long list of names. She says a name and then tells the kid what desk to sit in. When she calls my name, she tells me to sit in the first seat in the third row and that is right in front of her desk. I am walking in and as I pass in front of the teacher, she says, "Take off your hat."

Now this is something I do not wish to do. So I pretend I do not hear her. I just walk to the desk and sit.

The teacher says, "Take off your hat."

I look to my right, to my left, down to the floor and up to the ceiling like I am trying to find out who is speaking.

The teacher shouts, "I told you to take off your hat!"

I look at her and shake my head and say, "I do not see any rat here. Oh look! There! I see a cockroach but no rat."

She screams now, "Take off your hat!"

I say, "No, teacher, I do not say you are fat. You are but I do not say that. I do not say you are fat."

The teacher asks, "Are you deaf?"

I say, "Yes." But that was a mistake because, when I answer her, she figgers I am not deaf.

She says, "Go to the office. The Principal will make you take off your hat."

So when I get to the Principal's Office, I see a sign on the door what says, *Mr. Murphy*. This name I do not recognize because this is not the same Principal as last year. I get to know that Principal real good because we spend a lot of time together.

So when I walk into the office, Mrs. Kramer, the school secretary, who I know from many trips to the Principal's Office last year, shakes her head and says, "Earnest, you are starting off the school year in a bad way."

I nod my head but I do not say anything. I just sit in the same I chair I sit in many times last year.

Then the Principal's door opens and there is this old guy,

who looks a lot like a penguin, points his finger at me and says, "Take off your hat."

"OK." Since there are no kids around to laugh, I take off my hat. But when Mrs. Kramer starts laughing, I fast put my hat back on.

Mr. Murphy smiles and writes something on a piece of paper and says, "Give this note to your teacher. You can keep your hat on."

Well when I get back to the classroom and give the teacher the note, she reads it, looks at me and says, "I do not want to look at you with your hat on. Take a seat in the back of the room. Besides, I see from your permanent record card that you are not able to read or write so you can just sit in the back of the classroom while I teach a reading lesson to children who know how to read."

Well there are many empty desks with pull down seats in the back of the room mainly because so many kids transfer to St. Mary's School. So I sit in the corner desk near the window.

Well sitting all be myself can be pretty boring. I look up at the clock and the time is 10:15. I am getting restless more than somewhat. During the summer when I am not having an adventure of my own, I take out *Guys and Dolls* or *Tom Sawyer* and read about their adventures. But to take out a book and read it here in the classroom is definitely not a good idear. Reading a book such as one of these is sure to blow my cover. I want the teacher to think that I am still illiterated. I am thinking about such things for some time but when I look up at the clock the time is 10:20! Only five minutes goes by! I get to thinking about Tom Sawyer when he scribes about time slowing down and standing still. Time is stringing along and along real slow.

But then sitting by an open window is an invitation to do something what helps from being all that bored and maybe helps tempus fungus or something like that what Gutsy Gus says about time flying. So I open a desk top and find a few pieces of paper. I tear them up and make little balls. I put one on the center of the desk. I check out what the teacher is doing and she is at the board writing a long list of rules. She does not look at me. So I take my middle finger on my right hand and flick the paper ball what goes flying off my desk and out the window. First goal with the first shot! I look at the clock and it says 10:30. Only fifteen minutes and I am all already out of paper balls.

So I raise my hand and ask, "Can I go to the bathroom?"

The teacher says, "I suppose you can but you may not."

I remember that teacher game from last year. But the most important thing is to get out of here. I need a break. So I ask the right way, "May I please go to the labatory?" Now I know how it is supposed to be pronounced with a *v* and not a *b* but I like my way of saying things and besides the teacher does not hear me say it my way.

The teacher says, "That is the correct way to ask and since you asked the correct way, you may go to the lavatory."

So I get up and leave but, of course, I do not go the labatory or even to the lavatory. I go to the schoolyard and I climb the fence and then I swing over to the side of the building. I got a lot of energy and I gotta let it out! So I am sitting way at the top of the school yard fence and just about to swing over to another fence when I hear the teacher's loud voice, "Earnest! Get off that fence."

It is a sad thing when a teacher does not trust a kid. She followed me.

I explain as follows, "Teacher, I am doing a service to the school by picking up these pieces of paper what are blowing around here and there. And some pieces of paper got blown way up here at the top of this fence when some other kid, not me of course, has the nerve to throw them out one of the classroom windows. Thunder! Ain't it just suspicious?"

That incident ended with my second visit to Mr. Murphy.

After about an hour sitting outside his office, Mrs. Kramer tells me to return to my classroom. The teacher does not seem happy to see me.

Well for the rest of the morning time is stringing along and along real slow. But after lunch things get somewhat more exciting. The teacher asks each kids in the class to tell what they do during their summer vacation. Most kids talk about going swimming at McCarren pool and some went to camp. Real boring!

Then my turn comes. I stay in my seat and I begin by saying, "I spend a lot of my time on the stoop this summer just watching people go by." But then I decide to tell the truth and I stand up and say, "See it all starts out with my wanting to have an adventure this summer. Actually, I do have quite an adventure or two or three because me and my friend, Nicholas, who many of you know from the neighborhood, investigate many mysteries and suspicious goings on what with Commies and other bad guys infilterating the Catholic Church but that leads to killing about twenty bad guys, give or take one or two. So it really begins when this guy who we call Seabiscuit bumps into Nicholas and two big bags filled with C-notes, you know, one-hundred dollar bills, bust out of the bags and go all over the street and then a bag full of relics, what are gold and very powerful for doing religious magical miracles, goes flying across the street and falls down into a sewer on the corner of 34th Street and the Avenue of the Americans. So a few days later we go back and fish these relics out of that sewer. Then these bad guys are trying to kill …"

Unfortunately I do not get to finish my sentence because the teacher says, "Stop! You are lying. I have had enough of you."

"No. I am not lying. I know I have a bit of a repertation for some exaggerating but this is the truth." I continue telling the class more about my summer adventures. I say, "Then there is this problem what we have with Lucky Luigi who is also trying to …"

Then the teacher yells, "Stop! Just sit down and keep quiet. I have had enough of your lies."

Sometimes it does not pay to tell the truth. But at least I get to keep my hat on.

Then in a very short time I am back in the Principal's Office where I spend the rest of the afternoon watching the slow hands on the clock. Time is stringing along and along real slow. The only thing that happens is that I can hear Mr. Murphy talking on the phone. He is talking for a long time to his sister and then he gets to talking to his mother. I think it is wrong for him to be talking to his family when he is using the school phone but I do not say anything about that. At least it gives me something to think about. Time is stringing along and along real slow, stringing along and along real slow.

Finally the clock says three o'clock and Mr. Murphy tells me to go home. Then I think I hear, barely hear, him say under his breath, "And don't come back!"

Well when I get home from school today, my mom looks at me but then she squints when she looks at my hat. She says, "It is warm today and you have a hat on. Hmm? I wonder." Then she lifts my hat off my head. She puts her hand to her mouth. She is trying not to laugh. Next she says, "Sit down right here at the kitchen table. I have some repairing to do." She gets a scissor and gives me a real short haircut, really short. It still looks pretty bad but nobody better laugh at this bald headed kid.

Dear John,

This morning, after I get out of bed and walk into the kitchen, I see my mom standing at the kitchen table. She pours milk into my cereal bowl what is going snap, crackle and pop. My mom is smiling and she says. "I got a phone call this morning and I am really happy about it."

I ask, "What are you happy about?"

Mom says, "You are not going back to P.S. 18."

I think that is pretty good because me and that teacher don't hit it off all that good but then I get to thinking about what that really means and I start to ask, "Uh, oh! What school…?"

My mom says, "Mother Mary Celestine called. You are transferring to St. Mary's and you start today."

"But, Mom, just last week the nun says they got a very long list and I am way at the bottom of the list."

My mom says, "They got to the bottom of the list."

The End